SECRET of the SIRENS

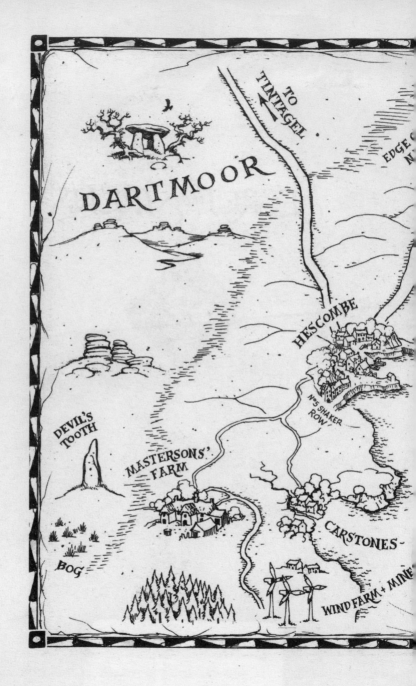

BOOK ONE
THE COMPANIONS QUARTET

SECRET of the SIRENS

JULIA GOLDING

OXFORD
UNIVERSITY PRESS

OXFORD
UNIVERSITY PRESS

Great Clarendon Street, Oxford OX2 6DP

Oxford University Press is a department of the University of Oxford.
It furthers the University's objective of excellence in research, scholarship,
and education by publishing worldwide in

Oxford New York

Auckland Cape Town Dar es Salaam Hong Kong Karachi
Kuala Lumpur Madrid Melbourne Mexico City Nairobi
New Delhi Shanghai Taipei Toronto

With offices in

Argentina Austria Brazil Chile Czech Republic France Greece
Guatemala Hungary Italy Japan Poland Portugal Singapore
South Korea Switzerland Thailand Turkey Ukraine Vietnam

Oxford is a registered trade mark of Oxford University Press
in the UK and in certain other countries

First published 2006
First published in paperback 2006

British Library Cataloguing in Publication Data
Data available

ISBN 978-0-19-275460-8

ISBN 978-0-19-275456-1 (hardback)

3 5 7 9 10 8 6 4

Typeset in Garamond MT by Palimpsest Book Production Limited,
Polmont, Stirlingshire

Printed in Great Britain by
Cox & Wyman, Reading, Berks.

Paper used in the production of this book is a natural,
recyclable product made from wood grown in sustainable forests.
The manufacturing process conforms to the environmental
regulations of the country of origin.

For Lucy

With thanks to those who helped shape this book:
Hannah and Ellie Siden, Alex Mylrea-Lowndes, Tom Lowe,
John and Rosemary Dickinson, Clare Bryden, the Pearson family,
Liz Cross, and Polly Nolan. And special thanks to Lucy
and Joss for listening.

Siren *(from Classical Mythology)*. One of several fabulous monsters, part woman, part bird, who were supposed to lure sailors to destruction by their enchanting singing.
In early use frequently confused with the mermaid.

(from *The Oxford English Dictionary*, by permission of Oxford University Press)

Contents

1
Seagulls

'GO on, I dare you.' The beady eye of the seagull twinkled at Connie from on top of the lifebuoy.

'But, Scark, I can't!' Connie whispered back, scuffing her trainers on a coil of blue rope on the quayside. 'What if someone sees?'

Scark cocked his head and opened his yellow beak in silent mockery of her cowardice. Connie glanced furtively over her shoulder. She really wanted to do it. No one was watching her. She was just another young girl spending her holidays hanging out by the marina. There was no one close enough to see that she was set apart from others by her mismatched eyes, one green, one brown, and by the fact that she talked to seagulls. The fishermen were too busy washing down their decks to notice the girl with ripped jeans and a mop of black hair. The parties of tourists by the coach park had eyes only for the straw hats and seashell mementoes in the gift shops. Nobody seemed to care that something extraordinary was about to happen a stone's throw away.

'OK, I'll do it!' Connie said, giving in to her desire. 'Bet I'll beat you this time.'

Taking a crust from her pocket, she threw a few crumbs into the air as practice runs. Scark flapped from his perch and caught them easily. Play begun, other herring gulls circled out of the sky and landed on the harbour wall, a row of eager spectators. White heads bobbed impatiently, waiting for the real fun to begin.

'Here goes!' called Connie to them. 'It's me against you lot. If one crumb falls to the ground, I win.'

The seagulls screamed their approval and flapped into the sky. Connie threw a handful of crusts high. Birds mobbed them from all sides, effortlessly plucking them from the air. Scark gave an ear-splitting mew.

'So, I can't catch you out that easily?' laughed Connie. She threw the bread faster and faster, spinning on her heels in an attempt to confuse her opponents. Gulls darted nimbly left and right, splitting their flock, spinning on the wing, diving, anticipating every feint, every low trick she could devise to outwit them. The billowing cloud of birds swarmed around her, responding to the movements of her body as if she was a conductor and they her orchestra, becoming an extension of her mood and music. She swirled them around her like a vast cloak, wrapping herself in their delight in showing off their skill on the wing. A power flowed from her to the birds: it seemed to them almost as if she had shed her human skin and become flight itself, the heart of the flock. The seagulls shrieked with joy, urging her to fly with them out to sea and join them in their raucous colonies on the ledges of the cliffs and rock stacks. The mass of birds formed into the shape of two vast wings extending from her fingertips. She felt that if she just tried a little harder, she too would lift from the earth and fly, but her feet could not quite leave the ground. Taking the last piece of crust in her fist, Connie threw it high into the sky.

'Catch!' she cried.

The seagulls zoomed upwards like Spitfires in a dogfight, vying with each other for the prize. With a beat of his broad, grey wings, Scark snatched the morsel from under the beak of a small white female and returned to the lifebuoy, ach-aching triumphantly.

'Hey, that wasn't very polite of you,' Connie scolded him affectionately, 'stealing it from her like that! Whatever am I teaching you?'

Scark bobbed his head in indignation, telling her with a puff of his wings that a mere chick— for so he considered her—could teach him nothing.

'I s'pose not,' Connie conceded. Sitting down on the cobbles beside him, she suddenly felt deflated. The other gulls drifted away on the breeze to seek new sport by the rubbish bins and fishing boats. 'I know I've got a lot to learn. I just wish I didn't have to go to school to do it. I hate school. I just know it's going to be a disaster.'

Scark shook his head sceptically.

'I haven't survived more than a term or two at my other schools. Something always happens: foxes start following me around, or mice invade the classroom, and it soon becomes pretty clear that it's all my fault. Why should it be any different in Hescombe? I don't stand a chance. At the other schools, it was only me that people found strange; here, there's my aunt as well.'

Connie threw a stone listlessly into the harbour. It plopped out of sight, leaving worried wrinkles to disturb the seaweed and the litter collected by the seawall. When her parents had moved abroad recently, they had considered sending Connie to boarding school but in the end decided that, in view of her terrible record in the classroom, she would be safer with a relative, even if that meant Mr Lionheart's strange sister, Evelyn. Boarding school had sounded grim, but now that she had met her aunt she wondered if it would not have been a better choice. Who else had an aunt who wailed mournfully from her bedroom window at five in the morning and disappeared for hours running on the moors dressed in a long black ragged cloak? As Connie had swiftly realized, Evelyn was strange, not to mention scary, but, unlike her niece, she did not wish to hide her oddness.

The tide was at its height. The multicoloured boats bobbed eagerly on their moorings, ropes ringing against masts, summoning their owners to set sail. Connie stood up and brushed down the seat of her jeans, which were damp from the fish-slick cobbles.

'OK, Scark, it's time to go. See you tomorrow.'

The seagull fluttered his wings once and shook his beak at her in farewell. She watched with admiration as he launched himself gracefully off the lifebuoy, heading out to the wave-flecked sea.

'Good fishing!' she called, her voice whipped away like an autumn leaf scuttling before the wind.

She wished she could go home with him far away from the humans who found her so odd.

Only when she turned from the sea did she notice the old man, long white hair streaked with ginger at the temples, half-hidden in a shelter ten metres away, equipped with a motorbike helmet, a thermos flask, binoculars, and a folded newspaper. By his side lay a pair of scarlet ear protectors, the sort worn by construction workers who use pneumatic drills, but there was not a piece of heavy machinery in sight and nor did he look anything like a builder. Had he been watching her all this time? Embarrassment flooded Connie in a hot wave: she hated to think that anyone had seen her playing with her friends. It always spelt trouble. People in Hescombe would soon be whispering that she was weird as they had in London. Mortified, Connie did not wait to return the warm smile he gave her when she met his gaze. She ran off, threading through a party of tourists boarding their coach, and pelted as fast as she could down the High Street in the direction of her aunt's house.

Dashing past the gaudy shops spilling plastic buckets, spades, and carousels of postcards onto the pavement, Connie collided with a group of people gathered outside the Anchor Tavern.

'Sorry!' she said, jumping back from an elderly lady, only to ricochet into a sturdily-built man in wellington boots. He caught Connie before she could fall and set her on her feet.

'Careful,' the man said. 'You'll do yourself an injury if you carry on like that.'

Connie's murmured apologies died on her lips as she stood pinned to the spot in the circle of people. They stopped talking and looked at her with polite concern. Connie hesitated, unable and unwilling to leave the group. She had caught an echo from them of what she had felt when playing with the seagulls. This was where she should be. The place was rightfully hers.

'Something the matter?' asked the man with a frown.

'No, no, sorry,' Connie said, shaking herself out of her paralysis. She was being stupid. Of course she shouldn't stand there all day. She didn't know any of these people—she had no business interrupting them like this. Their expressions told her they had not felt anything special as she stood there, other than entertaining vague doubts about her sanity. She backed off hurriedly. Yet, after running a few paces down the street, she could not help glancing behind her, feeling called back to the gathering of people. She was wrong: no one was looking at her, let alone calling her. They had all gathered around the elderly lady who was handing out scarlet ear protectors from her shopping bag.

Connie turned and ran all the way to her new home, Number Five Shaker Row, eager to be alone with her thoughts about what had just happened. Her aunt's house was the last of a terrace of fishermen's cottages that clung to the bottom of the cliff, seeking protection from the ocean that beat hungrily at their front-steps. Number Five shrank back from the waves, drawing itself taller and thinner than its neighbours, like the last person to enter a cupboard in a game of sardines. The house seemed to anticipate that the waves would at any moment rip the cupboard door open and that Number Five would be the first to tumble out.

Madame Cresson, her aunt's rather superior marmalade cat, was stalking down the path, tail purposefully erect. She miaowed when she saw Connie, who paused briefly to greet her before clattering into the kitchen to hang up her jacket. She stopped dead. There on the spindly umbrella-stand by the back door lay a pair of scarlet ear protectors. What was going on? Her first thought was that she should run straight back out again and keep on running until she had left all these strange people behind, especially her aunt. Then she changed her mind. Surely, as she had no real choice but to stay here, it would do no harm to find out more about Evelyn Lionheart and her odd goings-on? Perhaps the ear protectors themselves might give her a clue? She glanced over her shoulder to check she was alone and then picked up the headset to study it at close quarters. A small silver bird was stamped on both earpieces. She put them over her ears experimentally, and shut out all sounds so effectively that she did not hear the footsteps until somebody tapped her on the shoulder. Startled, she ripped them off.

'You know what they say about curiosity and the cat, don't you?' a voice asked smoothly—but with the smoothness of thin ice. Tall but light-footed, and dressed as usual in black, Evelyn Lionheart stood over her, her face ghostly white against her long brown hair. Madame Cresson padded in through the cat flap and wound round Evelyn's ankles, greeting her mistress.

'Er . . . no—what do they say?' Connie asked awkwardly, her heart pounding.

'That curiosity killed the cat,' said Evelyn lightly, taking the ear protectors from her to hang them back on the stand.

Madame Cresson yowled in protest, offended by this talk of death, and defected to Connie. She arched her back as she rubbed herself against Connie's jeans, seeking comfort from her special friend.

Connie stroked the cat's head. 'I'm sorry. I was just . . . It's just that I saw some other people in town with them today. I thought it a bit strange,' she ended lamely, thinking she must say something to excuse herself.

'Did you?' Her aunt's green eyes flicked to Connie's face with a shrewd expression, her silver-hoop earrings twinkling in the light from a small window in the back door.

'What are they for?' Connie ventured, blinking hard to shake off the mesmerizing effect of the glinting rings.

'That is none of your business,' said Evelyn, keeping her gimlet-gaze fixed on her niece.

Connie felt anger bubble up inside her, but it was almost immediately burst by a prick of fear when her aunt added, 'Forget you ever saw them.' Evelyn was so mercurial: at one moment full of wild laughter and enthusiasm, the next showing some alarming sparks of menace and temper. Connie did not know what Evelyn really thought about having her niece dumped on her. From the reception she had received so far she suspected that her aunt felt resentful and annoyed, and that only a sense of duty to the family had persuaded her to undertake the charge. Yet there seemed to be something else too—something Connie could not quite put her finger on. It did not help that, though they shared the same house, Evelyn shut herself away from Connie, keeping conversations to a minimum and inviting no confidences. Refusing to explain the ear protectors was all part of this behaviour and Connie was beginning to resent it. She wished that her parents had found a more sympathetic guardian for her, someone who at the very least would welcome her into their home. But she dared push the question of the ear protectors no further. The matter was dropped and the next time Connie passed the umbrella-stand, the headset had gone.

2
Sirens

Early the next morning, Connie was awoken by a keening sound coming from beneath her window. She slept up in a small attic bedroom with a sloping roof and a window overlooking the sea. It was the only place in the house where she felt comfortable: her own sanctuary. Slipping out of the covers and tiptoeing barefoot across the varnished floorboards, she tentatively pulled back the curtains. There, on the path in front of the house, was Evelyn, dressed in her black cape, and spinning slowly like a top, her arms outstretched but limp at the wrist, her head rolled forward. From above, the cape whirled in a perfect circle, the crimson band of Evelyn's headscarf forming a red pupil in the middle of the black eye. Her voice rose and fell in an ululating sob, as if she were mourning the passing of some beloved friend or despairing of ever finding hope again. The sound pierced Connie's heart: she wanted to stuff her fingers in her ears and block out her aunt's strange sadness. What had happened to make her act that way? As if Connie did not have enough problems of her own, she could do without living with someone who was so unorthodox.

'Shut up!' shouted Mr Lucas from Number Four. He thrust his head out of his window, flushed pink with anger. 'Some of us, with proper jobs, are trying to sleep! Practise your dance classes somewhere else!'

The wailing ended abruptly and the back door slammed. Connie leapt quickly into bed before she could be accused of snooping, but her aunt did not come upstairs to check on her. Turning over, Connie tried to go to sleep again. She fell into an uneasy dream that she was being driven over the moor by a howling wind, homeless and rootless, never at rest.

Her aunt made no reference to her early morning activities when Connie came down to the kitchen. It was as if the performance on the path had never taken place. Connie darted a disguised look at Evelyn as she poured herself some orange juice to see if there was any trace of the insane behaviour she had witnessed, but her aunt appeared calm, her expression calculating as she watched her niece. Being with Evelyn was like having breakfast on top of an active volcano: you never knew exactly when it might blow up.

'What were you going to do with yourself today?' Evelyn asked, studying Connie over the rim of her coffee cup. The sunlight was streaming into the warm fug of the kitchen. It passed over the cluttered sink to spotlight a bunch of flame-red chrysanthemums swooning from a vase on the table between Connie and her aunt. Every inch of the kitchen was filled with objects scavenged by Evelyn from her walks on the beach or moors: skeletal knots of driftwood jostled smooth pebbles; a mobile of feathers and multicoloured fragments of glass tinkled and twirled by the window. Connie found the collection unsettling— alluring with its magpie glitter and yet threatening to overwhelm her with its bombardment of the senses.

'Er . . . same as usual, I s'pose,' answered Connie defensively, fingering a fallen petal. She did not like anyone to interfere with her routine of visits to the animals with which she had made friends, but neither did she want to anger her aunt.

'Well, I want you to change your plans.' Oh no, thought Connie. 'A friend of mine, Lavinia Clamworthy, has a grandson who'll be in your class at school. I want you to meet him so you have at least one friend when you start next week.'

Connie was surprised that her aunt had even thought of the idea: it was the first time she had done anything to suggest she considered Connie as any more than a lodger, eating meals and sleeping under the same roof as her. But a boy who did not know her, who probably did not even want to meet her, had been destined by his grandmother and her aunt to be her 'friend'?

'I'm happy to wait till Monday,' Connie replied desperately.

'No, no: we will get this over and done with today,' her aunt said remorselessly. 'I've arranged to meet Mrs Clamworthy and Colin at a tea shop this morning. You're coming with me.'

Connie grimaced down at her bitten fingernails, shredding the petal into confetti: so her fate had been settled and there was no point in resisting. With a sigh, she looked up and gave her aunt a small nod.

The Copper Kettle was a fusty tearoom, much beloved by the senior citizens of Hescombe.

There were chintz frills and lace curtains to hide behind; plates of homemade cakes tastefully displayed on doilies; strictly no background music. Evelyn Lionheart stood out conspicuously from the other adults, like a black swan amongst ducks: she was forty years younger than everyone else and was dressed in a black denim jacket and red Doc Martens, her hair bunched back in a crimson scarf. Connie could not think why her aunt had chosen this for a meeting place.

Connie sat making a tower out of sugar cubes with a growing sense of doom. She had already pessimistically sketched out for herself the most likely scenario: anyone who agreed to accompany his grandmother to this place must be a sad geek whose friendship would be a social handicap from the start. She was destined to spend her first few weeks at Hescombe Primary School hanging around the computer room with him and his equally geeky friends, pretending she cared about the relative merits of PlayStation 2 versus XBox. That's if they let girls into their sad little club— which she doubted.

'Hello, Evelyn,' said a voice that fell like soft rain upon the hushed atmosphere. Connie looked up. It was the old lady she had run into only yesterday. With her was a boy wearing wraparound sunglasses. From his casual stance and the way he dressed, Connie instantly recognized him as someone with the coolness she had always lacked—the kind of boy with whom she would never normally exchange two words. There must be some mistake.

'You're looking lovely today,' the lady continued. 'Been visiting your friends?'

Evelyn gave Mrs Clamworthy the sort of smile that Connie would have loved to receive from her: both warm and affectionate. It made her look quite a different person—one that Connie might even like to live with. 'Thank you, Lavinia. Yes, I've been up to see them. How did you guess?'

'You don't get to my age without knowing a thing or two about these things, dear,' said Mrs Clamworthy, patting Evelyn's wrist. 'I'm not surprised. And this must be Connie? Didn't I bump into you yesterday in the High Street?'

Connie smiled and nodded shyly.

'I hope you like my favourite watering hole? Evelyn's too polite to tell me she hates it, but I was hoping I could make a convert of you.'

Mrs Clamworthy settled herself comfortably next to Connie, wafting the sweet scent of lavender into the air as she rearranged the silky stream of her scarf over her shoulders. Her round, good-natured face was surrounded by a cloud of white hair, like the halo encircling a moon seen through mist.

'And there are no prizes for guessing that this is my grandson, Colin—though apparently he prefers to be known as Col these days. He will be in Mr Johnson's class too, you know,' she continued, nodding encouragingly at Connie.

At ease even in these surroundings, the boy slumped down in a chair opposite Connie and took off his shades, slinging them on the table. He ruffled his short brown hair with both hands, yawning broadly. She raised her gaze to meet his eyes. To her astonishment, Connie found herself looking into one green eye and one brown. She could not stop herself.

'Wow, you've the same . . . !' She tailed off. Something odd was happening. The moment the four of them sat around the same table, new energy tingled through her, a feeling she normally only got when playing with her animal friends. She felt drawn to the Clamworthys—and even to her aunt, she realized with a shock—as strongly as she had to the group she had burst in upon yesterday.

Col laughed. 'Between us we make two regular pairs of eyes.' He jerked his head towards his grandmother. It struck Connie that he had the twitchy, darting movements of a robin. 'I blame the old lady: it's her genes that did it for me. How about you?'

Glancing quickly at her neighbour, Connie saw that Mrs Clamworthy also had different coloured eyes, but in her case the variation was less startling: a grey and a blue.

'Sorry?' she said, rather thrown by his question.

'Where did you get your eyes from: Mum or Dad?'

'No one as far as I know.'

'Great-aunt,' cut in Evelyn, pouring the tea matter-of-factly. 'And before that, her great-great-grandmother.'

Connie realized her mouth was hanging open. She shut it quickly.

'The hair as well,' Evelyn added as an afterthought.

Completely floored by this unexpected rush of information, Connie let the others conduct the conversation while she rearranged her thoughts. Why had she not been told this before? Come to think of it, what were the odds of meeting someone else with the same mismatched eyes? Her brain ached even to imagine the mathematics involved in working it out.

'It's one in ten million, I'd guess,' said Col.

'What?' said Connie, abruptly dragged back from her reverie.

'The chances of meeting someone else with the same odd eyes as me.'

'How did you know I was thinking about that?'

'I didn't,' he said with genuine surprise. 'I was just thinking about it myself.' There was a pause. 'Y' know what, Connie: I think we share quite a lot of things . . .'

'Like what?'

'Like stupid surnames for a start.'

She laughed. Yes, Colin Clamworthy was possibly even more embarrassing than Connie Lionheart. Maybe school would not be so bad after all.

When Monday morning arrived, Connie found she was looking forward to seeing Col again. The only problem was that Evelyn, under orders from Connie's father in case his daughter tried to bolt in misery as she had at her last school, insisted on walking her to the gate and even into the classroom. Fortunately, they were early so Connie did not have to go through this ordeal in front of the class.

The school was built round a Victorian building with separate entrances marked 'BOYS' and 'GIRLS'. Modern classrooms crowded around their more severe predecessor, their expanses of glass winking cheekily at the old high windows in the morning sunshine. Evelyn led Connie to one of the more recent buildings.

'Mr Johnson?' called her aunt to a short man with the comfortable girth and stature of a Shetland pony, who was writing the date up on the whiteboard.

'Evelyn! Delighted to see you. It doesn't seem so long since I had you in my class,' said Mr Johnson, rubbing the marker pen off his hands and coming forward to greet them. Evelyn gave a laugh like a silver chime, relaxing her guard in the presence of someone she knew and liked. Connie instantly warmed to the teacher, heartened by the effect he had on her aunt. 'I'd like to say you haven't changed a bit, but that'd be a lie. You never used to tower over me: I must have shrunk as you've grown.

'And you must be Connie? Welcome to Hescombe. There's a peg with your name on it outside in the cloakroom and your drawer is over there. We don't have particular places as we all move around a lot in my class, but why don't you start on this table here, near the pet corner? I seem to remember your aunt was particularly fond of sitting there.'

'Is that a good idea?' Connie murmured to Evelyn, panic fizzing inside her like froth out of a shaken can.

'Course it is. I told Mr Johnson when I rang all about your difficulties in your other schools. You can trust him not to make a fuss about animals liking you,' her aunt said breezily on her way to the door. 'He never did with me.'

There were no animals in the pet corner at the moment to look at so Connie sat down and waited for the human wildlife to arrive. There was a hard knot in her stomach—a dread that she was going to fail again. She had great difficulty answering Mr Johnson's questions about her favourite subjects as he walked around the tables distributing pristine exercise books. Just now she couldn't think of anything she had liked about school.

The room gradually began to fill up. Three girls came in and glanced curiously over at the new pupil. One gave her a hesitant smile but no one ventured to sit next to her. Connie felt her fragile early confidence ebbing away. It was going to be like all her other first days: she would soon be singled out and isolated because everyone would find her strange. Just then a dark-haired girl, dressed in a turquoise Indian tunic and leggings, staggered in carrying a gerbil cage, heading straight for the pet corner. Connie, sitting directly in her path, could not help but get up to assist her.

'Thanks,' the girl said, collapsing with a dramatic flourish into the chair next to Connie, her row of bracelets clinking merrily as she brushed her river of black hair out of her eyes. 'You're the new girl?'

'Yes, Connie—Connie Lionheart,' she replied tentatively.

The name passed over her neighbour without the slightest indication that she found it in any way amusing.

'I'm Anneena Nuruddin. My family own the Indian on the High Street. Do you know it?' Fanning her face with her slim tawny hand, Anneena looked at Connie properly for the first time. 'Hey, do you know that you've got eyes just like Col Clamworthy? Are you related?' Connie shook her head. 'Wow, the odds that the two of you end up in our class must be . . .'

'Astronomical—don't even think about it.' Connie was pleased to see that she had made Anneena smile.

On cue, Col came into the class and sauntered over to Connie's table.

'I see you've met Anneena. You're sorted then. Anneena knows everyone and everything about the school,' he commented. Connie hoped for a fleeting moment that he would sit on her other side. If he was close to her, would she feel again that strange energy she had sensed in the tea shop? But he turned and took a seat with some boys on another table as the register was taken and,

23

watching him go, she realized that she had probably been foolish even to think that someone like Col might sit near her.

'Col has his own pony and a boat,' remarked Anneena, following him with her eyes speculatively, 'well, his grandmother's boat at any rate.'

'What about his mum and dad? Doesn't he live with them?' asked Connie as Col shared a joke with a big lad with short blond hair, causing their entire table to explode with laughter.

'Simmer down, Col,' said Mr Johnson tolerantly, not even having to look up to know where the source of the disturbance lay.

'They don't seem to be around much,' said Anneena in a whisper. 'He lives with his grandmother. He's really popular.'

And thank goodness for that, for his strange eyes and odd name had made hers seem totally unremarkable; no one was going to notice her with someone like Col in the class. The tension she had felt since arriving in Hescombe eased a little. For the first time in her life, Connie dared to hope she was going to fit in.

At break, Anneena showed her round the school which was bustling with business as the children settled back in after the holidays—queues at the secretary's window, territorial disputes in the playground, gatherings for gossip in the girls' loos.

They finished up back in the pet corner as Anneena wanted to change the gerbils' water.

'I looked after them over the summer,' she told Connie. 'I love gerbils, you see, but Mum's always said they'd be too much trouble. I knew she wouldn't mind me borrowing the class ones though and I think I've managed to change her mind and she'll let me get my own. What about you?'

'Me?'

'Do you like them?'

Connie had never given gerbils much thought before, having had so many other animal friends. She knelt down by the cage to take a closer look, carefully breathing in the smell of sawdust and learning the creatures' secrets about their hoards of seeds. The gerbils immediately rushed to her side and began to weave around in what she knew to be their welcome dance.

'Hey, I've never seen them do that before!' Anneena exclaimed.

'No? I think they're just saying hello,' Connie replied, swaying slightly in response to the gerbils' dance, politely thanking them for their good wishes. Anneena looked at her strangely, a little unnerved by this unexpected behaviour.

'What are you doing?'

'Saying hello back.' As she said this, Connie felt her heart sink. Was this the end of her short friendship with Anneena? She kept her eyes on the intelligent faces of the gerbils, afraid to look up. But then Anneena began to copy her.

'That's cool,' Anneena said with delight as the gerbils raced to her side of the cage and bobbed up and down in front of her. 'You've got a real way with animals, you know.'

Meeting her new friend's admiring look, Connie shrugged and grinned.

Connie left school that afternoon quietly satisfied with the day. She and Anneena had got on well after the gerbil incident. Anneena had told the whole class in her breathless manner about Connie's handling of the class pets. Even Col had seemed impressed. Anneena had then introduced her to her group of friends at lunchtime. Connie had hopes that some of these might turn out to be her friends too. She particularly liked Jane Benedict, a tall, shy girl, one of the brightest in the class. Connie's only disappointment was that Col had kept his distance. She thought they had made friends at the tearoom, but it seemed this did not carry over into school. Pushing the gate of Number Five open, Connie decided that she could not blame him really. He was clearly way out of her league: so popular and funny.

She found her aunt rushing around the kitchen, packing what looked like a picnic.

'How was school?' Evelyn asked distractedly.

Connie sat at the kitchen table and helped herself to a slice of bread.

'Fine.'

'Good. Now, I have to go out again this evening. Mrs Lucas next door said she'd keep an eye on you for me. Find something in the fridge for supper and put yourself to bed, will you?'

After the effort her aunt had made that morning, Connie had expected her to be more interested in how things had gone at school. Did Evelyn ever spare a thought for her?

Silence fell, broken only by the noise of Evelyn's preparations. Connie measured out the moments, hoping her aunt would redeem herself by showing some interest in her. But as the seconds ticked by, it was clear that Connie's tactic of a dignified silence was not working. Her aunt did not seem to have even noticed.

'Where're you off to?' Connie asked in a hurt voice. Evelyn failed to register her injured tone.

'To a Society meeting,' she replied, ferreting in the fridge and pulling out a large cellophane-wrapped trout.

'What society?'

Darting to the back door, Evelyn added a

mackintosh and wellingtons to her pile and, as a final thought, the scarlet ear protectors.

'What society is it?' Connie repeated.

But her aunt disappeared out of the door to load her ancient Citroën and either did not hear, or did not want to hear, the question.

A small blue boat chugged out to the rocks guarding the entrance to the bay. The stone pillars dwarfed the vessel, towering like giants cloaked against the elements. Col cut the engine some twenty metres short and put on his ear protectors. His passenger, an elderly man with ginger-streaked white hair, sitting with a flask balanced on his lap, followed his example. They had rehearsed the next few moves back on shore in the safety of the Anchor Tavern. All they had to do now was wait for the other two boats to catch up—then they would be ready to face the worst, maybe even death.

Col watched Dr Brock calmly pouring himself some tea. It was a beautiful if breezy evening: the sky still light, though it was almost nine, a sign that summer was not yet forgotten. He wished he could enjoy it as serenely as his passenger, prove his readiness for the test by keeping his nerve under pressure, but he could not stop his heart galloping like a runaway horse as he contemplated the dangers ahead. Their mission was vital: they suspected that men had already lost their lives, lured to their deaths by the irresistible power of the creatures hiding in the rocks. There was a distinct possibility that neither he nor Dr Brock would return. In a few minutes, they might be driven out of their senses and drowned in the merciless waters that surrounded them. With this prospect before him, Col gave up on any attempt at tranquillity and allowed himself to shiver as he gripped the wheel.

Two more boats came into view. At the wheel of the first stood Evelyn Lionheart with Col's grandmother. Both already had their headsets on, taking no chances. Col thought back wryly to the discussion in the Anchor as to whether he was too young to come on such a dangerous mission. His grandmother had argued that Col should learn what he might be up against before he had his first encounter. On shore, Col had been flattered by his grandmother's recognition of his growing maturity; now at sea, bobbing about under the threat of a hidden peril, he had a creeping regret that he had argued so eagerly to come.

He waited as Mr Masterson, the skipper of the third boat, followed Evelyn Lionheart on a course avoiding the sandbars that fringed the Hescombe Channel. Mr Masterson was standing at the wheel in his wellington boots, ill at ease. He was far more at home steering his tractor on his farm than on a boat. His passenger, Horace Little, an elderly West Indian man with grizzled white hair, sat in the stern with binoculars clamped to his eyes, on the watch for any movement in the sky.

Once all the boats were assembled, Dr Brock stood up and reached for a loudhailer. The stiff breeze blowing inshore made it difficult for the skippers to keep their vessels in a ring around the huge stones, known locally as the Stacks. Col cursed under his breath as he revved the engine to nudge *Water Sprite* forward. He had to keep in formation; Dr Brock was depending on him not to let the creatures slip away unseen. Col hoped he would not have to hold position too long—just waiting here was unbearable. He grew very aware of himself: his quick, shallow breaths, his heart throbbing in his chest, the lick of the wind on his skin. If Dr Brock did not do something soon, Col was in danger of disgracing himself by doing something rash to release the tension—yell, laugh, or even leap over the side before the creatures had a chance to lure him there—anything but this awful stillness.

Dr Brock cleared his throat. 'Your Reverences,' he called out to the seemingly empty rocks. 'We are from the Society for the Protection of Mythical Creatures and we request an audience.'

Ear protectors clamped on his ears, Col heard none of this, but he knew what Dr Brock was saying. He scanned the rocks, a bead of sweat trickling from his brow, as he tried to spot the least sign of life.

Dr Brock repeated his call three times, but still there was no movement.

Was that it, wondered Col? After all this feverish anticipation, would they have to return home empty-handed? He could almost laugh at the indignity of their predicament.

'Shall we go?' Col mouthed to Dr Brock.

Dr Brock shook his head, and then bowed it as if in prayer, willing the creatures to respond. So much depended on this moment.

A flutter of wings—a flurry of activity on the rocks. Out of the lengthening shadows darkening the base of the Stacks, eight figures flew up to land—one on each crest. From afar, they looked like huge seagulls, but the members of the Society knew that each had the face of a woman. The sirens had come.

Dr Brock raised his loudhailer to his lips but, before he could speak another word, the sirens

31

launched themselves into the air, bearing down on them like storm clouds driven by a gale. Each siren had a vast wingspan, double that of an albatross. They skilfully cut through the air, white tails spread like fans, wings like scythes. Two headed for Evelyn Lionheart's boat, three to Mr Masterson, and three towards Col and Dr Brock. Skimming over the boats, they wheeled upwards to spiral high overhead, until they looked no more than distant white flecks in the sky.

Were they gone? Had they fled? Col strained to see what was going on, wondering if he could relax.

He got his answer: no. In unison, the sirens snapped their wings close to their bodies and plunged like darts aimed at the heart of each vessel. Col felt a stab of fear in his stomach, gaining unwelcome insight into how a rabbit feels when an eagle plummets out of the sky to pluck it from the ground. Approaching at great speed, the sirens were now close enough for Col to see that their crimson mouths were open in a scream, pale faces blazing with white-hot anger, their bird-claws tearing at the air. There was no need for Dr Brock's frantic signals: Col knew that it was time to turn tail and race for the shore. He revved the engine and swivelled the wheel.

Whoosh! He ducked as a rush of wind gave him a second's warning of the siren's approach. A claw flashed into view. Fiery pain. Something had caught him on the side of the face. He held on to his headset, ripping it away from the clutch of black talons. He glanced up to see the huge grey wings with white undersides swooping out to sea: beautiful but terrible.

Swiftly, Col turned to check his passenger was still on board. On the bow of the boat, Dr Brock was fending off the claws of two sirens. The creatures were mobbing him, intent on tearing the headset from his ears. Col glimpsed their human faces, their beauty distorted with rage: black eyes burning, blue-grey skin gleaming with sea-spray, the nostrils of their long beak-like noses flaring, all surrounded by tendrils of feather-like hair that blew in the air in curling white whips. If they succeeded in taking the ear protectors from him, Dr Brock would be lost. The song of the sirens, once heard, was fatal. It enticed the hearer to throw himself into the sea to reach the singers. No one could stop themselves. Screaming at the boat in terror, Col urged it forward as fast as it would go. Just a little further and surely their attackers must give up? A broad white wake stretched behind as he put as much distance as he could between the boat and the Stacks. At last, as the harbour came into sight, the sirens rose from their prey and hurtled past Col, back to their rocks.

Col pulled the ear protectors from his head and bellowed across to Dr Brock, 'Are you all right?'

Dr Brock staggered to his feet, having been knocked down as a parting gesture. Taking off his headset, he replied breathlessly, 'Unhurt, but I'm afraid I've spilt my tea.'

Shaken to the very core by what he had just witnessed, Col started to laugh with relief. Dr Brock was famous for his cool in the face of the most difficult creatures but this was the first time Col had seen him in action. He was glad Dr Brock would not have heard his terrified cries a few moments before. He was certain the doctor would never have lost control like that and he was ashamed of his weakness.

Back on shore, Col and Dr Brock had an anxious wait for the other boats to return home. Col tried not to think what might have happened to his grandmother and could barely be restrained from taking the boat back out again to find her. Five minutes later, a huge weight lifted from his heart as two boats rounded the harbour wall. Borrowing Dr Brock's binoculars, he saw that they had emerged from the attack without losing anyone. The sirens had been content to scare them away. Bar Dr Brock's ripped jacket and pulled hair, Col was the only one to have been hurt and he was sporting a nasty scratch on his cheek that his grandmother fussed over with some antiseptic cream.

'What do we do now?' asked Mr Masterson. Col noticed that, as the farmer sipped some hot sweet tea from Dr Brock's flask, his hands were still trembling. That made Col feel a bit better.

'I've never known anything like it,' said Mrs Clamworthy. 'Those sirens have been living perfectly peacefully on the Stacks for years. What could have made them turn on us now?'

'That's not so hard to guess,' said Evelyn sourly, kicking an empty petrol can on the marina walkway. 'Oil. It's no coincidence that their change of heart has come as Axoil invades their territory. Do you think the sirens could be behind the disappearance of the refinery workers, Horace?'

Horace Little, the most experienced among them with sea creatures, nodded. 'I think it's very likely, my dear.'

The verdict prompted Dr Brock to reach a decision. He put down his mug. 'This has spiralled out of our control. We don't have the resources in our local chapter to deal with the sirens now they've abandoned our ways. We've got to find out how we can stop them. They risk endangering everything the Society has sought to protect for centuries if they carry on like this.'

'So what do you suggest, Francis?' asked Mrs Clamworthy.

'I think it is time we called in the expert. Does anyone speak Italian?' he replied, raising one eyebrow quizzically.

3
Oil

ON Tuesday morning, Evelyn was subdued. She sat nursing a cup of coffee gloomily, not looking up from the local newspaper when Connie came in for her breakfast. Still angry at being casually abandoned the previous night, Connie was determined to make Evelyn acknowledge her existence for once.

'How was your meeting?' Her aunt only grunted. 'Bad news?' Connie persisted, gesturing to the newspaper as she helped herself to cereal, refusing to let her aunt get away with ignoring her so completely.

Evelyn gave in, perhaps realizing that she was going to get no peace until she replied. 'You could say that,' she said acerbically, pushing the paper over to Connie so she too could see the article that had caused a black cloud to settle on the day.

Connie glanced at the main picture—a group of grinning adults, one dressed in a fur-trimmed cape and chain of office, gathered around a model of a factory. '*Axoil entertains mayor,*' she read. '*Oil company opens its doors to local dignitaries.*' Sounded pretty boring to her but why had this upset her aunt? She looked harder at the photo and noticed one gaunt-faced man at the back staring at the camera as if he was about to strangle the photographer, his glare a strange contrast to the cheery smiles of his companions.

'What's wrong with this?' Connie asked cautiously, pointing to the article.

Evelyn gave a snort of derision. 'Well, it's enough to make anyone sick, but I didn't mean that story. Look at the bottom of the page—the small column in the corner.'

Connie did as she was told and spotted the article tucked away between an advertisement for stair-lifts and another for cruises in the Mediterranean. '*Third Axoil employee goes missing, by Rupa Nuruddin.*'

'Hey, I wonder if that's Anneena's sister!' Connie said excitedly.

Evelyn grimaced. 'Read on,' she said tersely.

'William O'Neill, 37, of Seabrook Caravan Park, failed to return home on Saturday morning. He was last seen by his family leaving for the night shift at the new Axoil oil terminal where he is employed as a welder. Maurice Quick, managing director of Axoil, told this paper that the company has "no record of O'Neill reporting for duty", though a number of O'Neill's colleagues told this paper that they saw him working as usual on the far end of the new sea defences guarding the harbour before the sea-fog obscured their view.

'O'Neill is the third person associated with the construction of the oil refinery to have gone missing in the past six months.'

Connie put the paper down. The article was very brief for such an important story. Surely the paper should have given more space to this than cheesy pictures of some mayor shaking hands with a bunch of suited businessmen? She thought she now understood her aunt's bad mood.

'That's very sad. Do you know him?'

Evelyn shook her head briskly. 'No, I don't. That's not the point.'

Connie swallowed. 'I'm sorry—I don't understand . . .'

She immediately realized that she had said the wrong thing. Her aunt leapt up from the table and marched over to the sink, irritably throwing her cup into the washing-up bowl.

'You're just like all the others, Connie: so shortsighted! Can't you see a disaster looming, even if it's staring you right in the face? How stupid can people get, building an oil refinery here of all places!'

'But what's that to do with the missing man?' Connie asked tentatively, looking back down at the paper. The gaunt man in the photo now seemed to be glaring at her.

Evelyn appeared not to have heard as she attacked her mug with the washing-up brush, shooting soapy water all over the kitchen floor.

'This is only the beginning—you mark my words. We just knew things like this would happen, but did anyone listen when we tried to tell them? And now they're talking about building a new road. Heaven knows with what consequences with so many crea—so many ready to take matters into their own hands.'

'Was that what your meeting was about last night?' Connie made a cautious guess, trying to steer the conversation into calmer waters.

'In a way, yes.' Evelyn gave no more details. She clanged her mug down on the draining board and returned to read the rest of her newspaper, allowing her anger to simmer down. After a moment or two, she added, not looking up: 'We'll be having a guest from Italy to stay, possibly next week, depending on how soon he can get away.'

'Who is he?' Connie was learning to accept the surprises that her aunt had a habit of springing on her without making a protest that she had not been consulted.

'Society member. Italian branch.'

'Is this society an environmental one, like Greenpeace or something?'

'Sort of.'

Connie wondered why her aunt was now smiling grimly as if amused by her question.

'Can I come along to one of your meetings sometime? I'm really interested in the environment.'

'That depends.'

'Depends on what?'

Her aunt thought for a moment, then said, with a sly smile, 'I suppose it depends on who you take after: me or your father.'

This cryptic reply puzzled Connie. What on earth did she mean? Why did she never give her a straight answer? She was fed up with having to tread on eggshells around her aunt without even having clear clues as to what she should do and say.

'And how am I to find that out?' she said, unable to keep the irritation from her voice.

'You don't—we do.'

Yes, Connie decided on her way to school, her aunt was definitely insane, and the Society members sounded equally mad. All that rubbish about them finding out about you before they let you go to a single meeting! She was not sure she wanted to be in their precious Society. In fact, the sooner her parents realized they had left her in the hands of a lunatic, the better. The only thing she would regret if she had to move again was the good start she had made at school. If it weren't for that, she would be on the phone to her parents today, demanding to be removed from Hescombe.

'Hey, Col, where d'you get that scratch?' Connie was standing only a few metres away from Col in the lunch queue and couldn't help overhearing his friends quiz him about his injury.

'Neighbour's cat,' Col replied, rubbing his cheek.

That wasn't right. Connie was sure he was lying. If it had been a cat, the scratches would have been smaller and in parallel. That ugly scar looked as if it had been made by something big.

'And why didn't you come to football club last night?'

'Oh, yeah. Sorry, Justin. Had to go to a Society meeting with Gran. You know, mega-boring, but she wouldn't let me out of it.'

Connie couldn't believe her ears. *Col* was in the crazy Society too?

Justin kicked the wall absent-mindedly. 'You seem to do nothing else at the moment, Col. You'll get dropped from the team if you're not careful.'

'You think?' grinned Col, supremely confident.

'Well, perhaps not,' laughed Justin. 'You're the only half-decent player the school has, Mr Johnson knows that. But he was mad at you.'

Col shrugged. 'I'll get Gran to talk to him. She'll explain.'

Society. Connie itched to ask him about it. Perhaps he'd be more informative than her aunt; at least tell her what she needed to do if she wanted to go along to a meeting. Deciding it was time she had another word with Col, she sought him out after lunch. For once, he was standing on his own, gazing out at the scrap of sea visible from the playground. She thought it would be best to broach the subject indirectly. Best start with a neutral question.

'So, Col, where did you really get that scratch? No cat could possibly make such a mark,' she said in what she hoped was a passable imitation of a cool, careless tone.

He shifted his eyes from the ocean, annoyed by the interruption. He was busy thinking about the sirens, wondering what had become of William O'Neill, and did not want to be bothered by Evelyn Lionheart's niece.

'Er . . . '

'The only thing that could make a mark like that would be something like a bird of prey.' She hoped she would impress him with her knowledge of animals.

Col flinched, reminded of the razor-sharp talons of the sirens and their furious attack. He was also unnerved by Connie's astute guess. 'You know a lot about wildlife, don't you,' he said, trying to move the subject away from his dark thoughts.

She refused the hint. 'Come on, Col: tell me. I know you're lying about the cat.'

'OK, OK.' Perhaps the quickest way to get rid of her was to tell her part of the truth. 'I got it at a Society meeting last night from a very large . . . seabird. We've been patrolling the waters near the Stacks to . . . er . . . to protest about the new refinery and I probably got too near its nesting site. Does that satisfy you?' He sounded exasperated with her and he quickly turned his back.

Connie was far from content: she now had many more questions she wanted to ask.

'How come you were allowed to join this Society?' she asked, dodging in front of him so he could not ignore her.

'What?' Would she not give it a rest, for heaven's sake?

'I asked my aunt if I could go along but she said it was invitation only.'

'You want to come along to the Society?' Col looked at her oddly as if she was talking to him in a foreign language.

'Yes, why not? I'm interested in saving habitats for wildlife too,' she said defensively, her courage beginning to falter under his intense gaze. She wasn't sure if he was laughing at her.

Col's face creased in the same odd smile her aunt had given her that morning. He looked at her properly for the first time.

'Sure. You seem the type—you'll know what I mean if you get to meet the others. We're a bit busy at the moment—bit of a crisis really—but when things settle down in a couple of weeks, your aunt can ask the assessors to have a look at you.' There—that should get rid of her.

The bell went for the end of break. Col hurried back to the class leaving Connie trailing in his wake. She wondered what it would be like to be a member of the Society after all. If Col was in it, it couldn't be completely full of weirdos—he was too cool for that. There was definitely something special about the people in the Society she'd met so far, not that she could describe what it was exactly. And a society that went on evening boat picnics sounded fun. She was sure she'd be able to tell them how not to upset the seabirds if they went out again. After all, understanding animals was the very thing she was good at.

Back in the classroom, Connie sat down next to Anneena. Mr Johnson called the class to order.

'Right, you lot, listen up. I want each of you this term to do a project on a subject of local interest for an end of term display. You can work in groups or singly as you wish. I've jotted a few sample ideas on the board. Copy them down and see if any of them take your fancy. I'll then ask if anyone has any ideas of their own that they'd like to pursue.'

'What were you talking to Col about, Connie?' Anneena probed, getting out her pencil case. 'What's going on?'

'Nothing's going on,' Connie whispered so as not to catch Mr Johnson's attention.

'Oh come on: it's clear you two were up to something,' Anneena hissed back. Connie realized that she was as persistent as a thrush bashing a

snail against a stone when she wished to crack a secret.

'I suppose you know about the campaign against the oil refinery?'

Anneena nodded. 'Of course. Rupa's been following all the local stories about Axoil. She thinks there's something fishy happening at the refinery.'

'I saw her article. I wondered if she was related to you.'

'You did?' Anneena glowed with pride. 'Well, Rupa had real trouble getting them to print even that short piece. She thinks her boss is scared of being sued for libel.'

'Well, my aunt and Col are involved in a group campaigning about the refinery—he's been helping out after school. They were on some kind of protest last night out at those rocks everyone calls the Stacks. I think it's where he got that scratch.'

'Oh, is that it?' Anneena asked, her eyes twinkling with curiosity. It wasn't only her older sister who had a nose for an interesting story. 'What was he doing?'

'Anneena, are you going to share with the rest of the class what you and Connie are whispering about, or are you going to do some work?' Mr Johnson said loudly, coming to stand behind them.

Connie had come to expect that Anneena would rarely be lost for words. Looking the teacher straight in the eye, she said a little cheekily, 'I'm very happy to share with the class what we've been talking about. It's very important—for everyone in Hescombe, that is.'

'Oh yes?' Mr Johnson said sceptically.

'We were talking about the Stacks and what we could do to protect them from Axoil tankers,' Anneena said piously. Connie flushed with embarrassment and glanced over at Col. He sat up as if he had been stung and looked daggers in her direction. The last thing he needed was for the whole class to be interested in the wildlife of the Stacks. It would be a disaster if they started asking questions that led to the discovery of the sirens. In contrast to Col's hostile gaze, Mr Johnson beamed down at the girls in delight, rapidly switching from reproof to praising Anneena's subject. As he turned away to address the entire class, Anneena grinned at Connie.

'Connie and Anneena are quite right: we should take an interest in these things,' Mr Johnson announced. 'That's exactly the sort of subject we need. Once it's finished, the new Axoil refinery is going to have a profound effect on our local community—that means on you and me. Let's use it as an example of how you can work up your

project ideas. I want you to divide into groups of four. Discuss what your group thinks would be an interesting way of covering the opening of the new refinery in our area. Put down your ideas to share them with the rest of the class. Off you go. You've got ten minutes.'

As quick as a flash, before he could be asked to join other groups, Col left his table and came over to Connie. Jane Benedict, sitting on the other side of Anneena, made up the fourth. Connie and Anneena exchanged surprised glances at Col's sudden move.

'Hi, Col. Nice of you to join us,' Anneena said. 'Don't usually see you this side of the classroom.'

'No. You don't usually have anything to say that I want to hear,' flashed back Col, giving Connie a poisonous look.

Anneena was momentarily taken aback, wondering what had caused Col to be so hostile, but she never let anything daunt her for long. 'Well, you might be surprised. Shall I write things down?' She picked up her pink gel pen and looked expectantly at her three companions. Connie and Jane readily agreed; Col stared out of the window, as if he was only half there. The others took his silence as agreement. 'Right then. Where shall we start? I think we should do something to find out what people really think about the refinery instead of all this brainwashing that Axoil is putting in the local press.' Connie watched with amazement as Anneena roughed out three columns, heading them: 'local government', 'media—radio and print', and 'local industry'. Jane chipped in with the addition of 'local community', making four headings.

'Hey, you two are good at this,' said Col with an ironic grin. 'Done it before, have you?' He had come over to hear how much Connie would say about his injury, but as she had not raised the subject, he was now enjoying himself watching his classmates doing all the work. Perhaps his decision to cross the classroom hadn't been so rash after all as it looked as if the girls were sparing him the effort of thinking.

'Of course,' said Anneena. 'My dad asked me to help him draw up a plan to publicize the restaurant last year. We had to start by finding out what people knew about it already. Jane helped with the web page.' She tapped her pad of paper with her pen, looking at what they had written down. 'What do you two think?' she asked, realizing that Col and Connie had been silent so far.

'Good of you to ask,' laughed Col, rocking lazily back on his chair.

Connie hesitated then said, 'But what about the Stacks? What I want to know is how can we make sure that oil tankers don't go too near and disturb the wildlife?' She was thinking about Scark and the other seagulls who she knew nested on these inaccessible rocks.

'Hmm.' Anneena thought for a moment. 'I think we'd have to go to the company and ask what they're doing about it—get a promise on record that they won't harm them. It may give us a chance to ask them about something else too.'

Knowing her friend well, Jane was not deceived by Anneena's throw-away remark. 'What else?' she asked suspiciously.

'Oh, I don't know. Like the missing men, for instance,' said Anneena, her light tone failing to disguise her excitement.

Col sat up with a clatter as his chair legs hit the floor. 'I don't think that's a good idea,' he said firmly. Hadn't Horace said the sirens might be responsible for the disappearances? Too many questions would put them at risk.

'Why ever not?' challenged Anneena. 'Rupa's not been able to get inside the building to ask them; they're no longer returning her calls; we could help.'

'No. Absolutely not.'

Connie stared at Col in astonishment. She had never seen him so serious about anything before. He usually treated lessons as a bit of a joke.

'What's got into you, Col?' mocked Anneena. 'Afraid?'

Col grabbed the pad from her and scored a thick line through 'Interview with company'. Afraid? If only she knew the half of it! 'I said no,' he said fiercely.

Anneena snatched the pad back and was about to make a tart response when the teacher called them to order.

'Right, time's up,' called Mr Johnson. 'Let's hear your ideas.'

The offerings from the other groups were uninspired. Nobody seemed to have thought of much beyond drawing a few boring pictures of ships and oil refineries. Mr Johnson turned to Anneena.

'My hopes rest with your group. Have you got anything else to contribute, Anneena?'

'Well, sir,' she began, standing up, reading off her pad. 'Col, Connie, Jane, and I thought we should find out what people think about the refinery and the local environment. To get to grips with all sides of the argument, we thought it would be a good idea to take a survey of local opinion, and then interview the company.'

'No we didn't!' Col hissed.

'Excellent,' said Mr Johnson as he scribbled Anneena's ideas down on the whiteboard. He stood back to admire them. 'I think this will really capture this moment in time in our local history.

'Do you know, girls—and Col, of course—I think you should take this on as a project for the term. I particularly like your idea of interviewing the company in person—that'll make a good centrepiece for your contribution to the display. I'll help you if need be. Draw up your list of questions for the company and let me see them next week. And now, who's going to take on the history of the lighthouse for me?'

The teacher turned his attention to the rest of the class. Col was fuming: Anneena had trapped him into doing the very last thing in the world he wanted. The three girls looked at him warily. Unexpectedly, they had become stuck with Col. The uncrowned king of the class had been partnered with some of its least cool characters. Well, it was too late to do anything about it now. They would have to get along somehow, even if he did look as if he was going to make a start by strangling one of his team mates.

The following Tuesday, an elegant leather suitcase by the back door announced that Number Five Shaker Row had a guest. Evelyn was serving coffee to the stranger at the kitchen table when

Connie came in from school, their conversation stopping abruptly on her arrival.

'Oh, Connie. Our guest has arrived today, as you see. This is Signor Antonelli,' her aunt said, waving the coffee pot in the direction of the newcomer. Looking uncharacteristically embarrassed, Evelyn sat down quickly behind an ostentatious bouquet of flowers, a gift from her visitor.

Connie nodded shyly to the Italian. Signor Antonelli was a short round ball of a man, with sleek black hair swept back from his forehead and a luxuriant beard. He bounded to his feet as Connie entered and swooped down on her to seize her hand.

'*Carina*, I am enchanted to meet you!' he said in broken English, bowing over her hand to kiss it. He pulled up, touching her fingertips with his warm fingers. 'But your leetle hand is frozen!' Then, quite bizarrely and unexpectedly, he burst into song. A powerful, beautiful voice boomed from his chest like the cry of the bittern. '*Che gelida manina*,' he sang, smiling into her bewildered face. He let the last note ring out in the kitchen and bowed again, this time as if to imaginary applause. He turned to Evelyn. 'Your daughter 'as no gloves, signorina?' He clucked his tongue disapprovingly.

'Niece, Signor Antonelli, she's my niece,'

Evelyn quickly corrected him with mounting embarrassment. She looked anxiously at Connie as if imploring her not to laugh at their guest. Connie had never seen her look so uncomfortable.

'Is she one of us?' he asked.

'No.'

'She 'as da look.'

Evelyn nodded. 'Perhaps. But we've not had time to find out. Connie's only been here a week.'

Somehow Connie felt sure they were talking about the Society. She was pleased that Signor Antonelli mentioned that she had 'da look'; Col had said something similar. Not knowing quite what to make of this strange little man, she took a seat at the table, wondering what was going on.

'When will we leave for boats?' he asked Evelyn, sitting down on the chair next to Connie with a flourish of his coat tails like a pianist taking his seat at a grand piano.

'A few hours yet. It's a busy time of day just now, what with the day-trippers coming back and the fishermen going out. We'll wait till the evening.' Evelyn threw a significant look in Connie's direction—Connie was sure she was signalling to him to be quiet.

'*Certo.*' He then tactfully but rather obviously changed the subject. ''Ave you ever been to Italia, *carina?*'

55

Connie shook her head. Signor Antonelli began to tell her about his home, Sorrento, a seaside town near Naples. He paused for a moment, rose to his feet, and then broke into a jaunty Neapolitan song, bouncing on the balls of his feet with every beat. Connie sat transfixed. She had never before met anyone who seemed to regard singing as interchangeable with talking.

Coming to the end of his rendition, he said in explanation: 'Now you 'ave a picture of my home—more good than words—more good than paint.'

Connie smiled encouragingly and helped herself to a glass of juice. Perhaps this nice man would give more details about the Society than she had so far been able to extract from her aunt? He certainly seemed less buttoned-up than Evelyn.

'And what does the Society do there?' Connie asked.

'We watch after an ancient temple,' he said, his warm brown eyes smiling back at her, but Connie thought she could sense a guard had gone up in their depths.

'Is that threatened too, like the Stacks?'

'No . . . but in a way, yes. My English is not so good enough to explain. I am sorry.'

The signor deftly turned the conversation to what Connie thought of Hescombe and what her family were like. Connie dutifully answered him but with growing frustration as she failed to get any more information. She doubted very much that Signor Antonelli's English was inadequate for what he wanted to say: Connie suspected that he had stopped because he would only tell others in the Society. And, as her aunt had made all too clear, Connie was still on the outside of these secrets.

Evelyn and Signor Antonelli departed at around seven to go to the quay, leaving Connie to another lonely evening with just the television for company. Even Madame Cresson was out hunting. Half-watching a programme about trainee vets, Connie wondered if Col would be allowed to go out again, feeling envious that he was in all likelihood part of this mysterious expedition. What did they hope to achieve by going to the Stacks a second time? They'd just disturb the birds again. How could that possibly help their cause? And what had the Italian to do with it anyway?

The boats limped back into port as the first stars came out. A chill breeze blew inland ruffling Col's hair like ghostly fingers. A light grey mist had settled over the sea like a shroud. Standing on the quay with his binoculars, Col could make out six figures in the boats. He heaved a sigh of relief: they were all back safely then. He had not been allowed to go out since the siren attack—too dangerous, his grandmother had said—so he had spent a frustrating evening keeping watch at the harbour. The boats seemed to take for ever to sail home. As he waited, an emergency siren sounded close by. He turned round to see a police car screech to a halt on the quayside right behind him, blue lights revolving frantically on its roof. Another siren wailed in the distance and a white ambulance emerged from the High Street.

'What the—?' murmured Col.

'Stand aside, son,' said a policeman as he began to unroll a reel of blue and white tape, cordoning off a section of the marina where *Water Sprite* usually had her berth.

'Hey, that's my grandmother's mooring!' Col objected. 'She's just coming in.'

'We know,' said the policeman as his colleague moved to push back the small crowd that was gathering. 'She'll no doubt explain everything when she gets here. Just stand to one side for the moment, please.'

Col fell back, but only as far as the mooring for *Banshee*. The boats were now only metres away. He could see Dr Brock standing on the bow of *Water*

Sprite in readiness to tie up; his grandmother was at the wheel.

Col waved to Evelyn in *Banshee* and caught the rope she threw to him. Signor Antonelli was sitting beside her, his head in his hands.

'Everyone OK?' he asked Evelyn anxiously, unable to see his grandmother clearly in the gathering gloom as the policemen jumped on board *Water Sprite*.

'Not exactly,' said Evelyn.

'What?' exclaimed Col. Horace—Mr Masterson: everyone seemed to be there. 'Did they attack again?'

'No,' she replied guardedly. She tapped Signor Antonelli on the shoulder to rouse him and Col offered him a hand as he climbed from the boat. Out of the corner of his eye, Col could see the policemen bending over a blanket mound on the deck of his grandmother's boat.

'We heard not a sound this time,' continued Evelyn in a low voice. 'Floated about for a good half hour before calling it a day. Signor Antonelli sang himself hoarse trying to raise them.'

'So what's all this about?' asked Col, gesturing to the police.

'Dey 'ave killed 'im!' burst out Signor Antonelli, close to tears.

'Killed who?' asked Col desperately, double-checking that everyone was safe.

'Col,' said Evelyn in a voice like steel as she gripped his arm, 'we did not see the sirens but they sent us a message this time—a very clear message. It's exactly as we feared. They've been killing Axoil employees. We've found one: they've sent us his body.'

Col turned his eyes back to the blanket just as one of the policemen lifted the corner to look at the dead man's face. Col felt sick: he could still see the expression of rapture that had been on the man's face as he drowned.

'Come,' said Evelyn, turning her eyes away.

'But how can they do this!' Col exclaimed in disbelief. 'And we're trying to help them!'

Signor Antonelli appeared to have regained some of his composure. He took Col's other arm to help Evelyn tow him away from the scene.

'It is *natura—la natura* of *le sirene*. Do you blame cat for killing mouse? No. We are mouses to them. Mouses who 'ave tried to drive them from their home.'

Col shuddered.

'I know it is 'ard—very 'ard to comprehend. But we deal with wild creatures—not pets. And they no understand that we in the Society try to help them.'

A quarter of an hour later, in Mrs Clamworthy's

kitchen, the Society members sat around the table in silence. The vision of the dead man hovered over them like a ghost. They all knew they had failed him. Dr Brock sighed deeply.

'Now you see, Luciano, what we are up against,' he said. 'The refinery opens for business very soon. Hundreds of tankers of crude oil will be passing through these waters unaware of the danger, flocking to a place where deaths have already happened—and the sirens are understandably angry. They feel they have been hounded from place to place. Now that their last sanctuary is being violated, they are refusing to move again. These three deaths are only the start: we're told by other creatures that the sirens have threatened to use their powers to bring about a catastrophe—an all-out assault on the refinery. The sirens feel they have nothing to lose. But we disagree. Not only do they threaten massive loss of life to unfortunate humans and innocent animals swept up in any disaster, the sirens also risk exposure: the very thing our Society was set up to prevent. Exposure of mythical creatures leads to investigation: investigation inevitably to eradication. We needed your help to persuade them. They won't listen to us any more. We've no idea why they've suddenly taken against our ways and opted for the path of violence.'

In the silence that followed, Col noticed the frantic ticking of a small clock on the mantelpiece. It was intensely annoying, unnaturally loud at this tense moment. He was tempted to get up and remove it from the room but dared not be the first to break the hush. Then Signor Antonelli spoke, his voice gruff after his recent fruitless efforts.

'They no come when I called. They are too angry and only a *vero*—a true—companion can speak to them in dis—'ow you say?—dis state. 'Ow do I know this? Each *colonia* of *sirene* is distinct. *Le sirene* from Capri: when they are afraid, they speak only to me—they want no one else. From what you say, dis ones are linked to your seagulls. I am no companion to that *familia*. But your *sirene*—I feel their fear: they are filled with a . . . with a *furia profondissima* . . . a terrible fury. They be a danger to anyone—*idiota*—who meet them at this time.'

The image of the most recent victim bobbed to the surface of everyone's thoughts—a grim piece of flotsam. Dr Brock rubbed his forehead as if trying to relieve the tension that had come to roost there. 'We seem to be at something of a dead-end. It's suicide for someone who isn't a siren companion to go out to the Stacks now. We have no one in our local chapter of the Society, as you must realize. The nearest we have is Evelyn: she's companion to the banshees—but if you can't talk to them, what hope is there for her? Col is as yet unassigned but we think his calling is to the pegasi. Sirens are very rare in England and I do not think I have met a companion able to speak to them since the last universal companion died ten years ago.'

Mrs Clamworthy clucked her tongue. 'And we can't pin our hopes on another of them coming along: we only see one in a century or so here in Britain,' she muttered aside to Col.

'What should we look for in a siren companion?' asked Mr Masterson.

'A rapport with the bird-species, the usual signs of a second order companion,' answered Signor Antonelli briskly.

Mr Masterson shook his head. 'That's no one I know,' he said.

Dr Brock dropped his hand from his forehead, a memory suddenly returning. 'There was this bird-girl though,' he muttered, half in thought. 'I saw her a few days ago. A day-tripper probably, but she was definitely at least a second order companion from the way she played with the seagulls. I was going to mention it but other events intervened.'

The others, who had been slumped in dejection, all sat up.

'What was she like?' asked Evelyn eagerly.

Dr Brock wrinkled his brow in an effort to remember. 'I'm hopeless at this sort of thing. Young—yes, definitely very young. Younger than Col, I'd guess. Dressed like all young people— jeans, you know the sort of thing.' He faltered.

'Great,' said Evelyn, unable to keep the hint of irritation out of her voice. 'A young girl in jeans, shouldn't be hard to find.'

Dr Brock looked apologetic. 'I warned you I'm not very good at remembering these details, but I do remember the birds.'

'Are you sure she wasn't local?' Evelyn asked.

Did she have to be quite so touchy, Col wondered. She had been in a bad mood ever since her niece had been dumped on her, cramping her freedom to see the banshees. And everyone knew that banshee companions were not the most sociable of people even at the best of times.

'We're a small community and I know nearly all the children. I'd not seen her before: that I am sure of,' Dr Brock reiterated patiently. 'Besides, I think she got back on a coach.'

A disappointed groan went up from all those gathered. Col thought for a moment of Connie: could it be her? But then, she was the same age as him, not younger, and her gift seemed to be with small mammals, like the gerbils at school. Should he say something? He cleared his throat to interrupt the adults, but his grandmother spoke first.

'There is only one thing for it. We must ask the seagulls themselves for a better description. My water sprites can speak to them for us.'

'Good idea, Lavinia,' said Doctor Brock. He checked his watch. 'If you would be so kind as to do that tonight, I suggest we gather here tomorrow evening to find out if there is any news. Will that be enough time?' Mrs Clamworthy nodded. 'Right. Thank you all for your good work tonight under very trying circumstances. I'll see you tomorrow.'

The meeting broke up and the guests began putting on their coats. Col felt the moment to say something had passed. It had probably been a stupid idea anyway—Connie could not have a gift both for four-legged and winged creatures at the same time, if she had any gift at all. Nobody could.

4

Water Sprites

AS it was already very late, Col went with his grandmother to keep her company on the dark paths out to the home of the water sprites. The sprites lived on the wooded slopes of the moors where the springs broke out from the escarpment above Hescombe. In these little valleys, the streams were particularly clear, containing nothing but rainwater and as yet unpolluted by farming or factories. Not that Col would see any of this tonight: it was pitch black under the trees and he could only tell the streams were there by the gentle bubbling of water running over stones. This expedition was a rare treat for him as his grandmother normally spoke to the water sprites on her own: the presence of another human—even her grandson—made the creatures wary and suspicious.

Mrs Clamworthy shone a flashlight onto a large stone that jutted out over the water.

'This is the place,' she said. 'Stand back a little, Col, and try not to move too much, there's a dear.'

Col did as he was told and stood apart to watch his grandmother. She switched off the torch and allowed herself time for her eyes to get used to the night. Once Col had also adjusted to the darkness, he realized that everything was bathed in a wash of pearly light provided by a nearly full moon. He could make out the water quite clearly now as it flowed from jet-black pools over sparkling miniature waterfalls. He watched with bated breath as his grandmother stepped out onto the stone and began to hum softly, her frothy white hair gleaming in the moonlight. The strange tune ran on with seemingly no beginning or end, gathering tempo then slowing to a gentle croon. It came to Col's mind that the tune was like the stream, ever-changing but somehow always the same. Mrs Clamworthy fell quiet and they both waited in the silence that followed.

After a few moments, Col's heart leapt—shapes were rising out of the stream. Though their substance changed continually, like water bubbling out of a fountain, the water sprites held the form of slender people, about two feet tall. Their bodies mirrored the dark sky but the moonlight reflecting from rippling skin revealed trailing hair, long fingers, and solemn eyes. Their faces were oddly distorted, as if their features were being viewed through a glass of water.

Mrs Clamworthy stretched out her hand, palm downwards, and the nearest sprite touched it lightly with its fingertip. The touch wrought a complete change: its flowing body suddenly turned to spiky solidity as if it had become ice. Its features became sharply defined: a long pointed nose and dark eyes like wet pebbles. It stepped out of the water to stand by the woman it acknowledged as a water sprite companion.

Mrs Clamworthy and the sprite began to sing together the same rising and ebbing tune she had used to call them to her. Col did not understand the words but he thought he could follow the drift of the singers. His grandmother's eyes were closed in concentration, her tone pleading and anxious. Col guessed she was explaining the need to identify the bird-girl. The sprite, whose song rippled underneath, supporting and supplementing the companion's tune, was soothing her, giving her a musical caress like a stream gently smoothing the tangled tresses of water weed. Col deduced that the sprite was willing to help, if only to take

68

away the disquiet felt by its friend. The song faded away; the water sprite broke its touch with the companion and flowed back to mingle with the stream, taking the other sprites with it.

'So, that's all right,' Mrs Clamworthy said to Col with relief when the sprites had gone. 'Issoon has promised to run down to speak to the gulls for me when they come to drink. We should have an answer by tomorrow.'

'That's great, Gran,' Col replied softly, still feeling awed by the meeting he had just witnessed. 'That's great.'

Taking her by the arm, he helped her carefully back down the shadowy paths to where they had left the car.

Connie, Anneena, Jane, and Col met in Anneena's kitchen after school on Wednesday to devise their questions for the oil company. Col had been difficult to pin down, pleading a prior commitment, but finally had admitted he could spare the girls a few hours.

'I have to be somewhere at six,' he said moodily as he flung his sports bag into a corner. 'I only came to tell you that I don't think we should do this.'

'Come on, Col,' urged Anneena, 'this is really important. Mr Johnson has said he'd try and get us in to see the company if we come up with some good questions.'

'That's what I'm afraid of.'

Connie felt a flash of annoyance towards him. Like everyone else in that Society, he seemed to forget that there were other people interested in doing something to save their local wildlife.

'I'll come only if you lay off questions about the missing men,' he said, throwing himself into a chair.

'Col!' protested Anneena. 'That's the most interesting stuff. Didn't you see Rupa's article about them finding the body of O'Neill?'

'Course I did,' muttered Col. 'I was there, wasn't I?'

'You were there?' asked Jane, turning her eyes towards him with an appalled expression.

'Yeah. It was Gran and her friends that pulled him out of the water. It was sick.'

Connie was stunned at this news. Evelyn hadn't said anything but she must have been there too— yet another secret her aunt was keeping from her. The revelation momentarily silenced Anneena, but it would take more than a drowned man to deter her when she had her mind set on something.

'Well, then: now you know how important it is to get Axoil to own up to the problem. They're pretending it's nothing to do with them—they claim that the men never even made it to work—but Rupa's sure they're lying.'

'But why lie about something like this?' asked Connie.

Anneena looked at her in disbelief.

'Because it's terrible publicity for them, of course—hardly the jolliest background to the opening of a new oil refinery. And if it turns out the men are falling into the sea at work, the employer is responsible. Health and safety. Surely even you've heard of that?'

Connie nodded vaguely.

'They could be prosecuted or be sued by the families,' Jane explained quietly.

'And it's nothing to do with us,' Col interrupted waspishly. 'Let's make up some questions if we must, but we stick to an agreed list, OK? No detours into stuff that is none of our business.'

Anneena said nothing, but her lips were pressed tightly together. Jane, ever the peacemaker, looked from one to the other. 'OK, Col, we won't ask if you're not happy about it.'

'Oh, won't we?' muttered Anneena.

'No, we won't,' said Jane firmly. 'We work as a team, remember, Anneena? We can still ask them about the Stacks and the local protest—there's lots of interesting things for us to cover.'

With bad grace, Anneena gave in. 'All right. Here's what we've come up with so far.' She put a list of questions down on the table. Col pointed to the first one.

'Let's start with an easy one—something to get them to think of us as silly little kids—it might help us get better answers to the real stuff on the Stacks.'

Connie wrinkled her nose at his suggestion. 'Silly little kids? Are you sure we want them to think we're stupid?'

Col nodded. 'Quite sure.' The others agreed, so Connie fell silent.

'How about,' Jane suggested, 'some dumb question as to what a refinery does?'

'Good idea,' fired back Col.

'What *does* a refinery do?' Connie queried.

Anneena and Col groaned.

'Turns crude oil into stuff you can put in your car,' explained Jane patiently. 'You can't use it straight from the ground—it has to be processed to be any good.'

'And Jane should know,' Anneena butted in, 'because her dad works in it, doesn't he?'

Jane nodded. 'Yes. I told him about our project: he was really interested. He suggested we write directly to Mr Quick, the managing director.'

Connie hadn't known this before. She looked sideways at Jane, wondering if, with all these missing men, she was worried for her father. If it were Connie's father who worked there, she would be worried sick that one day he wouldn't come home.

'Won't it be a bit awkward for your dad if we turn up asking difficult questions?' ventured Connie.

Jane shrugged. 'I don't think so—not unless we're rude or something—and we won't be, will we?' She looked confidently around at Anneena and Connie and then with less certainty at Col.

'Course not,' Col remarked. 'You can count on me to be the soul of discretion—as usual. After I've taken the managing director in a headlock and told him how rubbish his company is, I'll be sure to apologize very politely,' he joked.

The girls laughed nervously. His presence in their project team added a maverick element they could not control.

It did not take long to finish the questions. Col bolted for the door at the first opportunity, leaving Jane volunteering to word-process them that evening at home.

'I'll look up the company on the web,' she said, gathering the notes together, 'see what they say in public about the environment, wildlife, and all that stuff. We might find something to quote back at them.'

'And don't worry about Col,' Connie said reassuringly to Jane now that he had gone. 'I'm sure it'll be just fine. He may be a bit . . . a bit . . .'

'Full of himself?' suggested Anneena. Col's blocking of her plan to investigate the missing men still rankled.

'Yes,' said Connie, 'that's it—but his heart is in the right place. He won't get your dad into trouble.'

'It has to be her!' Evelyn exclaimed. 'Who else in Hescombe has hair like that?'

Col was standing outside the back door of his house, eavesdropping on the conversation within. He had heard excited voices and had paused to listen to what was going on.

'Yes, indeed, the sprites were quite clear about that.' That was his grandmother's voice, bubbling over with joy. 'I knew there was something special about the girl the moment I set eyes on her.'

A murmur of voices followed as the meeting broke up into the buzz of separate conversations. After a minute or two, Mrs Clamworthy called them to order.

'However, there is something I want to add. The sprites also said that the seagulls are angry with us. It seems they do not want us near the Stacks. I don't know why, but once they found out from the sprites that it was us who were asking after a companion to sirens, they quite dried up and would not tell the water sprites any more. That's why we've only got this sketchy description to go on.'

'But it's enough from what you say, Evelyn,' interjected Dr Brock. 'We'll have to ponder the mystery of the seagulls' anger another time. We have lives to save. Now we must send for your niece.'

Col chose this moment to clatter into the kitchen.

'Col, you've arrived at a most exciting time,' his grandmother said eagerly. 'My water sprites have given me a description of a girl just like Evelyn's Connie. It has to be her—the family connection, everything, seems to point that way.'

Col was silent for a moment. Connie Lionheart—that shy protégée of Anneena's—a companion to sirens? He'd thought of it first, he remembered, but had dismissed it as ridiculous. And what about the gerbils?

'I wouldn't be so sure,' he said with forced casualness. 'It seems to me from what I've seen at school that Connie's gift lies with the four-legged creatures.' He had their attention—the jubilant faces were beginning to dim.

'What do you think, Evelyn?' Dr Brock asked, turning to his neighbour.

Evelyn Lionheart nodded. 'It's true—I was getting carried away. Connie clearly has a special relationship with my cat. Perhaps Col's right: she might have a gift, but not the one we need right now. She may well fall into the Company of the Two-Fours. Perhaps, Dr Brock, you did only see a day-tripper: we may have been leaping to conclusions on the slimmest of evidence.'

Dr Brock turned next to the Italian. 'What do you think, signor? Have you sensed anything about the girl?'

Signor Antonelli scratched his beard thoughtfully. 'I 'ave no 'eard 'er sing. Does she sing?'

Evelyn shrugged. 'Not that I've noticed. She keeps herself to herself at home.'

Horace Little leant over to Evelyn and patted her wrist.

'We must assess her—put the matter to rest once and for all,' he said in his velvet-toned voice.

Col remembered his own assessment only the year before—the mystery, the confusion: only trust in his grandmother had made him go through with it. 'But how are you going to explain all this to Connie?' he asked. 'She's said once or twice she's interested in the Society but she doesn't have a clue what that really means. Won't it be a bit much to spring it on her?'

'Can't we tell her something about all this?' queried Evelyn, looking to Dr Brock.

He sighed. 'The rules of the Society forbid us to explain our business to others—even a prospective member—before they have been assessed. We all know the reasons for this, of course: for the protection of those creatures we have sworn to defend.'

Mrs Clamworthy made a noise that sounded very like 'pish'.

Dr Brock raised a bushy white eyebrow. 'I agree, Lavinia: the Society is apt to be rather bureaucratic and secretive in its approach these days.'

'Bureaucratic!' burst out Mrs Clamworthy. 'The new breed of officials are so tied up in red tape, I'm surprised they can even get out of the boardroom without tripping up! It wasn't always like that.'

There was a murmur of assent from Horace Little. 'Before I retired, we assessors never worried so much about the rules when we needed more latitude,' he added.

'We could get someone to test her at the encounter weekend,' suggested Mrs Clamworthy. She turned to Signor Antonelli to explain. 'A number of our young members—including Col here—' (she looked at her grandson proudly) 'are having their first encounter this Saturday. One of the mentors is an assessor, I believe.'

'What do you think, Evelyn? Col? Will it work?' Dr Brock queried.

Col shrugged. Connie's aunt shook her head doubtfully. 'I don't see we have much choice,' Evelyn said at last. 'It's a long shot but lives are at stake and we need to know.'

'Right. I'll leave it to you and Col to prepare the way. We'll suggest Sunday to the assessor—if that's convenient?'

'Why not?' Evelyn agreed; with those two words deciding her niece's future.

Cycling home from Anneena's, Connie called in at the quay. There was no reason to hurry, as she was sure she would be spending another evening alone with the television while her aunt was off on some adventure with her Society, sparing not a thought for her. She leaned her bike against a bollard and doubled over to regain her breath: she'd just finished an enormous curry, wickedly hot and incredibly filling.

Straightening up, she looked around for Scark but he was not there. Strange, this was just the time of day she would expect to see him hopping around the quay, pecking at the bits of bait and sandwich crusts left by the tourists.

Then she heard the rush of wings and cries from a flock of seagulls coming in from the ocean.

Connie turned with delight to meet them and saw that they were not flying in their usual looping dance above the waves, but heading straight for shore with fierce determination. She ducked as they swooped down and wheeled around, like so many silver arrows guided by a single purpose, raking the foreshore.

'Stop! Stop!' Connie yelled, running into the midst of the flock. What had caused them to behave in this angry fashion? On seeing Connie, the birds began to circle around her in a spiral. Their mood changed. Connie looked up and saw their exultant dance. Instinctively, she raised her arms, turning slowly, yearning to fly up through the funnel of wings over her head and go with them out to sea. If Dr Brock had been in the shelter today, he would have seen Connie, barely visible in the blizzard of birds, her long black hair shaken back and sparking with its strange static energy. She was transformed: gone was the quiet, shy schoolgirl and in her place was a being of power. But Dr Brock was at this moment sitting in a kitchen, unaware that the Society's questions could have been answered by a short stroll to the sea.

The whirling birds untwisted themselves from the dance and settled on the ground and on the water around Connie. The largest one came to rest on a lifebuoy. A smaller gull, still with remnants of a chick's grey plumage speckling her wings, glided to perch beside Connie.

Scark fluttered his wings once before tucking them away. His daughter followed his example.

'Why did you do that? Fly in like that, I mean?' Connie asked him. Scark shook his beak angrily. 'What? You're angry with someone?' The seagull tapped the lifebuoy with a foot—a sign of assent. 'Who? Not that boy you attacked the other day?' Scark tapped his foot. 'He only went to your nesting sites because that Society of his was trying to help.'

On the mention of the Society, Scark suddenly spread his wings, flapping them madly, sounding his mewing cry.

'I know they've been disturbing your nesting sites out on the Stacks, but I can help them with that—I'll tell them not to get too close. Besides, all your young have grown up by now, haven't they?' Connie scratched the head of Scark's daughter, a gull Connie had named Mew, as she nuzzled her hand, searching for crumbs.

Scark shook his beak again and then began a series of moves Connie could not follow. He seemed to be pointing at the other seagulls and then at Connie, repeating it over and over.

'Oh, Scark, I don't understand. But I think you're not happy that the Society is going out to the Stacks. Am I right about that at least?' A foot tapped. 'I'll tell them not to. But you know they are only trying to save the rocks from a worse danger. Men will soon be bringing great ships through the Hescombe Channel. Your nesting sites are at risk.'

Scark lifted his beak and shook it in the air. Was this despair? Anger?

'I'm sorry, Scark. I feel so powerless. But there's nothing I can do about it.'

The seagull fixed her with his beady eye. Connie felt speared by his uncompromising stare.

'You mean I haven't even tried?' she said gloomily. 'You're right, of course, but at the moment I really can't see what I can do about it.' Scark wailed. 'You think there is something I can do?' He tapped his foot. 'But what is it?'

She got no answer. Either it was too difficult for the bird to sign to her or he was not ready to tell. Scark flapped his wings and launched himself off the lifebuoy. On this signal, Mew and the rest of the flock rose like a curtain of beating wings and followed him back out to sea.

5

Pegasus

The few days that followed were strangely calm: there were no more mysterious disappearances, no sign of the sirens, but Col still feared it was the calm before the storm. In any event, he had his own personal storm cloud on the horizon: his first encounter loomed ever nearer and, as a consequence, he found it difficult to concentrate at school. Everyone noticed—even Mr Johnson.

'What, no quips this week, Col?' the teacher asked, catching Col at the beginning of one break. 'I've got used to your jokes and—despite me usually being the butt of them—I find I miss them. Nothing wrong, I hope?'

Col knew what Mr Johnson was thinking. Col's

parents, both extreme examples of members of the Society, had the habit of breezing into Hescombe and disrupting everyone's life—and if they happened to arrive at the same time, all hell was let loose. He felt resentful that they both treated him like a hobby that they could pick up and put down as it suited them, and yet he knew they were too thick-skinned to notice the effect this had on him. But that was not this week's problem—this week he was wondering if his gift would be confirmed on Saturday or not. He felt a painful lump in his throat whenever he considered the possibility that he might fail: there had been cases like that in the past—maybe he would be the next one?

'No, nothing's wrong,' Col replied evasively. 'Just a bit busy with something, that's all.' He left the classroom quickly before Mr Johnson could ask him any more questions, leaving the teacher looking after him with a worried frown.

Even with his own encounter to think about, Col had not forgotten that he should be helping to prepare Connie for the assessor. He would leave the introduction of the subject to her aunt, but he decided to take particular notice of her. Despite all his grandmother's words of reassurance, he had found his own assessment a bewildering experience last year. He felt a bit sorry for this stranger to Hescombe who did not know that she was about to be thrown in at the deep end. Perhaps he should try to be a bit more friendly towards her? This was the chain of thought that led him to drop an invitation to tea that Friday like a lightning bolt out of clear blue sky.

Connie was astonished. She had got used to Col ignoring her at school.

'You don't have to come if you don't want to,' he added carelessly, mistaking her bewilderment for reluctance, 'but Gran is expecting you.'

'Then I'll come,' Connie replied swiftly, more because she liked Mrs Clamworthy than because she felt particularly welcomed by Col.

They left school together that Friday afternoon and walked along the seafront to Col's home, conversing awkwardly about progress on the project. Connie was doing her best to defuse Col's anger towards Anneena who had again manoeuvred him into doing something he didn't want to do. Much to Col's chagrin, an appointment with Mr Quick had been made for the following Wednesday. Mr Johnson, who made the call for them, was surprised that they were going to see the 'chief honcho' himself—as the teacher termed Mr Quick.

'Well, I'm not surprised,' Anneena had said smugly to Connie and Col as they packed up to go home. 'As soon as my sister rang up the Axoil publicity people to offer coverage of the interview in the *Hescombe Herald*, I guessed Mr Quick would agree to see us.'

'What!' exploded Col. 'But you promised!'

'I didn't promise that I wouldn't ask Rupa along—I only promised that we'd ask nothing about the missing men,' said Anneena with a feeble attempt at injured innocence.

'But Rupa might,' said Col angrily.

'She might,' acknowledged Anneena with a shrug, 'but that's not our business, is it?'

Col and Connie turned into Windcross Street and paused to let construction vehicles rumble by on their way to Chartmouth, leaving a dusty diesel smell in their wake. As they crossed the road, a green Land Rover gave two toots and pulled up beside them. A pretty girl with fair hair, sitting in the passenger seat, wound down the window.

'Hey, Col!' she called, flicking her hair back with a feline shiver of her shoulders. She beckoned him over as if she was reeling in a fish.

'Oh, hi, Shirley,' Col said, immediately leaving Connie and crossing to the car. Connie watched closely as a rapid conversation ensued in lowered tones also involving the man in the driving seat.

'See you tomorrow then! Ciao!' the girl said loudly in conclusion. The Land Rover sped off out of town.

'Who was that?' Connie asked curiously, grateful for the opportunity to change the subject. 'I've not seen her at school. Is she older than us?'

'Just a bit—but she's at a private school in Chartmouth so you wouldn't have seen her around. Her name's Shirley Masterson. Her dad owns a lot of land up on Dartmoor. I'm going there for a riding lesson tomorrow—a Society thing.' Col avoided meeting her eye, pretending to be interested in the strap of his bag.

'Oh,' Connie said, feeling envious of him. Why were he and this Shirley girl allowed to go riding and on picnics and not her? It seemed so unfair. 'I'd love to learn to ride.'

'Perhaps you'll get the chance. Hey, Connie, has your aunt said anything to you about an assessor?' He turned to look at her expression. She shook her head, her face puzzled. 'Never mind then—come in and see Gran.'

Walking back after tea, Connie thought that Col and his gran had behaved very strangely. Col had been more restless than normal, as if he was on the verge of saying something but then thinking better of it. Mrs Clamworthy was also unusually agitated: she kept stroking Connie's hair and fussily pressing more tea and cake on her. Connie had found the whole thing deeply embarrassing but, despite this, she still felt that strange excitement being with them that she had at their first meeting. There was definitely something about these Society people.

At home, a long email had arrived for Connie from her parents: they had bought her a computer before they went away to ensure she stayed in touch. It was strange to read about their impressions of their new home in Manila—humidity, traffic, beauty, poverty—when she was absorbed in such a different new world of her own. She wrote back, wishing her little brother good luck at the international school. It was great to be able to assure her parents that for once she was enjoying her class. She told them all about Anneena and Jane, the project, the gerbils, and Mr Johnson: all in all it sounded a happy life in Hescombe. Perhaps they did not need to know about her aunt's strange goings-on with the Society—it would only worry her dad, who prized conventionality above all things.

Driven out by the warblings of Signor Antonelli in his bedroom, which were vibrating up through the floorboards, Connie came down from her room and found her aunt waiting for her with a box of family photographs. She was so surprised by this that she looked over her shoulder, half expecting someone else to be following her into the kitchen.

'There you are, Connie,' her aunt exclaimed. 'I thought you'd got locked in your bedroom or something—you've been up there so long!'

That was rich, coming from her, thought Connie bitterly, seeing that she had left her to entertain herself every other evening.

'Here, I've something to show you.' Evelyn hunted through the box until she found what she had been seeking. It was a sepia photograph, liver-spotted with age, of a severe-looking woman sitting by a potted plant. There was a blur on her lap, which could have been a cat.

'That's your great-great-grandmother, Enid Lionheart. And I think that is Madame Cresson's distant relative on her knee.'

Taking the photo suspiciously, Connie looked at it, wondering why Evelyn had sprung the family collection on her tonight. So this was the one who was supposed to have the same hair and eyes as her. To be honest, it was hard to tell if this was so from the picture because great-great-grandmother Enid's hair was fastened back in a bun, not a lock out of place, and the sepia print did not reveal eye colour. You could tell that her eyes did not match—but that was all.

'And here's one of your great-aunt—my Aunt Sybil—from her honeymoon, I think.'

This was a more recent picture taken in Sybil Lionheart's youth, some seventy years ago. It showed a young girl in a swimming costume jumping over the waves, laughing at the camera. Yes, you could definitely see the hair in this picture: it was flying all over the place. The eyes were not clear as Sybil had her face screwed up as she looked towards the sun.

'She was the one who introduced me to the Society. This was her cottage, which she left to me.'

Connie wondered why her father had never told her about these relatives before. She couldn't remember him ever mentioning a Sybil or an Enid. Intrigued, she decided to take full advantage of her aunt's expansive mood. 'So was Sybil in the Society too?' she asked.

Evelyn looked sombre. 'Yes. She married a man in the Society—it must have been him who took the photo—but he died in circumstances that have never been fully explained, on a mission for the Society during the war. She never married again. She gave me a roof over my head when it became clear that I'd also been chosen. Your gran and grandad were against it all—seeing what happened to Sybil's husband—but Aunt Sybil knew that, if you had the gift, you had to follow your calling, whatever the consequences.'

There she goes again, thought Connie, intrigued, talking about being chosen—having a gift. What did she really mean under the veil of this mumbo-jumbo she spoke? What exactly was this Society of hers all about? And what did she mean about Sybil's husband dying in mysterious circumstances? What had that to do with the Society?

'What do they think happened to her husband?' she asked.

'He disappeared in Finland while on Society business. All that the survivors would tell Aunt Sybil was that it wasn't the human war that had killed him, but something else.' Evelyn fidgeted with the edge of the photo as if disturbed by a memory connected with it.

'Does this happen often—Society members getting killed, I mean?'

'Not often. Perhaps I shouldn't have told you that just now.' She sounded sad. 'It was the wrong place to start. Don't you go worrying about that story. Every family should have a mystery or two: it keeps the rest of us on our toes.'

Evelyn got up to put the photos away. Connie wondered if that was going to be it.

'The wrong place to start what?' she asked, hoping her aunt had more to say.

'To start your introduction to the Society,' Evelyn replied, returning to her seat.

'My introduction?' Connie felt a rush of excitement. Finally she was going to be let in on Society events: to go on picnics—maybe even learn to ride. Everything she had wondered about and hankered after since she first stumbled into Mrs Clamworthy and her friends was about to be revealed to her.

'I wanted you to see that it runs in our family and that it could be part of your destiny too.'

'Could be? I don't understand.' She sensed there was a catch.

'No, you don't now—and I cannot guarantee that you ever will. But if you want a chance to find out if you are one of us, you'll have to trust me.' Evelyn laced her fingers nervously together, watching Connie intently.

Connie did not know what to say. To be honest, she did not trust her aunt—not *really* trust her like she did her parents. In fact, she wasn't sure she even liked her. For her part, Evelyn certainly seemed to have very little regard for her niece: this assessment thing was the first time she had shown any interest in her.

'I just need you to take a test on Sunday,' Evelyn continued. 'You can't know the details in advance as it wouldn't work if you did, but if you pass it, you'll have been selected for the Society. I promise I won't let anything bad happen to you.'

Lying in bed that night, nursing a headache brought on by a weird buzzing in her head, Connie was not so sure. With her parents far away and Evelyn so obsessed by the Society, Connie was feeling distinctly vulnerable, as if she was standing on the brink of a great drop with only a flimsy safety rail to stop her from falling. She had agreed to take the test on Sunday, of course, as she was still eager to be part of this Society. But if she failed, what then? And if she passed?

Ivor Coddrington, Assessor for the Society for the Protection of Mythical Creatures, New Members Department, arrived on the ten o'clock train from London. It had been arranged that Evelyn, Dr Brock, and Col would meet him so they could explain the situation to him en route to the Mastersons' place where the encounters were to take place.

'A companion to sirens, you say?' Mr Coddrington asked in a nasal voice that made everything he said sound like a sneer. Col, sitting behind him in Evelyn Lionheart's Citroën, inspected the assessor's dandruff-flecked collar with distaste, relieved that the visitor was Shirley's mentor and not his. He hoped his would have a bit more street cred than this dull man.

Mr Coddrington cracked his bony knuckles. 'They are exceptionally rare—almost as rare as I am myself: a companion to weather giants.' He gave a proud, thin-lipped smile. 'But why all this fuss? Can't she be assessed in the normal way after an application has been submitted and references given?'

Dr Brock explained for a second time the situation with the sirens and the need for speed.

'But you have no idea if this bird-girl is one and the same as the applicant?' Even the news that men were dying did not appear to ruffle Mr Coddrington.

'No,' Dr Brock replied shortly. He was clearly beginning to tire of the assessor.

'It would save you a second trip,' Evelyn cut in. She had the measure of the man rather quicker than Dr Brock and had realized that appealing to his self-interest would be more effective than any other tactic. 'The trains are horrible from London and you wouldn't want to have to come down a second time so soon.'

'Hmm,' muttered Mr Coddrington. 'True. I suppose I have come equipped.' He gestured to his strange collection of luggage, which included three cages and a black bag.

'I'll cook you lunch, of course,' she added. Col smiled: if Mr Coddrington knew any better, the promise of a Lionheart lunch would be a reason to take the early train home. Evelyn was known to be an atrocious cook. But Mr Coddrington had not been forewarned.

'In that case, I suppose I can fit the young lady in at, let's say, eleven o'clock tomorrow?'

'Then it's agreed,' she replied, risking a ghost of a wink over her shoulder at Col when Mr Coddrington was not looking.

The Citroën bumped over the broken tarmac road leading to the Mastersons' farm. The farmhouse, an isolated double-fronted building, lay at the end of a wooded valley, several miles from the nearest village. Behind the farm climbed hills leading on to Dartmoor where the Mastersons grazed their flocks of sheep as well as allowing less conventional activities to take place. The Mastersons had been staunch members of the Society for generations: every Masterson in living memory had had the gift. But even with this family history, today was a special day: the youngest member of the clan was to have her first encounter with a weather giant. As Mr Coddrington told Dr Brock pointedly as they approached the house, to have two companions to weather giants in England at the same time was like lightning striking the same spot twice. He then proceeded to laugh at his own joke, making Col groan.

A small crowd of people was already waiting in the farmyard as Evelyn Lionheart parked her car. Col scrambled out of the back, pleased to escape Mr Coddrington's company. Mr Masterson swept up the assessor and took him into the house to meet Shirley.

'What do I do?' Col asked Dr Brock nervously.

'Just wait here. Your mentor will find you,' the doctor reassured him while scanning the crowd for his pupil. 'Look for the lapel badge with the golden horse.' He was already pinning on his own badge with a black lizard, sign of the Company of Reptiles and Sea Creatures.

Col searched the thinning crowd apprehensively. He recognized only a couple of the people there. There were fewer Society members these days so many of the mentors had had to come a great distance to be there for their pupils. He saw Evelyn Lionheart lead a terrified-looking girl off towards the woods for her first encounter with the banshees; he could already hear the high-pitched wailing of the creatures raised in greeting to their new companion. Dr Brock was heading in the direction of the moors with two young dragon companions—twins by the looks of them, dressed in slick black leathers and gauntlets. Col was beginning to fear that his mentor had not shown up, when he felt a sharp rap on his arm. He swivelled round quickly to come face to face with a man wearing an old-fashioned brown leather flying-jacket, goggles, and helmet, upper lip adorned with a sandy handlebar moustache, and an ebony cane tucked under his left arm. He had a golden horse pinned to his lapel.

'Colin Clamworthy?' he barked out.

'Yes?'

'Captain Graves, Companion to Pegasi. Follow me!' He strode off down the lane, vigorously swiping the air with his cane, taking the heads off an overhanging crop of nettles.

'I have organized for you to meet a young pegasus called Skylark,' Captain Graves called briskly over his shoulder as Col hurried after him. 'It will be his first encounter too so you must not expect much of each other. It will feel strange, perhaps a little frightening to begin with. If things go well, he may permit you to sit on his back, but remember, he has never been ridden before!'

'I'll remember,' Col interjected.

'But first I want you to understand something of the magnitude of what is about to happen to you.' The captain swished his cane at his charge and Col instinctively flinched back, not wishing to share the fate of the nettles. He felt he did not need to be told: his stomach was already knotting itself like a game of cat's cradle. 'You have been chosen to befriend and protect one of the most magical and amazing creatures in the world: it is a great privilege and one that carries with it responsibilities.

'Mythical creatures,' the captain continued loudly, as if addressing a whole squadron of men, rather than one boy, 'are only mythical because men have made them so by driving them into hiding. They could perhaps better be described as representatives of all that is most wild, most wonderful and most strange in nature. Their survival shadows the fortunes of other creatures, so we have a duty to protect all created things and not just our special charges: the pegasi.' He gave emphasis to his last words by prodding Col twice on the shoulder. Col nodded energetically to show he understood. Satisfied, Captain Graves resumed his march and led Col up a farm track to a large paddock set back from the road, sheltered from onlookers by a bank of dark green oak trees.

'I remember my first encounter,' mused Captain Graves, his eyes taking on a faraway look. 'Me and old Flighty were scared witless. He bucked me the moment I climbed on his back. Very apologetic afterwards, of course—he'd just panicked.'

Taking a silver whistle from his jacket pocket, Captain Graves blew a shrill note on it three times. For a few moments nothing happened, but then, as if answering a call themselves, Captain Graves and Col turned towards the hills. Out of the clear blue sky, beating powerful swanlike wings in unison, came two magnificent winged horses: the pegasi. Col's heart began to race. Seeing them for the first time, he realized that he had just found the piece that had been missing in his life until that moment. Though he had gazed at pictures of pegasi in books as a young child, wishing that the images would come to life before his eyes, nothing had prepared him for their grace and pure beauty: it was as if they were the essence of all other horses, distilled and granted wings in recognition of their fleetness. The larger one—a chestnut stallion with glossy, muscular shoulders—landed expertly by Captain Graves; the younger one—a sleek grey—hit the ground with a thump, kicking up clods of earth on impact, showering the captain's spotless flying suit with speckles of mud. Col smiled to himself, finding the grey's lack of experience a comfort as he fully expected to make his own clumsy mistakes any minute now.

Unperturbed by the young creature's entrance, Col's mentor laid his hand on the chestnut's mane and bent his head, eyes closed in concentration.

After whispering in the horse's ear for a few moments, Captain Graves turned back to Col.

'This is Firewings: he is Skylark's mentor.' Col bowed his head as a sign of respect. 'Now, I suggest you take your first steps,' said Captain Graves, waving Col forward with his stick. 'Do what comes naturally to you. I will only intervene if you run into difficulties. Remember, you are about to find out if you are a companion to the pegasi. If so, you should not have to be taught the basics: you will find that you already know them.'

As he had done so often with his own pony, Col took a few paces forward, stretching out his hand to reach for Skylark's nose, longing to feel the bristles beneath his fingertips and the warmth of a fellow being. At first the grey seemed to hesitate, and even took a few steps backwards, then, gaining in resolve, he stood still and permitted Col to touch him.

Col gasped. It was as though someone had set off a battery of fireworks inside him. Energy was running from the creature before him, through his fingertips, and travelling into every inch of Col's being. His limbs felt light and powerful; he felt he could bound across the sky and leap the clouds. He arched his spine: there was a tingling in his back as if he had budding wings just waiting to break through his skin. Snorting in wonder, shaking his hair, feeling the energy zing from it like water droplets flung into the air, Col buried his head in the grey's snowy white mane. The horse felt it too and snorted in surprise. Slowly, as if a mist was lifting, Col found he could discern thoughts amidst the current that connected them. Skylark was overjoyed but wary; afraid of making a connection with the human world but fascinated by Col. The initial intensity of energy as they flailed about to connect with each other subsided as the two found each other's mind, like a radio tuner working its way through the static to settle on its chosen station.

'Hello,' said Col silently, the words running in his mind, but not needing to pass his lips.

'Greetings, human child,' came the reply.

'I'm called Col.'

'Greetings, Col, Companion to Pegasi.'

Col's heart was leaping for joy. This was the moment he had been waiting for: recognition of his gift by a mythical creature. His doubt and fear vanished: he knew through and through what his destiny was to be. Flying horses were his lifeblood; the pegasi, and no other creature, were to be his companion species.

'This is so right; this is how it should be,' thought Col as he recognized in Skylark a kindred spirit.

'True,' said Skylark. 'You and I have so much to learn from each other. You are so strange, so wonderful to me. Will you ride?'

'May I?'

'I'd be honoured.'

Col clenched his fist around a lock of Skylark's mane to swing himself up.

'Not so fast, young man,' called Captain Graves, who had been deep in talk with Firewings and not noticed the rapid progress his pupil was making. 'What about a helmet—what about goggles?' But Col did not heed him, so spellbound was he by his union with Skylark.

'Let's show the old folk what the youngsters can do!' Skylark snorted, flicking his tail disdainfully.

Col crouched low and gripped hard with his knees as the horse cantered to take off. At first, Col felt himself being bumped along the ground, but suddenly that all changed as rough grass was replaced by smooth air. Skylark's wings wafted either side of Col, who could now feel the strain in his mount's neck muscles as they worked hard to raise the added load from the earth.

'Am I too heavy?' Col asked anxiously.

Too proud to admit he was having to work more strenuously than ever before, Skylark panted: 'No, it will be smoother in a moment. Just wait.' He dragged them both up with laboured thrusts of his white-feathered wings.

Finally, once Skylark had gained altitude, he rested his wings in a glide, legs lifted up beneath his body as if caught in mid-leap. Col whooped with delight as he looked down over Skylark's flank and saw the farm spread out below, the tiny sheep and antlike people. The wind chilled his hands and cheeks with its cool touch.

'Shall we dive?' asked Skylark, spirits high.

'Why not?' answered Col, eager to prove to his new friend that he was ready for anything.

Skylark folded his wings so the tips were pointed backwards and plunged down towards the treetops. It was an incredible ride: like being on the most extreme roller coaster. Col found himself yelling with exhilaration, not the least bit scared. Indeed, he so trusted Skylark he would have been happy to attempt a loop-the-loop if the horse had suggested it.

Levelling out again, Col saw that Firewings, with Captain Graves on his back, was approaching swiftly.

'Come down, boy!' called Captain Graves, gesticulating wildly with his cane. 'That's quite enough for your first ride.'

The mentor was far enough away for Col to pretend he had not heard him. Skylark kicked his heels to head towards the hills: he was determined to keep Col with him as long as possible, despite the harsh neigh his behaviour evoked from Firewings.

'Once round the hills and then we'll go back,' Skylark promised Col.

The hills rolled like a counterpane beneath them, glowing emerald where the sun broke through the clouds to light upon a field. The sheep, disturbed by the strange shadow cast by the pegasus onto the grass, looked like white sand running through an egg timer as they followed the leader from one field into the next.

'Weather's turning,' said Col, seeing a black cloud the shape of an anvil looming ahead. 'Best go back.'

'No, just once around,' said Skylark, heedless in his elation.

They flew straight into the storm cloud. Col lost sight of the hills as heavy drops of rain splattered into his eyes. Perhaps goggles would have been a good idea after all. He was beginning to feel a little frightened. Did Skylark really know what he was doing? No, Col sensed the wave of doubt wash over his friend. A flash of lightning too close for comfort brought panic to Skylark and he began to rear and buck, neighing with fright.

'Steady, steady,' cautioned Col, clinging on for dear life as his mind too vividly imagined the consequences of falling from this height.

'Hold fast, boy!' came a shout close by. Captain Graves and Firewings hove into view on Col's right, flying swiftly and strongly despite the gusting wind. Firewings swooped up to Skylark and headed him off, guiding him back out of the storm. Emerging into blue skies again, Skylark began to calm down, his alarm succeeded by deep embarrassment at his behaviour.

'Sorry, Companion, I'm so sorry,' the grey said again and again, as the pair flew back to the paddock.

Landing with a thump, Col tumbled off over Skylark's nose and sat up, rubbing his knee. Above, he saw Firewings and his rider coming in to land with the storm still raging on the hills behind them. Now he was back on firm ground, Col had time to notice that the storm looked strangely unmoving; it was not affecting the rest of the fine day at all and the paddock was bathed in sunshine.

'Now we're in for it,' muttered Col to Skylark as Captain Graves swung off Firewings and strode over to the boy and his chastened mount.

But to Col's surprise, Captain Graves was far from angry.

'Very good: a very promising start. You have a natural seat, my boy,' said Captain Graves, clapping Col on the shoulder. 'Such things are to be expected on your first ride. I should have told you the hills are out of bounds today as someone is encountering their first weather giant. It could have been much worse, believe me: you could have run into the giant himself amidst his clouds.'

Col grinned with relief at Skylark, who nuzzled him affectionately in return. They had passed the first test, not with flying colours perhaps, but they had made a flying start.

6
Assessor

AT half past ten on Sunday morning, as Connie lay on her bed, she heard the Citroën spluttering down the lane. Her aunt had said she was not supposed to meet Mr Coddrington until it was time for her examination and Connie could think of no good reason why she should not play by her aunt's rules today. Trying to make herself smart, she sat up and brushed her hair in the mottled mirror, seeing her mismatched eyes staring back at her, fear in their depths. Why was she doing this? She did not need to put herself through it if she did not want to, so why? Curiosity, she supposed, but then, what had her aunt said about curiosity and the cat? Was she wrong to let her aunt enter her for the

Society's entrance exam? Might it even be dangerous?

The preparations had been solemn enough. Signor Antonelli had sung a soulful verse of *Panis angelicus* to her that morning on his way out, kissing her hand as if he might never see her again. Evelyn had even been spotted with a duster in hand, checking over the front parlour: a sure sign that something serious was afoot, as she never normally did housework. The parlour was a cold, little-used room that smelt of damp and dust, unchanged since Sybil Lionheart's day. It was still decorated with Sybil's wedding photos in tarnished frames on the mantelpiece, flanked by a white marble statue of a horse leaping from the waves and a figurine of a bronze bear. To Connie, it felt more like a mausoleum than a living room.

Well, it was no good regretting her decision to undergo the exam now. The assessor was on his way. The tests were to start at eleven so she had half an hour to kill.

Suddenly rebelling against her aunt's insistence on secrecy, Connie decided that even if she was not supposed to meet the examiner that would not stop her peeking at him out of the window as the car drew up.

A dark-suited man with straggling brown hair climbed awkwardly out of the passenger seat, his legs far too long to fit comfortably inside. Connie caught a glimpse of a pale, thin face looking with disapproval at the ramshackle cottage, but then he quickly disappeared inside to enjoy her aunt's hospitality in the kitchen. From this brief glimpse, he looked to Connie more like a bank clerk or insurance salesman, and not at all how she imagined someone with the august title of 'Assessor'. She did not fancy letting him test her on anything.

Her nerves were beginning to overwhelm her. She had better distract herself quickly before she chickened out of the whole thing. Connie tapped on her computer to while away the time, searching the web for information about the environment. Was the test going to be a written one like exams at school? She doubted it very much but no one had told her what was involved, saying it had to be kept secret from the candidate in order for it to work properly. Perhaps they'd be testing her to see if she was up-to-speed on local environmental issues? With this in mind, she decided to look up recent stories about oil disasters and found the references spread across many pages. Her heart sickened as she saw the pictures of seabirds tarred with black oil, dying lingering deaths as the stuff prevented them from feeding, or poisoned them slowly. It made very grim reading.

She was almost relieved to see her aunt, looking even more flustered than she had when Signor Antonelli had arrived, appear at her door and invite her to come down.

'Is it time already?' Connie asked breathlessly as the stomach-churning recollection of what was to come flooded back. Her aunt nodded curtly. Connie followed Evelyn down the steep staircase from her attic bedroom to the glacial hallway. Her aunt ushered her forward, avoiding her eye, and then disappeared into the kitchen without a word.

Taking a deep breath, tapping softly once, Connie pushed the door open, grimacing as it creaked on its rusty hinges. The room appeared empty. Stepping quickly inside, she collided with Mr Coddrington who had been out of sight, lurking behind the door. She started, apologized hastily and backed away. Close to, he looked even less like an environmental campaigner for a protest group. He had the pallor of someone who spent most of his life indoors; his hair was lank, his hands restless as they fumbled with his pocket-watch, revealing long, ink-stained fingernails.

'So, you are the cause of all this fuss and bother,' he said, giving her a look as if the very sight of her was distasteful to him. 'I hope you are not wasting my time.'

Indignation dispelled her fear. That was hardly fair, Connie thought, she had not provoked the rush: that was down to her aunt and her friends.

Mr Coddrington gestured to an upright chair placed in the centre of the room.

'Sit down, Miss Lionheart,' he said, pacing to and fro like a lynx in a cage. Connie sat down, folding her arms resentfully across her chest. 'Now, nothing that I say or ask you to do must leave this room. If you fail,' he gave a thin-lipped smile, 'then it must be as if it never happened. Do you agree to my terms?'

Connie nodded.

'I must have your signature, please—to avoid later complications.'

'OK,' said Connie, scribbling her name on a clipboard he handed to her. Taking it back, the assessor examined her signature carefully, checking that she had not cheated and signed some other name. Still feeling angry with him, she looked defiantly around and noticed that her chair was surrounded by four strange objects, laid out on what she realized were the points of the compass: north was a crystal, east a raven, south a green lizard, and west a white mouse. What was going on?

'I see you've noticed my fellow assessors,' Mr Coddrington said in a voice that slithered insidiously over the space between them. 'An assessment is conducted by objects and animals that never lie. Each represents one of the companies of our Society: the mouse for two and four-legged beings and beasts; the lizard—reptiles and sea creatures; the bird—winged beasts; and the crystal—those drawn from the four elements of water, earth, air, and fire.'

He was clearly talking rubbish: how could you have creatures made of the elements? It was like a game of 'Animal, Vegetable, or Mineral?' gone wrong and they expected her to play it. Waiting for him to continue, Connie looked at the three creatures; they were staring at her intently. Of the crystal, she could discern nothing: it just sat there—a lump of grey rock. This was all so odd, so nonsensical, but there was something about the creatures that unnerved her. Fear returned, smothering her anger; it fluttered in her chest like a bird trying to break out of its coop.

'Now, when I tell you, I want you to stand up and hold out your arms, palms downwards, and slowly point them at each object or animal in turn. Do not stop until you have completed a full circle. The response should indicate in which company your gift lies—if you have one, that is.'

This was stupid! Should she walk out? But her aunt would be waiting outside; what would Evelyn say if she left without even trying? Attempting to calm down, Connie reminded herself that she had heard of clubs with strange rituals for new members, which were supposed to be quite sane otherwise. Perhaps this was just the Society's way? Or was it all some elaborate joke? Still undecided whether she should do what he asked, she could hear her heart thumping as Mr Coddrington left an uncomfortable dramatic pause.

'Begin,' he said.

In a split second, her decision was made: she would play. She stood up, her arms trembling, and began to pivot around the circle as he had instructed, feeling sure she looked ridiculous. As soon as her outstretched arms pointed to the first of the objects, the atmosphere suddenly changed. The crystal began to glow and hum like a hive of bees.

'Good, good,' muttered the assessor, scribbling on his pad.

She continued to turn and now the bird flapped its wings, uttering harsh ear-splitting croaks. Mr Coddrington looked up, his mouth open in astonishment. Next the lizard started to chase its tail in a frantic circle. The assessor dropped his pencil and clipboard with a clatter. Finally, the mouse weaved to and fro, greeting her, begging to be picked up. Connie completed the circuit and dropped her arms; the humming stopped and the animals returned to their implacable scrutiny. She raised her eyes uncertainly to Mr Coddrington and saw that he was staring at her in horrified amazement. When he noticed her questioning gaze, his expression swiftly changed, as if he had brought the shutters down smartly to hide his feelings. Scrabbling on the floor for his clipboard, he broke into in a rapid volley of disjointed sentences.

'I'm afraid we can't continue. The assessors have never behaved like that before.' He hurriedly put the crystal in a velvet bag with a vicious tug on the black silk cord. 'You clearly have no settled gift—I doubt you are even a second order.' He shut the animals back in their cages, ignoring their cries of protest. 'It was a grave mistake to bring you this far. I'll have to speak to my superiors about it.'

Connie was dumbfounded. 'Do you mean I've failed?'

'Completely.' He gathered his belongings in an untidy bundle under his arm.

'But why did they make all that noise?'

He paused for a moment with his hand on the doorknob, considering his words—or was it his excuse? He was acting more as if he was scared of her than anything else.

'Only one object is supposed to resonate with the aspirant companion. That cacophony of sound was a sign of confusion—lack of a real bond with any one of them.' He opened the door. 'I'll send a full explanation of my assessment by post. I must leave immediately.'

Mr Coddrington bundled his belongings out of the parlour, calling loudly for her aunt. His desire to quit her presence so quickly made her feel as though he had just diagnosed her with the plague and feared to catch it himself. Alone in the cold room, Connie could hear words such as 'dangerous', 'rule-breakers', and—worst of all— 'quite without a gift' echoing from the hallway. She slumped back on the chair in shock, listening as Mr Coddrington made a point of refusing the lunch that had been prepared for him and demanding to be driven to the station.

Connie sat still as the front door slammed. He had been so abrupt, so cruel even, but his verdict was plain enough: she could not be a member of the Society. What would Col Clamworthy say when she had to admit her failure? Her brief moment of regret passed, to be replaced by anger: stupid, stupid Society! Why had she even tried?

By the time Evelyn returned from taking Mr Coddrington to the station, Connie was clattering around the kitchen in a red rage but no longer knowing with whom or what she was angry. One glance at Connie's strained face and Evelyn set about making some tea for her. Connie was too humiliated by what had passed in the assessment even to notice that it was the first time her aunt had made such a caring gesture towards her.

'It's not your fault, Connie,' Evelyn said softly, handing her a mug of milky tea. 'If anyone was at fault, it was us older members: we should've known better than to try and rush things through. But then, I was so sure that there would at least be something about you,' she added reflectively.

'I don't care anyway,' Connie blurted out, pushing the mug away. 'I'm going out.' The last thing she wanted was her aunt to come over all sympathetic now. She preferred the earlier treatment when she had barely existed in her aunt's eyes. At least then she did not have to worry what Evelyn thought of her failure.

Banging the door behind her, Connie ran off down Shaker Row, hardly knowing where she was going. The trouble was, she did care: she found she cared very much. From the turmoil of emotion one thought had emerged uppermost: she was never going to belong to the Society, never fit in even when she so desperately wanted to.

Connie did not want to meet any of the Society members in her present mood of bitter disappointment so she stayed away, walking the beach until night fell, despite the onset of foul weather. The darkening, storm-tossed waves scrabbled at the stones like tentacles trying to suck them down into the hidden depths of the Hescombe Channel. The black mood of the sea suited her bruised feelings and she was comforted to know that the natural world around her was restless and tormented too at that moment. Finally, cold, hungry, and tired, Connie walked slowly back to Number Five, her anger now dulled to a despondent ache.

Lights were on in the kitchen. Connie quietly let herself in the little used front door to avoid being seen by anyone. Kicking off her boots and socks, she padded along the hall to peek into the kitchen. Thank goodness she had done so for there was a collection of all the people she least wanted to meet: the Society members, even Signor Antonelli, were gathered around the table, discussing her.

'Tell me again exactly what happened. He can hardly have given her a fair trial if he was here for so short a time!' exclaimed Mrs Clamworthy.

Connie could see Col sitting, head bowed dejectedly, at his grandmother's right hand. In front of him was a present wrapped in shiny paper with 'congratulations' emblazoned all over it. That would not be needed now.

'I've not spoken properly to Connie about it—she was too upset,' her aunt was saying. 'But he invited her in and next I heard there was a great rush of noise from the objects and he bolted out as if she had stung him.'

An elderly man, his white hair streaked with ginger, looked up sharply at Evelyn. Connie recognized him immediately: it was the man from the quayside.

'Noise—you say the creatures made noises? What do you make of that, Horace?'

'I never met anything like that in my career,' replied a second man who was out of sight. 'Are you sure?'

'Yes, a lot of noise: it was very alarming,' said Evelyn. 'I can't imagine what Connie made of it all. Then Mr Coddrington dashed out, saying she'd failed the test, had unsettled gifts, possibly not even a second order, and demanded to be taken to his train. He said we'd receive his written judgement in the next few days and that his superiors would be contacting us about "our flagrant disregard of the rules". Can't say I warmed to Mr Coddrington.'

'That man was always a cold fish,' said Horace. 'Not a drop of warm blood in his body—he's got cold ink in his veins. We were mighty unlucky to get him for assessment.'

'The man 'as ink, no blood?' asked Signor Antonelli, confused.

'In a manner of speaking, Luciano,' explained the white-haired man.

'He should have spent more time with her. There's something odd about this assessment,' Horace continued.

'But it means my niece is no use to us. What do we do now?' asked Evelyn.

Connie turned on her bare feet and ran quietly back up to her bedroom.

7
Song

The storm had passed. The last fat raindrops spattered the window and trickled down to the sill. Connie breathed on the pane and drew a seagull in the mist. Downstairs the meeting was still continuing.

Useless, she wrote on the window. *I am useless.*

The scraping of chair-legs alerted her: they were leaving. Scampering back to the bed, she threw the duvet over herself and pretended to be asleep. She was just in time for, a moment later, her aunt quietly opened the bedroom door; a shaft of light from the landing streamed into the room, striking Connie's head hidden under a mass of hair on the pillow. With a sigh, her aunt clicked the door softly to, her footsteps fading as she went downstairs.

Leaping out of bed, Connie ran back to the window. The party from the kitchen was now gathered on the path waiting for Evelyn to come out.

They must have decided to go on another of their foolhardy expeditions, or why would her aunt be going out at this time of night? Waiting till she saw her aunt join them, she opened the window a crack to eavesdrop.

'She's OK. Asleep.'

'I'm worried for her, Francis,' said Mrs Clamworthy to the white-haired man. 'It must have been a terrible disappointment for her. What do you think we can do to help her?'

'I think we must leave that up to Connie,' he said, looking up at her window. Connie ducked down. 'There are more ways than one of demonstrating that you have the gift. We rely too much these days on these tests. If she is the girl I saw on the quay, and I feel convinced that she is, I would prefer to put my faith in her abilities than in those of Ivor Coddrington as an assessor.'

His words were the best comfort Connie could have received. He had seen her with Scark; he believed that she had the gift, whatever that meant. Perhaps it was a special relationship with animals? Well, if that was so, she definitely had it in spades.

So it need not be the end. Mr Coddrington could be wrong. She might not be useless.

As her mood lightened from dejection to defiance, she remembered the assessor's strange behaviour. He seemed to have wanted her to fail from the moment that bird had squawked and had certainly left no room for a second opinion. What had he seen that had scared him so? There was a way to find out—the old man had hinted as much—and she very much wanted to prove Mr Coddrington wrong and her family inheritance right. But what did she have to do? The man had not said. Well, perhaps it was time to play by her rules rather than theirs. The only way she could think of to prove herself was to stick close to them and see what they actually did. Then, she'd show them she could do it even better. That was it! She'd show them how to approach the seagulls without scaring them. If that didn't convince them, nothing would. But she'd better be quick if she was going to go with them to the Stacks tonight.

Connie dashed downstairs and pulled on her anorak and boots. She had already decided what she would do: if she ran fast enough, taking the lane behind the garage rather than the High Street, she might be able to beat them to the quay.

There was no one about to see her running through the dark backstreets of Hescombe, except a marmalade cat strutting along a narrow fence. Sensing something unusual afoot, Madame Cresson bounded down as Connie passed, dropped the limp mouse from her mouth, and padded swiftly after her on velvet paws.

Connie came to a halt on the cobbles of the quay.

'Which boat?' Connie gasped, bent double with a stitch, as she realized that her plan had a hitch. She remembered Col talking about his grandmother's boat last Friday: it had a strange name—something to do with water. Glancing nervously over her shoulder in case the others were in sight, she ran down the walkway of the little marina. *Bessie*, *Ocean Pride*, *Selkie*. Come on, quickly! Ah! Here it was: *Water Sprite*. Only a small boat, it did not offer many hiding places. Clambering on board, Connie wrenched back a tarpaulin tucked under a bench, creating just enough space into which she could squeeze. Ignoring the trickle of freezing water soaking her jeans as she crammed herself in, she was about to pull the cover back when a cat thumped down into the boat, causing her to jump with surprise.

'Madame Cresson,' Connie hissed, 'don't try to stop me!' The cat blinked her yellow eyes coolly and purred, her tail flicking slowly from side to side. 'So you're just here to keep an eye on me?'

The cat yawned and strolled over to tuck herself neatly beside Connie. 'That's fine by me—just don't make me sneeze!'

A babble of voices on the walkway told Connie that it was time to pull the tarpaulin back into place. It was fiendishly uncomfortable cramped under the seat: she wished they would hurry up and take to sea before she literally got cold feet.

'Right, Signor Antonelli,' came the voice of the white-haired man, 'you go with Horace and Evelyn in *Banshee*; Col, you take your grandmother and me in *Water Sprite*.'

Connie felt the boat lurch as two people climbed on board: one at a leap, the other more carefully. The engine erupted into life sending vibrations juddering through Connie's numbed body.

'Cast off there!' She recognized Col's voice.

The boat lurched again as someone jumped in with the ropes. The sound of the engine changed to a smoother tone and the boat started to move. A minute later a deeper pitch and roll told Connie they had emerged beyond the harbour walls. Madame Cresson yawned again and slipped out from Connie's side. She made a grab at her but the cat's fur slid like silk through her fingers.

'What's that cat doing on board?' she heard Mrs Clamworthy exclaim.

'Haven't the foggiest. I didn't see it when we got in,' said the man.

'Er . . . Dr Brock,' said Col from the wheel-house, 'do you think it's a good idea letting it come along? I mean, the sirens are part bird, aren't they?'

'Yes, that's true—but we're not going to turn back now,' Dr Brock replied.

'This whole expedition is not a good idea, Francis,' said Mrs Clamworthy fretfully. 'I doubt Signor Antonelli will get anywhere with them. He's told us already: only a true companion to these sirens can hear their song and not perish.'

'There's no choice: we must give it one more try. I don't know about you, but I can't live with the thought of more O'Neills bumping against our hull,' said Dr Brock firmly. 'Has everyone got their ear protectors?'

This last remark passed unheeded by Connie who had stopped listening when she heard the word 'siren'. She knew she had once before come across the name used about a creature; it had caught her imagination a few months ago when her old class read some stories of ancient Greece. She had liked the topsy-turvy chain of association that had led the name of a mythical peril being given to the wailing sound used to warn of danger. But the sirens—monstrous beings that lured

sailors to their death with their beautiful songs—
were just a fable, weren't they?

The next quarter of an hour seemed an age to
Connie cooped up under the bench. She could see
a pair of red wellingtons through a crack in the
tarpaulin—Mrs Clamworthy's, she guessed—she
must be sitting on the bench above. It began to
dawn on Connie that it would be very difficult to
make a dignified entrance now: what was she
going to say to them? How was she going to
explain her presence? Gatecrashing a Society
outing had seemed a good idea on dry land; now it
seemed plain madness.

Col cut the engine.

'Ear protectors on, everyone!' ordered Dr
Brock. Connie saw Mrs Clamworthy's hand reach
down into a bag at her feet and pull out a familiar
pair of scarlet ear protectors. 'And perhaps we had
better take cover with Col by the wheel.'

'Didn't help me last time,' she heard Col shout
back.

'No, but at least it gives us something to duck
behind. They almost lifted *me* off the bow.'

The bench creaked and the red boots
disappeared. Connie risked a quick glance around
the deck in front of her: no one. They must all be
at the back of the boat. Crawling painfully out on
her elbows, Connie emerged from her hiding

place, but still kept to the dense shadows away from the light on the wheelhouse. She need not have worried; they were not looking her way: the three of them were standing close together, staring up at the eight black rocks which loomed to starboard. Dr Brock had his binoculars out and had them trained on the top of the tallest of the Stacks. Another boat bobbed in the sea not far off, its passengers also watching intently for any movement coming from the rocks. Signor Antonelli was standing on the bow, his arm outstretched. He took a deep breath and started to sing a new song, one whose words were lost on the night breeze, but the soaring tune carried to Connie. There was something not quite right about the music: it was out of tune with the moan of the wind and the lap of the waves. It put her teeth on edge like the squeak of chalk on a blackboard. He fell silent and Connie was grateful, for now the discord had ceased and the world could return to its previous calm.

Connie waited to see what else they would do— to see if she could discover how they were annoying the seagulls. Her anxiety about what she was going to say when they spotted her ebbed away and she felt surprisingly calm as she sat down to watch, stroking Madame Cresson rhythmically. The rocking motion of the boat, the sound of the waves breaking against the fenders, had a soothing quality. She began to hum to herself; the hum turned into a song without words—more a croon, rising and ebbing with the motion of the sea. Gathering confidence, she sang louder—after all, none of them could hear her as they were wearing those ridiculous ear protectors and she was seized by the conviction that it was the right thing to do. Unbidden, the notes poured out of her, springing from some hidden source of music deep within she had not known she possessed. Unlike Signor Antonelli's song, she knew that hers was in tune with her surroundings, gliding effortlessly up to the stars and dancing joyously over the waters. Everything worked together to magnify the song; the whole of nature thrummed like the soundboard of one vast instrument, resonating with her notes. She brought the song to a crescendo, rising slowly to her feet, and then she waited. The world seemed to have fallen silent with her: the wind died down, even the waves subsided.

Then it came: at first so soft she was not sure she was hearing it. As it gathered strength, she perceived it more clearly: an answering song sung by many voices, a tune that looped and wheeled like a flock of seagulls skimming over the moon-flecked water, graceful, intricate, and beautiful. As she watched, eight huge birds spiralled out of the sky, each one landing on a crest of one of the rocks, their white-grey wings glimmering in the moonlight. At first she thought they were herring gulls. But no, she realized they were not gulls at all: they had human heads thrown back, wings half-extended, calling to the stars, to the moon, to Connie.

She gasped in wonder: never before had she heard anything so wild, so magnificent. She desired to soar upwards to join the singers—to go with them as they glided over the waves, daring the sea to catch them in their mastery of flight over its ever-moving surface. But even as she felt this urge, she knew that at the centre of all her whirling emotions there was a calm place. Though she felt the song's keen edge slicing through her soul, its blade could not wound her. She was in control.

A shout on her right—Connie turned to see Col lunging out from the wheelhouse, eyes wide with horror, scrambling towards her over a pile of rope, tripping in his haste and falling heavily on the deck.

'Connie—block your ears! Get down!' he yelled at her. But he seemed very far away to her, irrelevant to the song that coursed through her veins like silver fire. When she turned back to the sea, two of the sirens had taken flight, heading in her direction. Madame Cresson bristled at her heels, spitting and hissing as they landed skilfully at her side, brushing her with their wing tips.

'You have come,' said one simply, her voice a continuation of the haunting song that still echoed in Connie's ears.

Connie found herself gazing into two dark eyes, ancient and solemn, but 'other'—though they seemed human in form, their expression belonged to a different world, an earlier time.

'I have come,' Connie replied in a whisper, awed by the wild beauty of the siren's silver-grey face, the pure lines of nose and cheekbones blending seamlessly into the feathered neck and head. Downy white hair fluttered in the breeze, whispering against Connie's skin.

'Now you must fly with us,' the siren declared. As if in a dream, Connie nodded, mesmerized by the deep dark eyes. She felt she could fall into them like the sea, plunge down and never hit the bottom.

The creature raised a clawed foot. Connie heard Col shout, the cat yowled, but she had no time to reassure them as her jacket sleeves were grasped by two sets of talons and she was lifted from the deck. Climbing steeply over the water, her feet dangling precariously over the waves, she hung like a rag-doll in the sirens' grip for the short journey between the boat and the rocks. She closed her eyes tight, terrified of the drop below. The two sirens set her down on the tallest of the Stacks. The other six flew to her, surrounding her, murmuring their greetings, their eyes glinting fiercely in the moonlight. Then the one who had first spoken ushered Connie to follow. The siren led the way down some crude steps, cracked and sprouting sea-grass, carved in the side of the liver-red rock. Connie edged down them, half paralysed by her fear of heights, and these steps were slippery and steep, giving vertiginous glimpses of the waves below. With relief, she reached a small chamber scooped from the cliff-face. Screened by the other rocks, the boat was not visible from the cave and she wondered for a fleeting moment what Col and her aunt would be making of all this. However, she did not have long to consider them as she found herself in the middle of a circle of sirens.

'We have been waiting for you,' the leader said.

Connie felt as though her wits had been scattered like the grains of sand on the floor. 'For me? How could you know I was coming?'

'We were told.' The siren picked her way delicately across the cavern floor, her feet leaving arrow-headed marks in the sand, until she came to perch on a stone. Her sisters looked up at her expectantly, rustling their wings, filling the air with the scent of salt.

'Are you sure you've got the right person? Maybe you are waiting for someone else? My name's Connie, by the way.' Connie fell silent, feeling her nervous babble of words dry up. Of course they were waiting for her; in her heart she had known this from the moment she heard their song.

'Connie.' The siren said her name with great care, as if it was a new sound that she wished to savour. She then continued, 'I am Gull-wing, and these are my sisters: Enchanter, Sea-echo, White-song, Spray, Shell-voice, Wave-whisperer and Feather-breath.'

The sirens bowed in turn as they were introduced. Connie could hardly see them in the dark of the cave; all she could make out were eight shapes with a glimmer of white where their downy necks caught the moonlight and the glitter of their eyes.

'Am I your companion?' she asked, thinking she now understood Mrs Clamworthy's comment in the boat.

'Not ours,' Gull-wing laughed, her soft voice rising into a mew like the distant call of the seagulls.

Connie's heart lurched. 'Not yours? Then am I going to die? I've heard your song . . .'

'Heard but not perished. You do not understand yet, Connie. You are not ours—and yet you are. You are a rare creature—rarer even than us. You are what they call a universal companion. You will never be bonded to one creature like most in that Society of theirs—you are free to move from species to species, from beast to being. We will all recognize you.'

'When I heard your song, I felt bonded with you.'

'And we, when you sang to us, but you will find many songs inside you to sing to many creatures. We are honoured to have been your first.' Gull-wing's sisters murmured their agreement, rustling their wings with the sound of wind moving through sea-grass.

'I don't understand.'

'Not now, but you will. It is your destiny—this is what brought you to us.'

Gull-wing's words spoke to something in Connie: yes, it did seem right that she should come here; it was as if everything in her life had been leading up to this moment, guiding her this way. But she also knew that there was a more urgent reason for her being here tonight. The Society had wanted to talk to these creatures. Hadn't Dr Brock said something about 'no more O'Neills'? With a horrible lurch in her stomach, she finally realized what he had meant. She was standing among murderers. Yet part of her also understood; the thirst for revenge running in their veins was as much part of them as their blood. Maybe a little of it had transfused into her bloodstream too when they had sung together for she could now feel the temptation to use the power they had kept in check for so long.

'But, Gull-wing, something else brought me— and those people out there' (Connie gestured out to sea to where the boats had been) 'to your rocks. Do you know about the danger you're in?' The sirens gravely nodded their sleek feathered heads. 'So you know about the refinery and the ships?'

Gull-wing croaked with a sound like pebbles crunching underfoot. 'We know. And we know what those fools from the Society for the Protection of Mythical Creatures would say to us. They would say that if we attack the polluting monsters at their abomination of a home or wreck a tanker on these shores, many will die and the ships will still keep on coming. They would threaten us with discovery!' The siren ruffled her feathers with disgust. 'And what do they counsel?' she sneered, her voice rising until it became almost a screech. 'Flight? Where should we go? We have been harried into exile too many times. There are

133

those in our world that say it is time we struck back. And we are striking back!'

'Who says this?' Connie asked, frightened but also intrigued by Gull-wing's words. 'Who's persuaded you to drown those men?'

'There is no harm in your knowing—you will meet him soon enough,' said the siren with a cruel smile that made her nostrils flare as if she scented blood. 'Kullervo.'

The name meant nothing to Connie, but she was alarmed to hear she would be meeting someone who urged them to resort to violence.

'Who is he? Is he a member of the Society?'

The sirens laughed their croaking chorus again.

'No,' said Gull-wing with an amused curve to her lips. 'He is one of us. He wants to liberate us from the half-measures and feeble-minded ways of the Society. They have ruled us for too long, but what have they achieved after centuries? Nothing. According to them, we still have to move—still have to make way for men. The Society is a human-centred sham in league with the polluters and the destroyers. It is time we creatures struck back. But do not fear, Connie; when we do, we will make sure that you are safe.'

'But I don't want to be safe if my friends are in danger. Gull-wing, you must listen. I think the Society really is trying to help you. Have you thought that maybe this Kullervo is wrong? He's telling you to do a wicked thing. There must be another way.'

'We have heard it: the Society has nothing to offer us.'

'But innocent men are dying! There must be something else we can do—something that means that you can remain here peacefully! Just give me time—I'll think of it!'

Gull-wing puffed out her feathers, looking to her sisters. Connie knew her fate hung in the balance—the merest breath could bring down the beam on one side or the other.

'It is like a universal to care even for those puny lives that fell so easily to our song. You have until the winter storms, Companion,' Gull-wing declared, moving to break up the circle. 'That is when Kullervo comes. That is when we declare war and will carry out our plan to attack one of those monster ships if no other way is found.'

'But I might need more time!'

'We can give you no more time. It has to be enough. Kullervo will not wait. Stay here. We eat now.'

'How am I to . . . ?'

But the conference was at an end. The sirens took flight one by one from the cavern entrance, off to fish under the cover of darkness.

Left alone, Connie wondered what would become of her. The sirens had said nothing about returning her to land and she could not get down from the rock unless she sprouted wings. Her aunt must be worried sick about her by now. She peered out to the patch of ocean she could glimpse from the rock ledge—there was no boat, nothing to be seen except the glimmering water, iridescent black like a jackdaw's wing, rolling peacefully below. She was sure that the sirens meant no harm to come to her, but if they had not met a companion before, perhaps they did not understand that humans had to have food and water too if they were to survive? She could not remain cooped up in this cave. Yet what could she do but wait for their return and beg them to take her to some deserted place on the coast from where she could get back to Hescombe?

Waking with a start, Connie found herself curled up in a nest-like bed. Twigs prickled her skin and she smelt strongly of fish but she was oddly comfortable. As her wits returned, she realized that this was because her back was lying against the warm downy side of a siren—Gull-wing, she thought—who was breathing evenly in a deep slumber, her head curled under her wing.

But what had woken her so suddenly? Edging her way out of the nest so as not to disturb her bedfellow, Connie crawled to look out of the entrance. She gasped and rubbed her eyes as a burst of flame revealed what had been hidden by the night. There, rising and falling on huge outspread wings, was a ruby-red dragon; on its back was a man with snow-white hair. This did not feel like a dream—though it should have done. A second eruption of flame—this time she saw that it was coming from the dragon's mouth—and there was Dr Brock urgently beckoning to her, pointing upwards. Frozen to the spot, stunned by what she had just witnessed, it took Connie a few moments to understand: he had come to rescue her but, as there was no way he could land in the cavern, he wanted her to go up to the crest of the rock.

Scrambling to her feet, she wondered if she should wake one of the sirens to explain where she was going. After only a moment's reflection, she knew that she could not predict their reaction: they were as likely to attack Dr Brock as to let her go—she could not risk it. It felt terrible to creep out like this—almost as if she was betraying them. Impulsively, she seized a stick and scraped a message on the sandy floor: *I will come back soon—Connie*. It seemed a banal kind of message to leave, she did not even know if they could read, but there was no time for long explanations.

Connie had not forgotten the perilous descent of the stone steps. In the dark, with no siren to follow, she was convinced she was going to miss her footing and fall. Dawn came to her rescue: about halfway up, in the trickiest part of the climb, a glimmer on the eastern horizon gave her enough light to struggle up the last ledges. She was immediately seized in a firm grip and hauled up the scaly sides of the dragon.

'Hold on to my waist—we're leaving,' said Dr Brock.

Connie was about to shout a reply, but saw that it was useless: Dr Brock had ear protectors on. Doing as she was bidden, she grasped his coat. It was fortunate she had a tight hold, as the lurch made by the dragon to take off would otherwise have unseated her. Creaking and groaning as the leathery hide strained against the wind, the dragon's vast wings propelled its burden up off the rock. Once over the edge, the dragon swooped downwards in a heart-stopping dive, before letting the air currents lift it when it was a mere whisker above the waves. Connie had shrieked with terror as they plummeted, but now, as they rose once more, she began to enjoy the incredible sensation of riding on dragon-back. In touch with the creature's joy in flight, she lost her own fear of heights. The wings whooshed and flapped, like canvas sails swelling with a stiff breeze. A sulphury smell from the dragon's intermittent blasts of flame stung her nostrils, she felt a glowing warmth from the body she straddled— she was astride a being of fire! The sea beneath mirrored the night sky, but when the dragon let out its breath she caught a glimpse of scarlet and gold, like a shooting star, reflected in the water below.

All too soon the dragon spiralled down to find a landing place on the cliff. Connie bumped heavily into Dr Brock as they touched down; the companion to dragons, however, managed to keep them both from tumbling off. Once on firm ground, Dr Brock slithered nimbly down and held out a hand to assist Connie.

'Home and dry, my dear,' he said with a smile, taking off his ear protectors.

'Thank you for coming for me,' she replied, not quite sure how to express her gratitude when he had taken such a risk for her.

'Thank Argot here,' said Dr Brock, gesturing to the dragon.

In the early dawn, Connie had her first good look at her steed. The dragon's red and gold scales were smooth like fish-mail; the leathery webbing

139

of its wings glowed with the sunlight behind it, showing the fretwork of veins; but it was the face which kept her gaze with its flickering forked tongue, powerful jaws, and yellow reptilian eyes. Argot was larger and more vibrant than any creature she had ever seen: like a shout from nature in a room of whisperers. Catching sight of the dragon's uncompromising stare, Connie knew she too was being measured up—she hoped she would not be found wanting after all the trouble she had caused.

'Thank you,' she said, respectfully bowing her head.

The dragon nodded twice—once to her, once to Dr Brock—and then launched itself off the cliff edge. Climbing out of its dive, it beat its wings, heading towards the horizon. As it turned, the first shaft of sunlight broke from under a cloud and glanced off the dragon's flanks in a flash of gold. Connie felt a lump form in her throat: she had never seen anything so majestic as the sight of a dragon flying into the heart of a sunrise; it was a moment she would never forget.

8
Universal Companion

'AM I in trouble?' Connie asked.

She was following Dr Brock down the coastal path as they walked in single file between the dewy thorn bushes, brambles, and grasses. The air smelt of humus-rich mud leavened with the salt tang of the sea.

'For surprising us like that? Yes, you are in trouble,' he called back over his shoulder. 'Your aunt will have something to say on that score when we get you home. But for visiting the sirens?' Dr Brock paused to wipe his glasses with a silk handkerchief. 'No, you're not in trouble for that. It was a brave—if dangerous—thing to do, but that is the spirit of a true companion. You had to fulfil your destiny and discover that you were indeed a companion to sirens.'

'But I'm not,' said Connie.

'Not?' Dr Brock replaced his glasses and peered at her curiously. 'Of course you are or we would not be standing here now!'

'No—they told me I wasn't their companion—or not only theirs. I'm what they call a universal companion.'

Dr Brock swayed slightly as if she had just hit him.

'Those were their exact words?' he asked. She nodded. He rubbed his brow as if trying to adjust his ideas by physically pressing them into order. 'Well, that explains why Argot bowed to you—I wondered about that,' he said thoughtfully. 'But this news is extraordinary! Do you know how many universal companions there are at present, Connie?'

'No. How many?'

'One—and I'm standing with her. There have been no new ones for nearly a century. We've not had one in the British Isles for a decade or so since Reginald Cony passed away—and I am fairly certain that the last one in the world died at a very ripe old age in Argentina last year. Many in the Society have begun to think that the universal gift has died out with the fading of the last great mythical species.

'It's a very special gift, Connie, but it's one that comes with troubles and responsibilities,' Dr

Brock said soberly. He began to walk again, evidently wanting more time to take in her news before saying any more.

In the silence, Connie pondered his last words. She did not understand all this talk of mythical creatures—but then, she had stopped understanding anything when the world suddenly became populated with sirens and dragons.

Coming to a stile, Dr Brock paused, pulled out his thermos from his knapsack, and poured them both a cup of tea.

'I think it's time we broke our fast—it's thirsty work riding on dragons and I don't imagine the sirens were too generous with refreshments.' He perched himself on the top of the stile and handed her a biscuit to go with the drink. 'And I think I owe *you* an explanation too.' He patted the wooden bar, inviting her to take a seat beside him. She climbed up to sit next to him.

'We haven't been properly introduced, I believe. My name is Francis Brock. As you've probably guessed by now, your aunt and I are members of the Society for the Protection of Mythical Creatures. It's an ancient foundation established to protect these creatures from extinction.'

Connie looked at him quizzically. 'Mythical? But doesn't that mean that they don't exist?'

He laughed. 'Exactly, that's what you're supposed to think. We sound quite mad, don't we? Hear me out.

'Originally, the Society's main task was to prevent the senseless killing of mythical creatures by humans. Dragons, for example, had been driven to the brink of extinction by young knights in armour who thought it good sport to hunt even the most peaceable ones. As for unicorns, their horn became so prized by doctors and apothecaries that only a handful were left. Almost a thousand years ago now, our founder Trustees, that is to say the first universal companion, Abbess Hildegard, and eight friends, decided enough was enough. Something had to be done or none of the great species would survive. So they formed the Society with the aim of persuading people to disbelieve in the very existence of these creatures, making them no longer the target of huntsmen or poachers. Our Trustees used every means, from the pulpit to the market place, circulating the idea that these creatures were just the stuff of song and stories, silly tales for children. After all, you can hardly boast about killing an animal if people think you are mad for claiming to have seen it at all! Quite a brilliant strategy really.'

He gave her a broad smile, which she could not help but return despite her confusion and doubt.

Had she really just passed the night in a siren's nest and then ridden on a dragon's back? How could she not believe this kind old man and his tales of mythical creatures?

'These days, our job has become more difficult,' Dr Brock continued. 'In addition to maintaining the secrecy surrounding mythical beasts and beings, we also have to battle to preserve the last places in which they can survive. Humans have spread themselves so far across the earth that there are now few wild margins of uncertainty. Life for our creatures has become one long story of betrayal and flight until they are slowly dwindling away.

'There are some bright spots though. There are creatures that can exist in the heart of human settlements, thanks to people's amazing capacity to disbelieve the evidence of their own eyes— especially when it does not match a rational view of the world.'

His blue eyes twinkled shrewdly at her through his gold-framed glasses as he said this. She knew then that he sensed her doubt and how she clung still to 'rational' beliefs. An inner voice spoke up in support of him: there had definitely been a dragon—she had ridden it: how did her common sense explain all that?

'Aside from these beings, there are many creatures that can only survive in the wild.

Sirens—the creatures of most concern to us here—are one of these. They need inaccessible coastal sites,' (he gestured out to sea where the Stacks could just be seen, black needles on the horizon) 'far from the disturbance of human traffic, for their own survival and—I might add—for the safety of those who would otherwise cross their path. Not all creatures, you see, are harmless.'

'I can quite believe that,' Connie said fervently. And remembering the fierce eyes of the sisters, her doubts evaporated: it had happened so why should not all this about the Society be true too?

'Normally, in these cases, we would advise the creatures to move—our Society is nearly powerless to turn back the tide of industrial development. However, the sirens will not talk to us. I'm afraid they feel that they've heard enough about retreat from us in the past and have already decided on a more radical approach of their own. I think you know what that is. They want revenge. Those poor men are the first victims. But if the sirens think they can also scare Axoil away by picking off a few labourers, they are in for a shock. Too much money has gone into that place: the company will stick there like a limpet to a rock no matter what. They may not want to hear it from us, but the sirens will have to move.'

'They said you would say that,' Connie interjected, breaking open the wrapper of her chocolate bar. 'They said the Society was on the side of humans.'

'That we most certainly are not!' said Dr Brock indignantly. 'They've got us completely wrong if they think that!'

'They also said that someone was coming to them. They plan to wreck a ship.'

'A tanker is it? So that's what they're up to. I had my suspicions that something big was brewing but I wasn't sure. However, they're wrong if they think that will make a difference. I don't want Axoil here any more than they do but I know that the accident will be discounted as a freak of nature and tankers will keep on coming. How many accidents will it take before the sirens are discovered? What will be left of the coastline around these parts after even one "accident"? How many people and animals will have to die?'

'I don't know,' said Connie. She was beginning to feel quite hopeless as she listened to him. 'But they said it's war. They're waiting for someone—the plan to wreck a tanker has something to do with his arrival in the winter. They seemed to think he—this Kullervo—was their leader.'

'Kullervo!' exclaimed Dr Brock; his hand jolted, spilling his tea all over his dragon-riding trousers. 'Are you sure?'

Connie shrugged. 'That's what they said.'

Dr Brock went quiet; he did not even wipe away the spillage, which was now running down his thigh and dripping onto the grass.

'So,' he said at last with a shake of his head, 'the rumours coming out of the north are true then. I'd heard that some dragons had gone over to him, as well as some of the weather giants. Others too, probably. But I didn't want to believe it.'

'Who is he? Is he a siren?' asked Connie, her fear growing as she sensed his deep unease.

'It's a good question. He's not a siren but none of us is quite sure what he is because no one on our side has survived meeting him. He lives—or should I say has his roots—in Finland. We know that he is a mythical being—an evil spirit waxing stronger every day, feeding off the imbalance we humans have made in the earth's environment. Some say he is a shaman—one who can communicate with all creatures—not unlike you, my dear.'

'Is he a universal companion?'

'Oh no.' Dr Brock laughed bitterly. 'Universal he may be, but companionship is far from his mind. I think he is more like a whirlpool—or black hole—pulling all who venture near him inexorably into his wicked schemes. Once creatures go down his road, it is nearly impossible to pull them back. They get in too deep, falling for his lies that all humans are the enemy—the oppressor. It's tragic that while the sirens think that they are choosing freedom to act without restraint, they are in reality choosing captivity. They may believe he's serving their cause, but once he has his hooks into them, they will end up his slaves. He is only interested in them in so far as they further his goal.'

'His goal?'

'The eradication of humanity.'

Connie reeled, feeling as if she had just been punched in the stomach. Her mind couldn't take in the enormity of what she had just been told. 'But they said that it was the Society that had ruled them for too long—that he was helping them.'

'Our rule, Connie, is nothing to his iron yoke. We have laws—laws advocating peaceful co-existence where possible, and it's for these the sirens despise us. From the moment of their creation, their element has been chaos; we should perhaps only wonder that they have curbed these urges for so long.'

'They won't move: I'm certain of that—we must find another way to save them,' said Connie with conviction.

'I wish we could, but the Society cannot produce solutions like rabbits out of a magician's hat. For many years I have been forced to watch retreat after retreat of my dragons. I too on occasion have been tempted to counsel violent resistance—as Kullervo does—but I'm restrained by the knowledge that this would only bring more suffering and the end of the creatures I seek to protect. If dragons came out from behind the protective shadow of myth, how long do you think it would be before they were hunted into extinction? A few might linger as caged curiosities in a zoo—but not for long. Dragons cannot survive behind bars.'

Dr Brock hesitated over his mug, staring for inspiration in its remaining contents. 'I think it is time the Society woke up to the threat of Kullervo.' He looked at her, his blue eyes shadowed by her news. 'His adherents are growing: he is gathering on his side forces that could devastate whole continents if they are unleashed. The weather giants have already done a lot of damage. He's coming here in the winter, you say?'

'Yes, and I'm to meet him, according to the sirens—he's heard about me.'

Connie thought she glimpsed a flash of panic cross Dr Brock's face, but he swiftly mastered himself and gave her a reassuring smile. 'Then we should be ready for him,' he said resolutely. 'But promise me, you will not agree to meet him willingly—I know of no one who has survived that encounter.'

'I don't want to meet him at all,' said Connie. 'Who would if he's as terrifying as you say?'

'Good girl.' Hitching his rucksack onto his back, he added: 'Oh, and about you being a universal companion—I'd keep it to yourself for the moment. Allow the others to think that you're a companion to the sirens for the time being. I will write a letter to the Trustees of the Society. It is now clear that Ivor Coddrington was more than incompetent when he assessed you, but he will still be a difficult obstacle to surmount if we're to get you into the Society for the Orpheus programme.'

'Orpheus?'

'Your training. There is more to being a companion than you yet know—there's so much to learn about the creatures, about us. As a universal companion, I'd say you'll have your work cut out for you.'

Col did not get to see Connie until Tuesday as her aunt had insisted she take a day's rest at home from her ordeal. He was intrigued to find out how his shy classmate had got on with such violent creatures as the sirens. Part of him was still amazed that they had not eaten her for breakfast. He could not wait to hear what had happened so he sought her out at break-time.

'Connie, are you OK?' Col enquired as they headed for the picnic bench on the far side of the playground. He ignored the calls to come and join a game of football.

'I'm fine—I think.' She seemed a little dazed and was looking at him with an odd expression in her eyes. He was not surprised: it often took newcomers to the Society a few weeks to adjust to seeing the world properly for the first time.

'What happened?' Col glanced nervously over his shoulder to check no one else was in earshot. Justin was intent on kicking a shot towards the goal and no longer watching him.

'It went well.' She spoke as if each word was an effort. She was still coming to terms with the news that she had a gift—an extraordinary gift that set her apart from everyone. She had been used to being different, but now the reason behind her uniqueness had been explained, she had an inkling that her life had changed irrevocably. The knowledge that she was a universal would define what she did and who she became. It sounded so exciting: she wished she could share the news with Col and ask his advice, but she remembered in time that Dr Brock had told her to keep it secret. She therefore kept her description of what had happened to a minimum. She would save up her news for another occasion. She said instead, 'The sirens accepted me and we talked. Then I think they forgot that I might have to go home and Dr Brock came to my rescue on Argot.'

Col jerked his gaze back to Connie's face, struck anew by the strange contrast between the slight figure before him and the extraordinary adventure she had just had.

'What—you got a dragon-ride! You don't know how lucky you are! I've been waiting for years for my first encounter, and I never even dreamt I'd get on a dragon, and it all happens to you within weeks of learning about the Society!'

His outburst roused her and she laughed for the first time. 'But it was also quite scary, you know,' she added, as consolation for him.

'All the same—a dragon—and sirens!'

'OK, I have to admit: it was brilliant.' Her eyes now shone with excitement, reliving for a moment the thrill of dragon-flight.

'I'd give anything to have done what you did on Sunday,' he said, ruffling his hair into place, checking that no one was observing them. 'And I'm pleased we now understand each other properly.'

'So am I,' she agreed, though she felt a little guilty as she said it, knowing that she was holding the full truth back from him. 'And you told me that it was a large seabird that scratched you! I was so angry with you all.'

'It wasn't so far from the truth, was it? Anyway, I'm relieved you are a third order like me.'

'Third order?' There was clearly much to learn about the Society—so much she did not understand.

'Hasn't anyone explained yet?' he asked. She shook her head. He smiled. Now he had a chance to show her how much more he knew. 'OK then: you'd better hear it from me. The Society recognizes three orders.' He counted them out on his fingers. 'The first's the companion to everyday animals—this is what the world calls an animal lover. Second order is for those who have a special bond with one kind of animal: snake charmers, horse whisperers—all these belong to this group. The third order, only for those of us in the Society, are people who are companions to a particular mythical creature. Mine's the pegasi. Your aunt's is the banshee. Dr Brock, as you now know, is a dragon companion.'

'But how do they know which is your companion species?'

'Simple really: they look very closely at any special bonds with second order creatures—that's what the assessment was supposed to be about. They knew I might be destined for the pegasi because I've always had a special bond with horses. Don't know why yours went so wrong—never heard of that happening before. But that reminds me.' He dug in his school bag. 'Here, I got this for you.'

He thrust into her hand the present she had seen on the kitchen table. She ripped off the wrapping paper: it was an illustrated copy of *The Odyssey*; on the cover a picture of the Greek hero lashed to the mast surrounded by singing sirens.

'What else?' Col said with a smile. 'You'd better get reading if you're going to see your friends again.'

9

Axoil

Evelyn, in a new mood of protectiveness for Connie, surprised her by volunteering to drive Connie and her friends to Chartmouth for the interview with Mr Quick that Wednesday. Connie knew what her aunt felt about the company and was touched by the offer. She didn't realize that she was now under informal guard, thanks to a few hints to Evelyn from Dr Brock.

'I'll set foot in that building on one condition only,' Evelyn said, looking in her mirror at her passengers. Somehow, they had all managed to squeeze into her tiny car, but the three girls in the back were feeling distinctly cramped. 'And that's that this doesn't all turn out to be good PR for them. Make sure you get in there with your questions about environmental protection, won't you? Then I won't begrudge you the lift.'

'Oh, we will, Miss Lionheart,' said Anneena, rather too eagerly.

Col shot her a suspicious look over his shoulder. Connie shifted uneasily. She now understood why Col had been so keen not to draw attention to the missing men: he had been trying to protect the sirens. She just hoped Anneena would stick to their agreement and keep to questions on the environment.

The Head Office of Axoil UK was a flashy building—all glass and glistening paintwork—on an industrial estate called 'Harbour View Business Park', a short ride from the terminal building and port. The newly laid lawns and emaciated trees leading up to the entrance announced that the building had only just been finished. Evelyn parked her car by the entrance in a slot with 'Managing Director' written over it, next to a glossy black BMW.

'Miss Lionheart, you're not supposed to park there,' Anneena said, pointing to the sign.

'And why not?' Evelyn replied sharply. 'I'm sure I'm a director of something if I think long enough about it.'

Anneena turned to appeal to Connie, but she just shrugged, knowing her aunt well enough now to be aware when it was useless to argue.

Evelyn ushered them through the revolving doors into an echoing atrium draped with plastic plants to where a pretty young woman was sitting, minding the phones.

'Take a seat. Someone will be down to see you shortly,' the receptionist chirped, regarding them with a wide but impersonal smile.

The leather sofas squeaked embarrassingly as the girls sat down next to Rupa and the photographer, who had arrived before them. Connie gave a nervous giggle, attracting a frown from Anneena who was trying to look as if sitting in white marble foyers on designer furniture was something she did every day of her life.

Col remained standing to look at the photographs that adorned the walls showing the company's tankers decked out in their livery of blue and yellow. Hardly believing his eyes, he saw that the ships were named after mythical monsters: *Cyclops, Leviathan, Minotaur*. He nudged Connie and nodded towards the pictures. At first she did not get it, then her eyes widened with astonishment.

'That's ironic, isn't it?' he muttered.

After a few minutes, a sandy-haired young man, wearing a badge with 'Mike Shore—Customer

Care Manager' written on it, came to fetch them. He led them through several passages smelling of new carpets and lemon air-freshener to a door marked 'Managing Director'. The four friends glanced at each other apprehensively; Col gave Connie a quick grin.

'Into the lion's den?' he muttered behind their guide's back.

The children filed into a darkened room, oppressively full of black leather chairs and mahogany furniture. The managing director was a powerfully-built man with a suit so crisp that it looked as if you could cut yourself on the lapels. He dominated the room without even rising from his seat. His face bore vestiges of great good looks, high cheek bones and piercing grey eyes, but time had hollowed his cheeks and lined his forehead. Mr Quick greeted them coldly, his mouth pursed in a sour smile. Connie recognized him as the gaunt man from the photo she had seen in the newspaper and shivered. His bald head gleamed in the dull light from a skylight above his desk; the rest of the room was plunged into shadows, as the blinds were down on the windows. In this single pool of light, he sat enthroned in a huge black chair behind a desk trailing papers like a spider in a white paper web.

Mr Quick did not offer his hand. He merely said: 'Welcome to Axoil. It is gratifying to find there are young people who take the trouble to find out the truth about us, rather than swallow the lies some have been industriously propagating in the local press.' He shot a poisonous look at Rupa and her photographer, who had followed the children in. 'I have quarter of an hour now for your questions, then Mr Shore will show you the refinery.' He looked down at his notes. 'Which one of you has a parent who works for Axoil?' Jane shyly raised her hand. Col noted that Mr Quick had done his homework on them, which was a little alarming. 'I have asked him to accompany the tour. And Miss Lionheart?' Mr Quick looked over to Evelyn who was standing quietly by the water-cooler. 'I understand you're part of the local campaign against my refinery? I'm glad to have this chance to show you around as part of our dialogue on corporate responsibility.' He gave Rupa a sharp look to see she was getting all this down. Evelyn tensed but nodded her head courteously. 'Now, I believe you have some questions for me.'

As agreed, Anneena acted as spokesperson. Connie watched her closely, relieved to see she was sticking to their list.

'We've been told, Mr Quick, that you grew up in Hescombe,' said Anneena sweetly. 'As a local person yourself, what do you think the refinery will do for us?'

Mr Quick fixed each of them in turn with his grey eyes. Connie found his expression strangely blank. 'It will drag this place into the modern age, that is what it will do. Hescombe has always been too set in its ways. Superstition and old wives' tales put people off exploiting the natural advantages of the deep waters around the Stacks—the perfect highway for modern ships. An injection of the no-nonsense approach of big business was just what the region needed. It makes me very proud that I am the one coming back to introduce the change.'

He continued to extol the merits of his refinery in his dry monotone voice, assuring them repeatedly that the environment was safe with him, for a full fifteen minutes. Even Anneena was struggling to appear interested.

'Time is up,' he concluded as an alarm beeped on his expensive-looking wristwatch. 'I hope you'll find your visit educational.' He tapped his pen thoughtfully on his desk as they got up to leave, scrutinizing them carefully. Connie did not like his look: she felt he was dissecting them one by one, memorizing their faces.

'Oh, I'm sure we will,' said Anneena. 'Thank you.' Even her usual exuberance was quelled in this room.

'Good. Enjoy the tour.'

'No go with him,' Anneena whispered to Connie as they left.

'No go? What do you mean? Anneena? Anneena?'

But Anneena didn't answer. She had tripped after Mike and now struck up a conversation, first disarming him with an innocent smile, nodding and gasping with wonder as Mike continued Mr Quick's theme of the benefits of the refinery for the local economy, and mankind in general. Connie watched powerlessly as Anneena fed him dumb question after dumb question. She had him eating out of her hand. Col and Connie exchanged worried looks. What was she up to? This wasn't part of the script.

On arriving back in the foyer, Anneena beckoned her sister forward with a nod. Rupa casually sidled up to their escort. 'May I ask a question . . . er . . . Mike?'

Feeling very pleased with himself, Mike turned his attention from Anneena and smiled at Rupa. He was like an over-enthusiastic game-show host but he had evidently not realized what game the Nuruddins were playing.

'Sure, if the children don't object. This was supposed to be their tour, you know.'

'We don't object,' said Anneena quickly.

'But . . .' began Col.

'Thanks,' said Rupa. 'I just wanted to ask you about the death of Mr O'Neill. Do you know what caused Mr O'Neill to fall into the sea two weeks ago while he was working in the terminal?'

'Of course not,' Mike said, his eyes darting to the door as if he was contemplating making a dash for it.

'Then you admit that he was at work when he fell?'

'Yes—no,' Mike said in confusion. 'I mean I don't know.'

'You don't know if one of Axoil's employees was at work at the time he fell to his death?' asked Rupa, her black eyebrows arched in disbelief.

'Look, it's nothing to do with me. I'm public relations not personnel,' blustered Mike. 'But I do know this: Axoil maintains the highest safety standards at all times. Of course, if one of our employees is depressed, wants to take his own life when at work, it's impossible to stop . . .' His voice trailed off. He realized he'd said too much. His eyes flicked back to the children. 'Now, if the young people have any more questions?' The wattage of his smile had considerably dimmed.

Col scowled at Anneena. Connie clutched his arm, afraid that he might start an argument in front of the Axoil man. 'No, I don't think we have,' she said rapidly.

'In that case—let's go and see the refinery.'

Trying to repair his mistake, Mike kept close by at all times while he ferried them by minibus to the new refinery. Jane's father, every inch the scientist Connie had imagined with his lab coat, pebble glasses, and fly-away hair, greeted them at the door and led them into the vast hall that housed the refinery machinery. Connie was astonished by the scale of the enterprise. Amidst the gleaming pipes and vats, the white-coated technicians on distant gantries looked like worker bees in a hive, their scurrying lives serving a single purpose: the production of black honey.

'We opened the initial phase on Monday—you probably saw it on the news,' gushed Mike. With a slightly desperate enthusiasm, he directed his comments to Rupa while her photographer took pictures, trying to get her back 'on message' after his earlier indiscretion. 'But it will not go on-stream properly until the winter. We are training staff and testing the equipment at the moment. Axoil has worldwide experience of this process and we know we can't afford to make any mistakes when the tankers start coming, now can we?'

Rupa smiled politely, moving to the other side of a computer bank to where Mr Benedict was showing his daughter some technical drawings.

'So tankers will start to arrive in winter, will they?' asked Connie, making a quick calculation of her own.

'Around then, yes,' Mike answered.

'About the same time as the worst weather?' Col added, realizing where Connie was going with her enquiry.

'Yes,' Mike replied, a little put out by the implication of their questions. 'But don't you worry about that,' he said patronizingly, 'these tanker captains are experienced people. I am sure the worst that Hescombe can throw at them will seem like a fine day in the Atlantic.'

'I wouldn't be so sure,' muttered Connie aside to Col.

'Anneena, how could you!' Connie and Col were surprised to hear Jane was the first to speak. They were waiting in the car for Evelyn as she argued with the security guard who had clamped her front wheel. 'You promised.'

'That Mike's a real chump, isn't he?' said Anneena delightedly. 'Walked right into it!'

'So are you going to apologize to Col?' Jane asked.

'Apologize?' said Anneena innocently.

'Oh, come off it, Anneena, you can't pretend you and Rupa hadn't planned that,' said Col.

'So what if we did? I knew as soon as we walked into Mr Quick's office that we wouldn't get anywhere with him. I had to soften Mike up for Rupa instead. The answer was worth it, don't you think? It's opened the scandal right out.'

'You're impossible,' commented Jane in exasperation.

'I know,' grinned Anneena, 'but Rupa's got her story. People have got to know what's really going on.'

'That's what I was worried about,' said Col, speaking quietly to Connie. Anneena and Jane were now cheering as Evelyn approached the car in triumph, having won her argument. 'You'll have to warn your friends. Tell them they'll be found out if they attack anyone else.'

Connie nodded. The only problem was that she wasn't sure if the sirens cared if they were exposed. They were on a collision course with humanity and she doubted she'd be able to deter them from the path they had chosen.

10
The Trustees

The lead story in the Saturday edition of the *Hescombe Herald* was spread out on the breakfast table when Connie went down. *'Death at Axoil!'* the headline declared above a picture of Mr Quick behind his desk. *'Oil company confesses to school children that latest casualty may have died at work,'* it continued. Turning to an inside page, Connie found a longer piece about their visit, complete with a picture of the four of them on a gantry in front of one of the refinery vats.

'After months of refusing to come clean to the media, Axoil employee Mike Shore admitted to children from Hescombe Primary School that William O'Neill may have fallen to his death while at work. The exact circumstances remain shrouded in mystery, raising fears of a cover-up at Axoil. The local community, led by Mr O'Neill's widow, is now calling for an immediate inquiry.'

Evelyn entered the kitchen carrying Madame Cresson.

'What do you think of that, Connie?' she said, stroking the cat as she leant over her niece's shoulder to read the headline. 'When I asked you not to let the visit turn into good PR for them, I didn't quite have this in mind. That poor fool's bound to get the sack from Mr Quick for talking to a reporter without clearing it with him first.'

Connie grimaced. 'But you saw them— Anneena and Rupa were unstoppable. Col's not speaking to Anneena now.'

Evelyn gave a wan smile. 'Don't be too angry with the Nuruddins. They're right, of course. The families are owed the truth,' she said, stroking the cat with firm, even strokes just as Madame Cresson liked it. 'They just wouldn't believe the truth—nor can we afford to tell it to them. It would be the end of the siren colony if we did.'

'We must stop the sirens doing anything else. I don't know how long their promise will last—they're really mad at the invasion of their territory. Can I take this?' Connie asked her aunt, pointing to the paper.

'Of course, I expect your mum and dad would like to see it.'

'No . . . I mean, yes, of course they will, but I meant to send it to the sirens. I've got to warn them.'

Evelyn shrugged. 'Do as you wish. But I doubt this will change their minds. They won't understand what it means.'

'I know. But I've got to try something. And we should warn the company too—tell them not to let workers out on their own—put them in groups or something.'

'But, Connie,' said Evelyn gently, seizing her niece's trembling hands in her own as she folded up the paper. 'What's to stop the sirens taking whole gangs of men? They could, you know. And just how would you get Axoil to listen to you?'

Connie realized her feverish thoughts of warning the company were pointless. No one would take the Society seriously: they'd be laughed at, mocked for suggesting that the company take steps to defend their workers against a dangerous 'song'. It was up to her to persuade the sirens. No one else could.

Connie went down to the quayside, hoping to find Scark. Clutched in her hand was a tightly wrapped bundle with a string loop. Scark was there before her, wading on the strand just outside the harbour wall where the high-tide mark was usually littered with interesting flotsam and jetsam, much of which was edible—for a seagull. Connie jumped down onto the terracotta sand and crunched her way over to him, splashing through the rivulets of fresh water that made the pebbles shine like jewels. He was pecking at a dead crab with only half its claws still intact.

'Scark!' she called. He flapped over to stand at her feet.

'Good morning!' she greeted him. He bowed in response, his eyes shining with pleasure to see her. 'Were you saving that for your daughter?' She pointed to the crab. Scark tapped his foot.

'I'm really sorry to be a pain but would you mind taking this to our friends on the Stacks instead?' she asked, showing him the little bundle. He dropped the crab but stood with his head to one side. 'Are they cross with me?' she enquired, noting his hesitant stance. Scark shook his beak, ruffled his wings, and hopped from one foot to another. 'No? But they're excited about something?'

That was it, according to the seagull.

Perhaps the sirens were agitated after meeting a companion, or maybe they were anticipating the arrival of that creature Kullervo? Connie could not be sure and wondered if she could go to see them again to find out? Perhaps she had better wait to see what effect her message had? In her note she had both written and drawn pictures, trying to explain what was at stake if they were discovered. She had begged them not to attack any more men at the refinery. But she should definitely go out to them soon before any more lives were lost.

'Will you explain to them that I'm trying to help them?' she asked Scark.

He tapped his foot.

Connie held out the parcel. Scark took the loop in his beak and bid her farewell with a rapid volley of 'ach, ach, ach'. She watched him fly as long as he was visible against the cloudy sky, the parcel swinging to and fro like a pendulum suspended beneath him.

When Connie arrived back home, she was surprised to see that they had a visitor, or maybe visitors. An old motorbike and sidecar stood in Shaker Row outside Number Five. Clattering into the kitchen, she found two helmets but only one caller: Dr Brock. He was chatting with her aunt and Signor Antonelli over a mug of coffee and some tough, home-baked biscuits.

Dr Brock called out to her as she came in: 'Ah, Connie, I was waiting for you. I see you've been bearding the lion in his den with your trip to Axoil.'

'Yes,' she said, taking a seat at the table. 'Sorry about that. But it was Anneena and Rupa's idea.'

'So I've heard. You can't help what your friends get up to. After all, they're only following their nature as two very inquisitive young women. We'll have to hope that the sirens lie low for a time. But I haven't come on a social call. As I told you, I have written to the Trustees about the events of last week and they've replied asking to meet you.'

Evelyn could not keep silent, evidently convinced that Dr Brock was not giving the news its due weight. 'It's a real honour to be asked to meet the Trustees, Connie,' she exclaimed. 'I don't think I've ever heard of anyone else being invited to do so!'

'No, we companions of *le sirene* do not meet with Trustees, *carina*,' the signor beamed at her.

Dr Brock gave Connie a conspiratorial wink. 'Well, our Connie is special. And we have to have the highest authority to over-rule an assessor.'

'But to meet all of them: it's unprecedented!' said Evelyn.

'Indeed. But the long and the short of it is that the meeting is to take place tonight up on Dartmoor. We will need to get there before dusk, as I don't fancy trying to find the place in the dark.

Your aunt has given permission for me to take you, so if you agree, we'll have a quick lunch and be off.'

Connie could sense the excitement among the three of them. It made her eager to see what these Trustees were like. 'That sounds great. But I had been thinking that I should go and see the sirens today. Surely someone should go and talk to them?'

Dr Brock exchanged a quick look with Evelyn and Signor Antonelli.

'Er . . . we don't think that's a good idea at the moment, Connie,' he said, running his fingers through his hair. 'If the sirens have gone over to Kullervo . . . Well, let's get your membership of the Society sorted out first. Signor Antonelli is dealing with the sirens.' The Italian bowed to her.

'But . . .' began Connie.

'The Trustees are expecting you, Connie,' interrupted Evelyn swiftly. 'They've come a long way; you mustn't keep them waiting.'

An hour later, Connie was belted into the sidecar, zooming along the country lanes that separated Hescombe from Dartmoor. She could not see much, as rain splattered the small windscreen in front of her, but she gained a tremendous sense of speed crouched so close to the ground. When she glanced to her right-hand side, there was Dr Brock sitting on the bike, goggles over his eyes and raindrops streaming off him. It occurred to Connie that riding a motorbike might be the closest he could come through conventional means to flying on a dragon, but it was a poor exchange: no wings, no flames, no creaturely communication.

The bike slowed to enter a car park and jolted through some muddy puddles. Connie climbed stiffly out of the sidecar and stretched her cramped muscles. With the exception of one car, they had the place to themselves. Hardly surprising as it was a miserable day for a walk on the moor: clouds scudded across the horizon shedding grey showers on the hillsides; nearby a sheep bleated sorrowfully; and the wind tugged insistently at Connie's hair. Bronze bracken sagged over the path, weeping raindrops as they passed.

Dr Brock, however, seemed far from down-hearted.

'Good, good,' he said, locking the helmets away in the sidecar. 'This is perfect: no one else around so next to no chance of anyone seeing the Trustees.'

'Why don't they want to be seen?' asked Connie.

'Because half of them are mythical creatures—they'd create quite a stir if they pitched up in Hescombe, believe me.' He chuckled at Connie's expression of amazement. 'You didn't think I would drag you all the way out to Dartmoor on a wet day like this if we could all have met in your aunt's warm kitchen?'

Connie was not sure what she had thought. The ways of the Society were so new and so extraordinary, nothing Dr Brock suggested would have seemed odd to her.

'There is someone else around though,' she said, nodding over to the car.

'That's only Ivor Coddrington,' Dr Brock said dismissively.

Connie's spirits sank. 'I didn't know he was going to be here,' she muttered.

'He wants to put his version of events to the Trustees first after making such a scandalous mistake. Turning down the first universal companion for a century: not something he'll like to remember, believe me!'

Dr Brock studied his map for a moment before setting off in a northerly direction. Connie tagged behind, in two minds as to whether she wanted to go. The last person she wanted to see was Mr Coddrington. She was sure that their dislike was mutual. He had shown at the assessment that he didn't want her anywhere near his Society. Might he not turn the Trustees against her?

'Is it far?' she asked.

'About four miles,' said Dr Brock, glancing back. 'We've got plenty of time: we'll take it easy. Best foot forward, my dear.'

They set off across the green turf, winding around rocks that protruded like grey teeth breaking through earthen gums. The grass seemed to Connie to be only a thin layer concealing something that slept beneath, some nameless presence more primal, cold, and bleak than anything she had ever met before. In places the gorse had been hacked back or burnt away; grey roots writhed on the surface like twisted snakes. The silence and desolation crept into her heart, filling her with despair. Unbidden, the memory of her aunt's twirling dance returned to her mind and she felt all happiness leach out of her soul, spun off into the remorseless barrenness of the moor. It was only through a great effort of will that she kept putting one foot in front of another, doggedly following in the footsteps of Dr Brock.

Connie trudged on, wiping the rain from her eyes. It was uncomfortable walking in the wet: as she grew warm from the exercise, she longed to take off her anorak, but it was still raining. She wondered how Dr Brock could keep going with no sign of suffering in these conditions: perhaps dragon companions were made of stronger stuff? Just when Connie felt she could go no further, Dr

Brock stopped at a stone stile to take a short breather. It was already getting dark. The looming clouds made it blacker than normal at this time of day.

'Dr Brock?' she said.

'Yes, Connie?'

'There's something that has been bothering me since the assessment.'

'Oh yes, and what's that?'

'I think that Mr Coddrington might have known that I was a universal companion, but he failed me deliberately. He doesn't like me, you know.'

Now that she'd voiced the fear that was plaguing her, Connie expected Dr Brock to tell her not to be so silly. But he did nothing of the sort, just considered her thoughtfully, leaning against the stile.

'I suppose it's possible,' he said at length. 'Universal companions are both envied and feared by other members of the Society. Some see them as a threat to the system, as they cut right across all our neat little categories and arrangements. Ivor would be the sort not to want the boat to be rocked. After seeing the gift die out, it could be that it's his worst nightmare to find it reborn in the new generation of companions.'

Connie thought about this for a moment. Yes, it was plausible, except that she had had the impression that he had disliked her even before assessing her—as if he had already decided his verdict when she stepped into the room.

'But whatever Ivor Coddrington thinks is now irrelevant, Connie,' Dr Brock continued, standing up. 'You're to be assessed by the Trustees: there's no higher honour for a companion than that.'

Col was having his worst flying lesson on record. His father had turned up out of the blue to watch and the knowledge that he was there had sent all of Col's natural talents scuttling into hiding.

'No, no, boy!' rapped out Captain Graves. 'Lean to the left when he turns. You'll be off in a jiffy if you continue on that tack.'

Col grew even angrier with himself as he felt his face flush.

'What is the matter, Companion?' asked Skylark with concern. 'Parts of you are closed to me today. I cannot hear your thoughts.'

Good, thought Col sullenly, for Skylark would be shocked if he heard the tirade of angry words running through Col's head at that moment. He did not like himself in this mood and could not imagine that it would be forgiven and understood by anyone else.

'It's nothing, Skylark,' Col lied. The horse tossed his head, scepticism emanating from him like the beam from a torch, threatening to shine into places that Col would rather keep hidden. Such exposure was the last thing Col wanted right now so he leant forward and said aloud: 'Enough, Skylark. I'm sorry but I've had enough. Can we go down, please?'

Skylark had sufficient sensitivity to know not to push Col any further, so he glided silently down to land with only the merest thump on the grass near Col's father and Captain Graves.

'Don't know what's got into the boy today, Mr Clamworthy,' said Captain Graves almost apologetically, as if he felt responsible for his pupil's poor performance. 'He's not like this normally. He's a natural, as I was telling you, extraordinarily gifted on horseback.'

'It's all right, Captain,' said Col's father, casting a wary look at his son. 'We can't all perform on demand, can we? I believe you when you say he's good—after all, he's my son. I can hardly be surprised if he turns out talented, can I now?'

He said it as a joke, but Col winced: his father was always so sure of himself, so proud of his own obvious abilities as a companion.

Captain Graves led Skylark away, patting the young horse affectionately on the shoulder, leaving father and son alone in the paddock. The day had turned nasty—a cold rain flattened Mr Clamworthy's spiked black hair and spotted his designer-label jeans. Mr Clamworthy—or Mack as he preferred to be known, even to his son—always aspired to look younger than he was, to be one of the lads. Col thought that the rain-flattened hair somehow made him appear older, revealing lines around his eyes: in fact, making him look more like the ordinary dad Col often wished for.

'So, Col, having a bit of trouble, are you?' Mack Clamworthy asked none too subtly. Perhaps his father was trying to show interest in his progress but Col could not help but hear the unspoken words he had so often had to listen to, that success was due to Clamworthy genes, failure to those of Col's mother.

'I'm managing OK.'

Mack put his arm round his son's shoulders to steer him in the direction of the farmhouse. 'Has your mother been to see you recently?'

Col shrugged, feigning indifference as a painful image of his startlingly beautiful mother flashed into his mind. 'No.'

'Huh!' Mack laughed disdainfully, leaving the implication hanging in the air that somehow Col's trouble today was due to his mother's neglect. Col felt a wave of anger: he knew full well that, had she visited, that too would have been seized on as a cause of his poor showing. Eager to change the subject before he said something rash, Col asked the question he knew would always get his father on to a different track.

'What brings you down here? Is the Kraken in our waters again?'

'That's right. I went diving yesterday but everything's OK. It's well hidden—very deep.'

Col glanced sideways at his father, thinking that despite everything else he felt about him, it was really cool to have a father who was a companion to one of the most feared sea-beasts in the world. He could not even begin to imagine what that encounter must be like: it made his gift for the pegasi seem tame by comparison.

'I hear from Mum that you've been visiting our friends over at Chartmouth,' said Mack abruptly, surfacing to the present from the depths into which Col's question had sent him.

'Oh yeah. Did you see the newspaper too?'

'Yeah. Too bad you drew attention to what the sirens are up to.' Col flushed. 'You watch those guys, Col—I mean it. I've met their kind before in other parts of the world: they're real cowboys. Axoil is ruthless—no reason to expect their European branch to be any different. Don't go thinking that some two-bit paper and four kids will stand in their way. And as for that idiot, Maurice Quick—I know him. We were at school together. Axoil's welcome to him. He was a nasty piece of work as a boy—always boasting that he had a better watch or something than the rest of us. I bet he's just the same now he's been given even bigger toys to play with at the refinery. He must've loved coming back here to shove his success down our throats. You'd better pray our paths don't cross. It won't be pretty if we come face to face, I can tell you.'

Col suppressed his resentment that even here his father was claiming that he knew better than his son. He never seemed to be able to do anything that Mack had not done before—and done better. But perhaps for once his dad was right: Mack's vast experience of the sea might mean that he would be able to give them some advice as to what to do next. Was there any way to stop the sirens being exposed?

'Dad, do you have any ideas what we should do now?' Col asked when they reached the car park in front of the Mastersons' house. Mack paused in the act of buckling on his crash helmet and met his son's eyes for the first time. He hesitated, then took his helmet off and smiled, clapping Col on the back, looking very pleased to have been asked.

'Sure. When in doubt, I've always found it best to go back to the first principles of the Society. I think what you need is a diversionary tactic . . . '

Dr Brock and Connie reached the meeting place at about seven in the evening. The Trustees had chosen one of the remotest points on the moor: it was marked by a tor—a rock carved by the elements into a tortured shape, like a hooded man leaning into a strong wind, straining to remain upright. Wisps of low cloud curled around it so that the tor seemed to be moving, revealing glimpses of its dark, mysterious features between the rags of mist. It dwarfed Ivor Coddrington who was already there, taking shelter in the lee of the rock, struggling with a black umbrella. It had just blown inside out and he was wrestling to put it to rights; their arrival did little to cheer him.

'Hello, Ivor!' called Dr Brock heartily.

Mr Coddrington glared at them both. 'Fine fuss they are making about her,' he replied, shaking the umbrella violently so that it re-formed itself into a crumpled dome over his head. 'Dragging us all out here!'

Connie shrank back behind Dr Brock.

'Come now: Connie's quite a find for us,' Dr Brock said with a hint of amusement.

'Humph!' Mr Coddrington grunted, before turning his attention back to the umbrella, avoiding further conversation. Connie heard him mutter 'a danger more like' but not loud enough to make Dr Brock feel he had to respond.

It was a tedious wait. There was only one place that offered any chance of shelter from the rain—the leeside of the tor—which meant the three of them had to sit in unwelcome proximity. With Mr Coddrington within earshot huddled beneath his battered umbrella, Connie was disinclined to ask any questions. But they ran round in her head nonetheless. The wind moaned in the crevices of the tor like a demon imprisoned in the rock, fretting to be released. A steady, penetrating rain fell, casting a grey twilight over the moor, which stretched out on all sides like a dull green sea, rippling with restless waves of grass. Staring at the fading landscape, Connie once again felt desolate and afraid. Her gift set her apart, she was beginning to understand that, but would the Trustees let her into the Society after their assessment or would they listen to Mr Coddrington? And who or what were the Trustees? To distract her anxious thoughts, she passed the time casting stones at chosen targets. Dr Brock joined her in this desultory game and she cheered up as they got a fierce little competition under way.

'Ah ha! I win!' exulted Dr Brock, after hitting a clump of grass on the edge of the pool of light cast by their torch. Connie gracefully conceded defeat, having won six rounds herself.

'Again?' she asked, but got no reply. Dr Brock was looking up into the night sky. She could make nothing out—there were no stars or moon to be seen—but she sensed something too: others were approaching. The creak of leathery wings forewarned her—a burst of flame and a dragon with a brilliant green underbelly descended through the clouds right above their heads, circling down to land.

Dr Brock jumped to his feet with excitement. 'It's Morjik,' he cried.

'Morjik?' she asked.

He helped her up. 'Yes—the oldest and wisest of dragons—all the way from central Europe.'

The dragon landed with a heavy thump a stone's cast away, folding its wings into its gleaming body. It was then that Connie noticed a woman dressed in a brown leather riding-suit on his back. From the glimpse of her in the torchlight, Connie guessed the lady was around Dr Brock's age, and, like him, still quite up to the task of dragon-flying.

'Kinga!' Dr Brock rushed over to hand the woman down. 'It's a joy to see you after all these years!'

'And you, Franciszek—though I see you've lost your fiery top to age,' she replied in a throaty voice with a Slavic accent, gesturing to his white hair. She kissed him lightly on the cheeks three times. 'Are we the first?'

Dr Brock nodded and then turned to bow very low to Morjik.

'Wise One, we are honoured by your presence,' he said gravely. The dragon—with its vivid green hide, gnarled and knotted like tree bark, and startling red eyes—flickered its tongue gently so that it touched Dr Brock on the head. Connie sensed a bond of affection between the three and wondered what story lay behind this encounter.

The woman greeted Ivor Coddrington with the slightest bow of her head; the dragon paid him no attention at all. They both then turned in Connie's direction, but Dr Brock stepped forward to stand between them.

'Perhaps we should wait?' he suggested, thinking better of a premature introduction before all the Trustees were assembled.

'True, that is for later,' declared the lady. She pulled some faggots of wood off her mount's back. 'Come, let us make a fire to warm the others when they reach this miserably wet island of yours, Franciszek. You see I am prepared: a little present from the forests of my country.'

She threw the wood in a heap and, with the dragon's fiery breath, they had no problem starting a blaze despite the rain. Connie hovered on the far side of the fire, feeling awkward. When would the others arrive? She was eager to meet the newcomers properly, particularly the dragon, whose mesmerizing eyes drew her to it: she longed to touch its rough scales and feel the warmth coming from its body that glowed faintly in the dark like an emerald.

Then something made the hair on the back of Connie's neck prickle: more creatures were approaching. Quite unexpectedly, she was swept by three distinct sensations: first a silky calmness like standing in a shower of silver mist; then a troubling, dark mood; and finally a steely determination which gripped her so fiercely she gasped. She reeled as she battled with three conflicting presences; it was as if she was attached to ropes pulling in different directions. Dr Brock was swiftly at her side.

'What is it?' he asked with concern.

She could say nothing—indeed, she need say nothing because six figures stepped out of the shadows into the firelight. First came an animal that Connie recognized immediately as a unicorn. It was larger than she had imagined with powerful shoulders rippling with muscle; a gilded horn rose majestically from the centre of its forehead, and a silver mane foamed down its neck, scintillating with reflected flame. An African woman, dressed in robes of bright orange and with intricately braided hair, paced beside it, her hand entwined with a lock of the unicorn's mane as if she had just dismounted. Next into the circle of light came the most confusing creature that Connie had yet met. It looked like a great raven, the size of a man; as it lifted its wings, flashes of white light flickered forth accompanied by a deep rumbling. A tall, bronze-skinned man in a fringed suede jacket studded with blue stones strode beside the bird. His long black hair was streaked with white and he had a string of red beads around his throat. Finally, a stocky, manlike creature stamped into the light, face shadowed by a hooded cloak; all Connie could spy in the folds of the cloak was a dark, craggy hand carrying a mallet. With his other arm, he supported his elderly companion, a frail man in a yellow sou'wester who reminded Connie of one of the old sailors to be found seated over their fishing rods on Hescombe quay, face wrinkled like a walnut.

Kinga, as the first to arrive, assumed the role of host and stepped forward to greet them.

'Welcome, friends,' she said, her sharp eyes glinting in the firelight, her smoke-grey hair coiled at the nape of her neck. 'We meet on a great occasion for the Society—that is if what we all hope turns out to be true. First, let us introduce ourselves to our guests and thank them for coming to meet us at such short notice.'

She turned to Dr Brock, Connie, and Mr Coddrington, signalling that the meeting was in session.

'The Trustees are assembled: for the Company of Reptiles and Sea Creatures stands Morjik, oldest of dragons, and myself, Kinga Potowska, Dragon Companion; for the Company of Winged Beasts stands Storm-Bird and Eagle-Child, his companion; for the two and four-legged beasts and beings stands Windfoal, the greatest of unicorns, and her companion, Kira Okona; and for the creatures of the four elements, Gard, the rock dwarf, with Frederick Cony, Rock Dwarf Companion.'

The eight Trustees arranged themselves in pairs in a circle around the fire: north sat the dwarf with his companion, east Storm-Bird, south the dragon, and west the unicorn. The rain had eased off; the skies were clearing and one bright star shone through the fleeting clouds, glinting above the golden horn of the unicorn like a jewel on the pinnacle of a sceptre. The atmosphere was charged with energy: the feelings Connie had experienced before still lingered, mingled with the fiery presence of the dragon. She was confused, struggling to control her instinct to reach out to each creature: she had never been in the presence of more than one species before and was in danger of being overwhelmed.

Dr Brock said in a low voice: 'You do not look well, Connie: is something the matter?'

Connie tried to explain her confusion, but found her voice strangled in her throat: she felt suffocated with the flow of energy coming from the beasts—lashed with fire, drowning in a swirl of sensations.

Dr Brock stepped forward into the circle. 'Trustees, I must beg you not to send your thoughts out to the young girl. Four such powerful minds at once are more than a human can withstand.'

The four human companions looked at their creatures in wonder: none had been aware that their bond had been shared with another while they sat waiting. Then Connie felt a withdrawing of energy, like a tide creeping out, and found she was able to think clearly again.

Mr Coddrington had been watching her closely throughout this episode and chose this moment to step forward. His presence in the centre of the circle of creatures seemed all wrong to Connie.

'Honourable Trustees, may I speak?' Kinga nodded. 'This is what I found when I assessed the girl—confusion, chaos,' said Mr Coddrington, spitting the words out disdainfully. 'She may have unusual gifts but I stand by my judgement that they are unsettled, disorderly. It was as much for her own good as for that of the mythical creatures that I failed her. It is too late, perhaps, to eject her from the Society, now she has seen so many of our secrets, but I would sincerely advise that her activities be restricted to one species only.'

Connie, standing beyond the pool of light, watched the Trustees anxiously: did they agree with the official? In her heart, she believed that she could control her response once she had trained herself to focus, but if Ivor Coddrington got his way she would never be able even to attempt this.

Kinga looked round the circle. 'I know what Morjik and I think on this question, but perhaps others would like to speak first?'

Eagle-Child held up his hand, the fringe of his jacket swaying gently in the breeze like prairie grass. 'We would like to hear from Connie herself,' he said quietly.

The dragon companion beckoned Connie forward. 'Welcome, child, to our meeting. We know that it may be difficult for you to speak up before strangers, but if you have the courage, tell us what you wish to happen to you.'

A harsh deep voice—that of the rock dwarf—butted in from the northerly point of the circle. 'One doubt need not concern you: there is no question in our minds that you have the universal gift—raw and untried though it is.'

Finding her knees were shaking, Connie stepped forward nervously. She moved to the centre of the circle, displacing Mr Coddrington, searching instinctively for the point where the energy emanating from all four creatures was held in balance. She found it and stood still, and immediately no longer felt exposed and alone, but connected to the creatures, like the hub at the centre of a wheel. As if sensing a call, Morjik lifted his snout, releasing a tongue of fire; Windfoal whinnied; Storm-Bird's wings fluttered, flashing with needle-sharp points of white light; and Gard thumped the ground with his mallet so that it rang like a deep bell.

'I would like to develop my gift, if I may. I am sure . . . at least I think . . . I can learn to control it—settle it,' she added with a glance at Mr Coddrington.

'She is right,' came a penetrating growl. Connie wondered for a moment who had spoken, until she realized the voice had come from Morjik. The others seemed equally surprised that he had intervened, speech being a rare commodity amongst dragons.

Kira Okona added her voice to the debate, her soft voice like the scent of sweet melted chocolate rolling across the space between them. 'Windfoal and I are content for Connie to try. No one finds their gift fully-formed; each of us has to learn to use it; her task is similar, though greater in complexity.'

A loud croak from Storm-Bird and Eagle-Child said: 'Let the chick learn to fly—don't tie her to the branch.'

'Then it is agreed,' declared Kinga. 'We thank Mr Coddrington for his concern for the well-being of the Society, but in this case we believe caution is the wrong choice. Connie's membership of the Society for the Protection of Mythical Creatures is confirmed; the result of her previous assessment is set aside. We judge that her calling is that of a universal. She should begin her training at once.'

Connie felt a glow of pleasure alight inside her. She hadn't realized until she heard those words quite how much membership of the Society had come to mean to her. And to hear that the sirens had been right—that she was a universal—that was perhaps the best of all. It sounded such an amazing gift! Dr Brock came forward to shake her by the hand, clearly delighted; Ivor Coddrington sloped off into the shadows, muttering that he would return to his car. No one paid much attention to his grudging departure as the unicorn neighed and shook her mane, scattering silver sparks.

'Windfoal wishes to meet Connie,' said Kira. 'She wants to learn what is in Connie's heart.'

'What do I do?' Connie asked Kira as Dr Brock pushed her gently forward.

'Just wait: you'll know,' said Kira with an easy smile. The unicorn trotted over and came to a halt, towering above Connie. She could smell the beast's sweet breath and found herself looking up into eyes as black as the night. Windfoal bowed her neck to the girl's level, enveloping her in her spice-scented mane. Cautiously, Connie raised her hand to the unicorn's nose and leant her forehead against the animal's velvet cheek, whispering her name softly in Windfoal's ear. A calm mood stole over her, this time no longer fighting with other sensations. Connie was filled with peace as she slipped into the warm bath of the unicorn's gentle nature, and her eyelids grew heavy.

Kira spoke to the others: 'Windfoal reminds us that Connie is yet a child—she needs sleep. We have more things to discuss here tonight, but let

Connie rest now. Later, Windfoal will carry her to save her the long walk back.'

'Yes; when we have completed our business here,' said Kinga, 'Morjik and I will take Francis as near as we dare go to the road.'

Lying beside the unicorn, Connie was only vaguely aware of the conversation being conducted over her head. She knew that her name was frequently mentioned—and that of the creature, Kullervo—but there was something so intoxicating about the sleep sent by Windfoal that these now seemed of little matter to her. All she wanted to do was curl up on a blanket provided by Eagle-Child and drift off into dreams filled with sunlit streams, lush meadows, and the sound of laughter.

11
Mags

Connie had only a vague memory of the journey home as she was gently lifted from Windfoal's back into the sidecar. She woke next morning in her own bedroom and lay for a moment watching the dust motes swirling in the shaft of light coming through the curtains. The sprightly voice of Signor Antonelli floated up into the air like bobbing helium balloons released into the sky in celebration. *'Nessun dorma!'* he sang beneath her window. *'Nessun dorma! Tu pure, o Principessa . . .'* Fully awake now, Connie asked herself if last night had been a dream. Had she really ridden a unicorn and met three other extraordinary creatures? The trip to Dartmoor had been real enough because there, on the chair, lay her muddy clothes. She remembered Evelyn helping her out of them late last night when she had stumbled into bed.

A dustbin lid at Number Four banged discordantly.

'Shut up!' yelled Mr Lucas. 'Who do you think you are: Pavarotti?'

Signor Antonelli evidently considered the suggestion to be spot on for he held his concluding note defiantly. When he finished, Connie mentally applauded him—the song was just right for her delicious mood of content.

Stretching, enjoying the warmth of her duvet, Connie suddenly recalled the most important thing that had been said: her gift had been confirmed. She must tell her aunt. Throwing back the covers, she scrambled into some clean clothes and dashed downstairs. Her aunt was waiting for her in the kitchen and astonished her by folding her into a tight hug.

'Dr Brock told me!' Evelyn exclaimed, her voice quivering with emotion. 'A universal companion—in my own family! I am so, so proud.'

Connie pulled away to see that Evelyn had tears in her eyes. She had known from Dr Brock that her gift was special but witnessing her aunt's reaction drove home the magnitude of what had happened to her.

'We'd given up hope, you see,' Evelyn continued. 'Thought that the mythical world was failing. But you are a sign that it's not too late.'

Connie, only just having woken up, found the news that so much was expected of her rather daunting. 'But I don't know what I can do to change things,' she said.

'Of course not,' said Evelyn a little aggressively. 'But we all have to do something to save our companion creatures. When I think of how we have driven many animals and habitats to the edge of extinction—and even over the edge—well, it makes my blood boil!' Connie saw anger flash in her aunt's green eyes.

'But now, with you to help us, we can begin to set things right. And maybe there will be other universal companions again. Let us take it as a good sign and stick to that hope,' she concluded, twirling Connie around at arm's length, making the kitchen spin faster and faster. Connie shrieked, laughing at her aunt's fey mood. Evelyn released her hands and Connie flew away, dizzily staggering into Signor Antonelli who entered the kitchen from the garden at that moment.

'*Tranquillamente!*' he smiled at her as he caught her. 'We must take care ov da *universale*, no?'

* * *

When Col answered the door, he found Connie standing on the doorstep, her face radiant with excitement.

'How'd it go yesterday?' he asked. 'Did they accept you as a companion to sirens?'

'Can I come in? I've so much to tell you,' she said. She was eager to break the news, convinced Col would understand how amazing it was. He would surely be pleased that she would now even be able to share his delight in the pegasi?

'Of course,' he replied, stepping aside to let her pass. 'Gran's at church but she'll want to hear all about it too when she gets back. Come into the garden. In fact, it's high time you met my pony.'

Col led the way into the garden, wondering why Connie had not given him an answer yet. She looked so happy: surely they must have accepted her?

The garden was full of late flowers—the memory of summer had not yet faded here, creating a haven for bees and butterflies. Dragonflies danced over a pond, flashes of blue perfectly mirrored in the surface beneath. Connie was enchanted by the water lilies floating serenely on the pool, their cuplike buds the colour of buttermilk. Everything seemed especially beautiful and significant to Connie this morning. Her ears caught the sound of the bulrushes whispering in the breeze, and the tinkling music of a fountain playing in the sunlight. She would have lingered, but Col had not brought her this way to show her his grandmother's handiwork. He led her to a little stream that ran down the boundary at the far end. Col jumped over with Connie following and they continued on into the allotments that lay beyond. There amongst the rows of beans was one allotment that had been fenced off to make a paddock. Awaiting their approach was a handsome little chestnut pony.

'This is Mags,' said Col proudly, swinging himself over the fence. 'Don't be fooled by his sweet look—he can bite.'

Mags trotted meekly over to Col and nibbled him on the ear. Col dug in his pocket and pulled out a packet of Polos. He liked to show off his unique relationship with his pony to his friends. He had always considered that it marked him out as being special as it had been the sign of his bond with the pegasi—a calling that, since his encounter, Col was convinced put all other companionships in the shade.

'His favourite,' he said, holding out one for the pony to eat. 'But I have to ration them very strictly or he'd have the whole packet off me.'

Connie climbed into the paddock and held out her hand. Mags immediately left Col and the mints to come to her side. She laid her hand on his neck and whispered a greeting in his ear. Watching this performance, Col was torn by conflicting feelings of surprise and jealousy. Mags had never shown any affection to anyone else in Col's presence—so strong was their bond—but here he was nuzzling Connie as if she was an old friend. What was going on?

'So did the Trustees accept you?' Col broke into Connie and Mags's private conversation a little roughly, reasserting his seniority in matters regarding the Society.

Connie turned to him, her face lit with excitement. The moment had come to tell him. 'Yes they did: they set aside the failed assessment. And I can begin my training.'

'That's great,' Col said, coming to lay claim to Mags by taking his halter.

'But I've more news for you, Col. They told me something else: they told me that I'm a universal companion. That's what the sirens said but the Trustees confirmed it.'

Col choked with surprise. 'A what?'

'A universal companion, you know: someone who can bond with any . . . '

'I know what it means,' he said curtly. 'And you're one of them?'

'The only one at the moment.'

Col knew he should be marvelling at this astounding news, knew he should be pleased and proud for Connie, but instead he felt jealous. All his expectations had been rudely reversed. *He* was the leading youth member of the Chartmouth Chapter, not her. A wave of jealousy swept over him and, without thinking, he hit on the first thing he could think of to hold against her.

'And why didn't you tell me this before? I thought we were friends.'

That was rich coming from him when he had kept her in the dark about the Society for weeks!

'I would've done, but Dr Brock told me to keep it a secret until we were sure.'

'But you could've at least told me!' Col gave Mags a cursory farewell pat, not feeling too pleased with his pony either, and started to make his way home. Connie ran to hold him back.

'What's the matter, Col? What've I done? I thought you'd be happy for me.'

He said nothing, but shook her off and stomped back to the stream with Connie tagging behind. He was beginning to feel sorry that he had reacted so badly, but now that he had snapped at her, it was doubly difficult to admit that he was in the wrong.

'Look, your grandmother's back,' said Connie, pointing to a bicycle leaning against the wall.

'Good, you can go and tell her your news yourself then,' he replied sullenly. 'I'm off to see my mates. I'm playing football this morning with Justin.'

Kicking the garden gate open, Col ran off down the street in the direction of his friend's house, aware that he had just told Connie a lie. He had not arranged to play football with Justin at all, but he could not bear to be present when she told his grandmother. He knew his grandmother would overreact, probably cry and make a great fuss over her. His own gift paled into insignificance beside hers: who would be interested in him if Connie were there meeting creatures left, right, and centre? He had liked the idea of sharing the secret of the true business of the Society with someone in his school—but he had never imagined it would be on anything but equal terms.

It was worse than Col had feared. Not only did his grandmother chatter on endlessly about Connie all that day, but everyone else seemed to have become obsessed with the subject. Even Dr Brock, whom Col admired intensely, had caught the hysteria surrounding the universal and had gone to the unusual length of summoning a special meeting of the Chartmouth Chapter at the Clamworthys' that evening. Col sat moodily in a corner cleaning the mud off his football boots ready for school the next day. He gave everyone the minimal greeting he could get away with without being too obviously rude. His grandmother by contrast was alight with enthusiasm, showering her guests with champagne as she popped open a bottle she had kept back for a special occasion. His dad sloped in and ruffled his hair in greeting before moving swiftly on to take over from his mother as wine waiter. Col scowled and smoothed his hair back.

When Evelyn and Signor Antonelli entered—Evelyn looking uncharacteristically happy, the Italian kissing all the ladies' hands gaily—Dr Brock immediately leapt up and asked: 'Where's Connie? Is someone with her? She mustn't be left alone.'

'Don't worry, Francis,' said Evelyn, accepting a glass of champagne from Mack with a radiant smile, 'I've left her with a friend from school—the Benedict girl. You know the family: they live on the new estate.'

Dr Brock nodded. 'Oh yes, the Axoil scientist. She'll be safe there.'

Col dug angrily at the dried mud stuck between two studs, prising off a piece that looked like a slice of grey Swiss cheese. So, they were going to have minute-by-minute bulletins on the universal's movements now, text messages as to what she had for breakfast!

'Now, I've called this meeting not only so that I can share the great news about Connie. In fact, I see from your faces that that would be quite redundant as you all seem to know already. Someone is going to have a very large phone bill at the end of the month.' Dr Brock cast an amused look in Mrs Clamworthy's direction.

'Well, Francis, it's not every day I get the chance to spread such a lovely bit of news,' she replied defensively.

'Indeed not. But that's left me with the task of having to share only the bad news with you. That's why Connie's not here to join in the celebration. I needed to speak to you all without her being present and I would be grateful if you keep what I say from her for reasons you will soon understand.' Col's ears pricked up. 'The shape-shifting creature, Kullervo, has heard about Connie's gift. In fact, he knew about her even before we did—and the sirens say he is coming for her.'

Kullervo! Col was still reeling from hearing the name of the mythical creature, who, it was rumoured, could assume any shape he wished.

Ever since he could remember he had heard his family mention that creature with awed fear. He knew that during the last World War, Kullervo had taken advantage of the chaos created by humanity and led an attack on the Society from the north, under the cover of war. He had wiped out nearly a generation of members of the Society as he directed his followers to turn on humans. Creatures loyal to the Society had eventually succeeded in stopping his forces on the edge of the Arctic Circle. Thankfully, the Society had managed to hide the two living universals from him so that he was unable to unleash his own formidable powers as he intended. Yet the threat had never really gone away—'contained but not defeated' was how Col's grandmother had described it—and she should know, for she was of the generation who had protected the universals by stopping him, and had lost many friends in the struggle.

The happiness on Evelyn's face drained away, replaced by pale fear. 'So that's why you asked me to keep a close eye on her until she met the Trustees,' breathed Evelyn. 'And I thought it was just to stop her trying to see the sirens again.'

'There was that too. We can't risk letting the universal within a mile of followers of Kullervo.

'I hardly need tell you what danger he would pose to our world if he managed to persuade the universal to join his side. His power is locked in the mythical world—at the moment he uses others to do his dirty work for him—but with a universal by his side the door opens, and humanity would be hard pressed to survive his onslaught. It would be like the meteorite that brought an end to the dinosaurs.'

Col put his boots down, his attention now riveted on Dr Brock's earnest face. And he had been jealous of Connie! He now realized he should have been terrified for her.

'That's one reason why universals have always been so important to the Society. They are a blessing; but if they go wrong, they could be our curse.'

'But *la signorina*, she no go wrong!' protested Signor Antonelli. 'She is *gentila*.'

Dr Brock nodded his head in agreement. 'Of course, Luciano, I have no fear of her: I fear *for* her. She is so young, so new to the Society. She can't possibly be ready to hear all this about her calling. That is why the Trustees have decided that Connie should only be told in stages what she needs to know, so that she can be slowly prepared for the full truth. For now, she is aware only that it would be dangerous for her to meet him.

'Therefore, we have to find him before he finds Connie. We must also ensure that he has no chance of meeting her—at least not until she has been fully trained to resist him.'

Mrs Clamworthy looked worried; the bubbles had gone from her champagne mood. 'But how can we do that? There are no universals left except for Connie. None of us know their secrets.'

'But we each know something about our own gifts: Connie can learn much from us. When she is ready, she'll be given the key to the deeper knowledge of her company.'

Evelyn, who had been silent for a long while, stood up suddenly. 'I must go and fetch her. What if she's under attack right now?'

'No, Evelyn!' said Dr Brock sharply. Mack, who was leaning against the back door, blocked her exit, and received a stony glare in payment. 'You must not panic. The Trustees were quite clear that we have to let Connie live a normal life—as far as it is possible for a universal to live a normal life. Think, Evelyn: Kullervo will not attack her when she's in the midst of other people—that's not his way. He'll be looking for an opportunity to get her when she's on her own and vulnerable. We must not let that happen.

'That's why you've all been allotted tasks. Evelyn, obviously you must ensure that Connie is safe at home. Col . . . ' (Col sat up with a start; he had thought that he had been completely forgotten) 'you are to keep an eye on Connie at school. Signor Antonelli, if you are willing to stay a little longer, we'd like you to lead a task force to deal with the sirens. We cannot risk letting Connie go out to them again, not now we know they've gone over to Kullervo's side, but we still have to deal with the threat they pose to the refinery and to shipping.'

'*Certo*,' agreed Signor Antonelli with a deep bow.

'The rest of us are to participate in the hunt for Kullervo. Remember: we must all treat Connie normally. It seems we have a couple of months to prepare both her and ourselves—the sirens said that Kullervo was coming in the winter storms. We'll have to make the most of the time that gives us. Do any of you have any questions?'

Col had loads of questions buzzing around in his head. What was he supposed to do to protect her? He wasn't suited to being a babysitter but it sounded very much as if Dr Brock expected him to follow her every step. And what could he do if Kullervo did suddenly surface in the playground? How would he even recognize a shape-shifter?

'Er, Dr Brock?' he said, raising a hand.

'Yes, Col.'

'What do I have to do exactly—at school, I mean? I don't even know what Kullervo looks like.'

'As I said, treat her as normal but just look out for anything unexpected, anything suspicious. Make sure she's not alone.'

At least that last one was already covered: he never saw her out of the company of Anneena and Jane.

'OK,' he said with a shrug, though his casual demeanour hid an inner turmoil. He did not want to have to admit in this company that he had made a very bad start by falling out with the universal at the first opportunity.

'Good,' said Dr Brock, looking round the room at the sober faces before him. 'If we all pull together on this, I'm sure we have nothing to fear. Remember: it's still a great day for Hescombe—the first universal in a century, the first of the new millennium.'

When Col arrived at school on Monday he had almost made up his mind to apologize. Despite having to bear endless discussion of Hescombe's universal companion, he had felt the resurgence of his better nature and resolved to try to control his jealousy. It was a good thing the universal gift had come back; it was just bad luck that it happened to be his friend who had it, and not him. He now had a serious duty to perform to protect her: he should not waste time on petty quarrels, particularly now he knew what was at stake.

With these thoughts in mind, Col watched for an opportunity to say sorry as soon as possible. His resolve was strengthened by the fact that Connie looked quite miserable when she traipsed into the room and studiously avoided his eye. But before he could have a word with her, Anneena breezed in and barged her way between Col and Connie. She soon cheered Connie up with a torrent of stories about her weekend at a family party. Her sister, Rupa, had announced her engagement, much to everyone's delight.

Mr Johnson came in carrying the register and the buzz of conversation died down. Always sensitive to the feelings of others, Connie noticed that the teacher wore a worried expression this morning. After checking off their names, he looked down at a sheet of paper and cleared his throat to speak.

'Mrs Hartley's asked all the staff to make an announcement to our classes. We've had some good news.' He said these words in such a flat tone that Connie wondered why. 'A rather unexpected development has taken place. It seems that the visit to Axoil by four pupils in this class has reawakened happy memories of Hescombe Primary School for Mr Quick, the managing director. He has approached Mrs Hartley with the most generous offer of a donation to redevelop our playground and install some state-of-the-art play equipment.' An excited murmur ran round the class. 'Mrs Hartley hopes this will be the first step in a happy friendship between this school and the local business community.' Jane glanced at Connie and raised her eyebrows. It was clear what Mrs Hartley hoped, but what about Mr Johnson? 'Every class has been invited to send in ideas for the new playground which will be built during the Christmas holidays. Mr Quick himself will be here to announce the winning design at the end of term assembly.'

Mr Johnson glanced across to the register briefly before making the next announcement.

'That's all I've got to say on that but could I see Anneena, Jane, Connie, and Col at break, please?'

The four of them spent the first part of the morning wondering why Mr Johnson wanted to see them. It did not take a genius to work out that it had something to do with Mr Quick but Col could not imagine what it would be. Staring at his maths textbook, the numbers swimming before his eyes, he remembered what his father had said about Axoil being a cowboy outfit that liked to play dirty. Building a new playground seemed to suggest Axoil had changed. They'd surely only get a little local publicity for this, nothing that would really count? But then, they needed every positive story they could get now Rupa had splashed the story about William O'Neill's death over the front page. And when Col remembered the cold gaze of Mr Quick, he could not swallow the explanation that 'happy memories' were the reason. No, whatever was going on, Col would eat his flying helmet, goggles and all, if it was coming from the goodness of Mr Quick's heart.

The bell went for break and the classroom quickly emptied as the children dashed outside to start planning their new playground. Col hung back, standing apart while the three girls clustered around Mr Johnson's desk.

'Right,' said the teacher, 'I want to have a brief word with you about the end of term display.' He paused, letting the meaning of his words sink in. Everyone in class had been working on a display to go up in the entrance hall to show what they had been doing as their project for the term. The four of them were putting together material on the local debate about the Axoil refinery, including their visit to the company.

Anneena was instantly suspicious. 'You're not going to ask us to drop it, are you, sir?'

Mr Johnson shook his head but looked uncomfortable. 'Of course not: that would be a deplorable thing to do. No, Mrs Hartley has just asked me to ask you to make sure you stick to your theme about the impact of the refinery on the local environment. She wanted me to reassure her that you'll take a balanced approach, which I said you would, of course. You must understand that she's worried that Mr Quick might be offended when he comes to the assembly if he sees something about recent tragic events or that shows his company in an overly negative light.'

Col could not believe what he was hearing. Not that he had any intention of letting Anneena bring yet more attention to a subject that he wished she had let well alone.

'He's not going to care what some classroom display says about his company!' he burst out.

'On the contrary, it appears that he does. The article following your visit has not passed unnoticed in the business press. I'm afraid he thinks that you've ... er ... complicated his life somewhat. I think he would like the opportunity to restore the balance with some positive news coverage. That's why the presentation of the cheque and announcement of the winning design is going to happen in front of the local media.'

It all began to slot into place for Col. Axoil's publicity office had made a mess of the first interview; Mr Quick was moving in to tidy up the public relations disaster and was doing all he could to control the event in advance. Of course the local press would seize on any mention of the missing men by the children if it were prominently displayed in the entrance hall when they came to the presentation. Mr Quick didn't want that particular story to have a second airing.

Mr Johnson, looking round the little circle gathered at his desk, added hurriedly: 'I promise you that I will put up whatever you feel you want to include. I just want you to understand that Mrs Hartley—and I—expect you to take particular care that what you choose to display is accurate and fair to all concerned.'

Anneena, Jane, and Connie nodded, more ready to trust Mr Johnson than Col. He felt annoyed with them for this—and annoyed with their teacher.

'It's not fair!' he burst out rudely. 'You know it's not!' Axoil sticking its nose into their project was almost enough to make him think that Anneena and Rupa had been right to make life as difficult for Mr Quick as they could. He turned on his heel and left the classroom, kicking the door open angrily. Mr Johnson let this pass. Connie realized that the teacher must not feel too good about himself at that moment and probably part of him agreed with Col.

'Sorry about that,' said Anneena primly, as unofficial leader of the project team assuming responsibility for Col's behaviour. 'We'll do our best, but we may not have a message that Axoil wants to hear.'

Mr Johnson sighed. 'I know, but as long as you can show that you've tried to be even-handed, I'll fight this all the way with Mrs Hartley.' A combative light appeared in his normally mild eyes. 'I will certainly not let our class display be chopped and changed just because some local benefactor might take offence. What sort of lesson would that be to teach you all?'

The mood amongst the four when they continued work on their project was miserable. Col would barely talk to them, saying they had sold out and he reacted angrily when Anneena told him not to be so stupid, pointing out it had been her and Rupa who had got the company on the run in the first place.

'I wish I'd never started this,' Jane confided to Connie as they leafed through some photos of the Stacks. 'I'm afraid Dad's going to lose his job—and all because of me. He seems really unhappy at work now and won't say why. It was OK before our visit to Axoil.'

Connie secretly thought that *no* job at all must be better than working for Axoil, not with Mr Quick for a boss and the sirens after the employees, but she couldn't say this to Jane.

'If he loses his job,' Jane continued, 'where else will he be able to find work around here? There's not much work for an organic chemist in these parts outside the oil companies. We'll have to move.'

Guilt filled Connie: she did not want to be the cause of Jane having to leave Hescombe. They had already talked about going up to Chartmouth Secondary School together next year, about trying to get in the same class. It would be a disaster if their attempt to save the Stacks ended up forcing Jane's family to leave.

'You think we were right to do what we did, though, don't you, Jane?' Connie asked anxiously.

Jane smiled sadly. 'Of course, but I can't help worrying. Sorry for moaning at you about all this.'

Connie squeezed Jane's arm shyly. 'You can say what you like to me,' she said. 'I understand.'

At the beginning of the following week, Connie received a bulky letter through the post. Evelyn seemed to know what it was, but said nothing as Connie ripped open the envelope. Four badges tumbled out onto the floor as she turned it upside down. Scooping them up, Connie saw that each was different: one was shaped like a pair of silver wings, another a crystal droplet, the third a black lizard, and the fourth a golden horse.

'So,' said Evelyn, 'they've sent you all of them.' She turned her lapel over and showed Connie her shiny horse brooch. 'Each company has their own symbol. My banshees are in the company of two and four-legged creatures so this is my brooch. I suppose, as a universal, they didn't know what to do with you and thought this was the simplest solution—though I thought the universals used to have their own sign.' Connie pinned them on to her school jumper. 'Better not wear them openly,' cautioned her aunt. 'People may ask awkward questions.'

'I'll take them off before I leave the house,' said Connie quickly, touching each badge in turn, admiring their beautiful shape and finish.

Connie then picked up the letter. It congratulated her on her membership of the Society and announced that the first phase of her training would take place over the next three weekends at the Mastersons' farm.

'Where's that?' she asked.

'Not far from here. The Trustees are staying there for a while. Plans are being made to counteract the threat from Kullervo.' Evelyn glanced across at Connie. 'Dr Brock told me what the sirens said. I know you can't possibly understand what this means, but I want you to trust us when we tell you to avoid meeting that creature at all costs. Look at your great-uncle if you need any proof . . . ' She stopped and cleared her throat.

'What do you mean?' prompted Connie, feeling as if ice-cold fingers had just brushed against the back of her neck at the mention of Kullervo.

'Connie, not all mythical creatures choose companionship with humans. Some have set themselves against us. Kullervo is our greatest enemy—our greatest threat. It was rumoured,' said Evelyn slowly, as if picking her way over a minefield, 'that your great-uncle died because Kullervo took him.'

'Killed him?' Connie asked fearfully.

'Took him,' her aunt repeated. 'They say that Kullervo can force his way into your mind. He can take you over and drive you into madness and death. But he doesn't do it quickly. He plays with you first—like a cat with a mouse.' She fell silent. Then, shaking herself as if to banish these dark thoughts, she added in a brighter tone, 'At least you're the first to benefit from the Trustees' decision to stay here, for they're to undertake the preliminary stage of your training themselves while they are in England. So we'd better start getting your things together.'

'What sort of things?' Connie found it difficult to dispel the fear that had grown as she listened to the description of Kullervo torturing his victims.

'A leather flying-suit for one: you can't learn to ride a mythical creature in jeans, Connie, particularly not a dragon.'

'Learn to ride?' The promise of riding lessons jolted her mind off the subject of Kullervo as nothing else could.

'Well, you didn't think you'd be shut away in a classroom for your Orpheus training, did you?'

12
Storm-Bird

After a miserable week at school avoiding Col, Connie looked forward with relief to the weekend and to her first training session on Saturday: an encounter with Storm-Bird and a chance for her to begin to use her gift. She felt a door to a new world was about to open for her and she was determined to do her best to live up to her calling. The meeting was to take place in a secluded valley behind the Mastersons' farmhouse and she had been asked by Eagle-Child to bring with her two strange items: rubber gloves and rubber-soled shoes.

The sun had barely risen when Connie was dropped by her aunt in the farmyard; a pale pink wash stained the sky and the birds sang tinnily, their song shrill in the moist, cold air. As Connie and Eagle-Child climbed the hill behind the farmhouse to reach the higher ground of the moors, they found a changed world spread out before them. The hills rose above the sea of mist like the humps of whales emerging from the waves. The human world of houses and roads was lost down in the fog. Connie followed the companion through a five-bar gate and into a wooded dell. The lichen-covered trees were shedding their leaves in drifts. Mossy grey boulders were strewn on the slopes, jostling for space with the tree roots. The air was very still. Connie waded through the fallen leaves and brambles which were still heavy with dew netted on gossamer webs; droplets brushed off against the legs of her jeans, making them stiff and heavy. Eagle-Child, by contrast, moved as if he barely touched the earth in his moccasined feet, having the liquid motion of a mountain lion.

'Eagle-Child?' Connie asked, at last daring to break the silence. 'Can you tell me what the rubber gloves are for? I can't imagine you wearing them.'

Eagle-Child's laugh sounded as if it came from deep stores of joy hidden behind his impassive face.

'No,' he said, 'but at the beginning I would have perhaps benefited from them. The storm-bird is a difficult companion species, Connie: complex, mercurial, and dangerous. If you fail to make a complete connection, you are at risk of an electrical shock.'

'And if you make a complete connection?'

'Ah, then—then you are more like a lightning rod than the tree struck down: you'll feel the energy pulsing through you harmlessly.'

The storm-bird was waiting for Connie and Eagle-Child in the deepest, most secret part of the dell, its massive crow-like form perched on a boulder, brooding. Its beak was like polished ebony, its feathers glossy pools of ink. Seeing them approach, it opened its wings and glided down to land at their feet, white shards of light crackling from its outstretched wings, as if its feathers barely hemmed in an explosive force ripe to leap forth. Standing by the bird's side, she gazed up into its black impenetrable eyes, dark globes that reflected the world around but let none read their expression.

'Now,' said Eagle-Child softly, crouching beside Connie. 'Understand that Storm-Bird rarely links with anyone but me. Storm-birds are unique creatures—born of the fury of the thunder as it mates with the lightning. You should see them, Connie: in my country, they fly before the rolling storm clouds, riding the turbulence recklessly, flocking to the lightning strike. My tribe has produced the only companions to storm-birds known in the world, and there are few of us left in America: we too are dying out. Come, let us begin. Put your gloves on and then hold out your hand.'

Feeling completely unworthy to meet so extraordinary a creature, yet eager to do so, Connie did as she was bidden and stretched out a bright yellow fist. The bird fluttered its wings and croaked angrily. Eagle-Child frowned.

'Hmm,' he said, 'Storm-Bird objects to the gloves.'

Reaching out, Eagle-Child placed his palm against the bird's black beak and, after a few moments, entered a trance, swaying rhythmically. He remained like this for some minutes, before dropping his arm and saying to her: 'We shall have to do this without the gloves. The shoes will help in case of need, but Storm-Bird has promised to lead you to find the right path to bond with him. But I must warn you, Connie: you cannot proceed without danger to yourself. Are you willing to continue?'

'I'm not afraid,' she said. 'I'd prefer to take off the gloves: they aren't natural and would've only been in the way.'

Peeling them off, Connie dropped them onto the ground and held out her arm once more. This time, the bird leaned forward until her fingertips just brushed the edge of its feathers. She sensed the creature's life-force pulsing beneath her hand and gently increased contact until her palm was flat against the storm-bird's neck. With a riveting shock, she found her hand connected to the bird as if it were a powerful magnet and she an iron filing. She had the sensation that she was being inexorably drawn into Storm-Bird, of being swirled around with the energy fluctuating through the very marrow of its being, flying in a great whirl of power—it was as if she had become one bird amidst a great airborne flock, turning to and fro in response to a shared intuition. Each move was now guided by the earth's magnetic field; she could see it, glistening in the air like blue ripples on the surface of a lake. As she darted through the field, brushing it with her wingtips, she knew exactly where she was in relation to the globe below her, how far north she would have to glide to reach the regions of ice and snow, how far south to reach the burning deserts. She was exhilarated by this new-found skill, losing self in the identity of the group, mastering with it the air and elements. What could she feel, Connie asked herself in this spinning, twisting flock? Power, anger, moodiness. Storm-Bird had a nature as far removed from the unicorn as one could get. It was

kin to that of the sirens; it cut into her consciousness with a dangerous edge like a wing made of
sword-blades.

'What are you angry about?' Connie asked in
thought as the flock wheeled about in the sky,
skimming the clouds.

The answer flashed back, almost knocking her
over had not Eagle-Child been on hand to steady
her.

'Destruction. Dirt. Foul winds sullying the
upper air.'

She felt billowing storm clouds surround
her, fogging her inner vision, disturbing her
connection with the blue sparkling magnetic field.

'What will you do?' she thought, wondering
where all this rage would lead.

There was no answering thought, only an
answering feeling. Connie found a tingling
growing in her arm and down her body. She could
not see it, but later Eagle-Child told her that her
hair had risen on her head until it stood brush-like,
spitting out sparks of static. The tingling grew
painful, running down her free arm. Connie
clenched, then stretched her hand on that side to
relieve the tension and a shaft of white light
erupted from her fingertips, striking a bush some
metres away. It fizzed and burst into flames, swiftly
becoming a charred mess.

In her surprise, Connie abruptly broke her link and stared in disbelief at what she had done—or what the bird had done through her. Storm-Bird whistled shrilly, pleased with the havoc it had created.

Eagle-Child looked at them both in wonder. 'I have not seen that happen except in the most advanced companion-creature relationships—certainly not on the first encounter. I would have expected you to be injured: you are not, are you, Connie?'

Storm-Bird croaked irritably, as if the question insulted it.

'No, I'm just surprised,' she said, finding she was trembling uncontrollably.

Eagle-Child put his arm around her shoulders to stop her shaking.

'I was wrong to call you a mere chick on our first encounter: you have taken your first flight with Storm-Bird like a master.'

'I can see what you mean about the danger,' she said with a slight laugh, pointing ruefully at the scorched bush.

'You can only do that if Storm-Bird wills it, and so far, despite his anger, Storm-Bird has never aimed carelessly or with intent to harm the innocent. You felt anger, did you not?'

'Yes, indeed.'

'Then you begin to understand Storm-Bird. Like many creatures, he grows impatient with us humans.'

After his last disastrous training session, Col was determined to redeem himself in the eyes of Skylark and Captain Graves. His mentor, however, seemed to have passed the lesson over as an aberration; Col was flattered to find that Captain Graves was convinced his student was ready for the next stage.

'I sense you relish a challenge, my boy,' Captain Graves said gruffly. 'And you too,' he added, addressing the pegasus who was trotting patiently behind them with Firewings. 'Well, we've got a real corker lined up for you today!'

His eyes twinkled beneath his exuberant brows; he was twitching with excitement, eager to break the news. Uncertain as to what Captain Graves might consider a 'corker', Col questioned if he would feel as enthusiastic in a few minutes when he knew what was coming.

'And what's that?' he asked, steeling himself for the answer. Whatever it was he had already decided he would throw himself into it heart and soul and make up for his recent failures.

They were drawing near a line of trees that marked the edge of a pine plantation on the part of the farm closest to the sea. The wood stretched from the cliffs to the moor, a dark, dense patch between two open and airy expanses. The firs crowded together, killing the sunlight before it could reach the forest floor. Two people were emerging from the gloom, headed in their direction.

'I've arranged for us to share our lesson today with Miss Masterson and her mentor,' replied Captain Graves, gesturing to the figures approaching them. 'As we saw from your first encounter, you and Skylark need practice dealing with adverse weather conditions, a frequent hazard in our business. I understand from Mr Coddrington that the weather giant is happy to oblige.'

Col shrugged: that didn't sound too bad—a bit of wind and rain should not now put Skylark off his stride. Captain Graves noticed his pupil's reaction and smiled knowingly when he continued: 'And I've also asked Mr Coddrington if we can spice the lesson up a bit by introducing an element of combat training. Miss Masterson will guide the weather giant in using his powers to flush you out of hiding—your job is to avoid being caught.'

Col gulped.

'The giant's skilled and has been instructed not to use lethal means. He will only use his powers to disorientate you or to startle Skylark out of hiding. Now, how does that sound?'

It sounded terrifying.

'Fine,' said Col.

Shirley and Mr Coddrington had now reached them. She smiled at Col with a hint of triumph already glinting in her pale blue eyes.

'Heard what we've got planned, Col?' she asked. She seemed to be probing him for some sign of weakness or fear on his part.

'Yeah,' Col said with a studied air of unconcern. 'Should be fun.'

Fun for whom? Col wondered. He turned back to Captain Graves.

'Captain, you called this combat training?'

'That's correct.'

'Combat for what? Who are we fighting?'

'No one at the moment, Col, but all mentors are under new instructions from the Trustees to teach their charges how to take evasive action if attacked by Kullervo's forces. Now, shall we get started?'

Shirley nodded eagerly. 'Yes, let's—unless they're too scared to take us on, of course. Not going to chicken out, are you, Col?' She smirked at him. Col shrugged in what he hoped she would read as a nonchalant manner. 'Not going to *clam* up with fear, I hope?'

He gave her a humourless grin. 'Oh very good, Shirl, very original. Do they give you lessons in such side-splitting puns at your school then?'

She flashed him a matching grin. 'And I s'pose they give you lessons in sarcasm, the lowest form of wit, at yours?'

'Come, come,' interrupted Captain Graves. Col sauntered to Skylark's side, wondering what the pegasus made of it all. 'Ivor, would you like to explain the rules?'

'Certainly, Michael,' said Mr Coddrington with evident relish. 'We are role playing a situation where Team A—the pegasus and rider—have to carry a message to base—the farmhouse—without being caught by Team B, Miss Masterson and the weather giant. Mr Clamworthy, you and your mount shall start in there.' The assessor pointed to the wood. 'Your job is to return to the farmhouse from this location. As the weather giant cannot stop you by force, you will be counted as caught if he or Miss Masterson can pinpoint your location at any stage. It is fair to warn you . . .' (Mr Coddrington cleared his throat importantly) '. . . that the giant will be doing all he can to make your task harder by using all weather means at his disposal. You will, however, be assisted by cloud cover as making weather generates vapour, so the more active the giant is, the easier it is to hide.'

Great, thought Col bitterly, the worse the weather, the better for us, huh!

Skylark butted into Col's silent protests. 'Come on, Companion: we'll beat that windbag easily.'

Afraid that Skylark would think he was losing his nerve, Col swung into action, mounting in one swift movement.

'Right, Mr Coddrington, we understand. Let's get started,' he said resolutely. Col urged Skylark forward and the rider and his pegasus slipped into the plantation and were soon lost from sight in the darkness under the boughs.

Captain Graves shouted after them. 'You have two minutes to hide yourselves—then the hunters will be after you. I'll blow my whistle once and the pursuit starts. If you hear me blow it twice, that means the game is over.'

Skylark trotted light-footed over the uneven ground, Col bent close to his neck to avoid low branches.

'What shall we do, Companion?' asked Skylark, pausing by a fallen tree.

'Give me a moment,' replied Col, his face creased in concentration. 'We need a plan.'

The horse snorted as if to say that this was obvious, but all the same he waited silently, giving Col space to think. It was getting darker, as if a storm was brewing—which, of course, was exactly what was happening. Fat droplets of rain began to patter through the needle canopy. The air was warm and still, pungent with the scent of pine resin; fir cones crunched as Skylark shifted his hooves restlessly.

'Right,' said Col finally, pulling out his flying helmet and goggles as the rain fell more heavily. 'I know what we should do—we've got to do the unexpected—take the least likely road.'

'And what is that?' asked Skylark. 'Set out in the opposite direction and circle round?'

'No, they'll be expecting us to try something like that. Look, I don't have time to explain—just feel it with me.'

A pulse ran down the link between Col and Skylark as the creature probed his companion. He saw the plan laid out in Col's mind like a chess problem. He understood.

'A little risky, human!' Skylark exclaimed, but he gave his mane a twitch of pleasurable anticipation. Col knew that his mount was as keen, if not keener, on risk than him.

'He who dares, wins,' Col replied with a grin, urging Skylark forward.

Rain streamed down, forcing its way through the protection of the trees so that Col and Skylark were soon soaked through. Far away a whistle blew. Immediately, there was a great crack as branches gave way before the passage of some missile, followed by a dull thud ten metres from their position. Half buried in the forest floor was a hailstone the size of a football.

'Non-lethal means, huh?' Col swore. If that had struck them, they were unlikely to have lived to complain to their mentors. The game had suddenly assumed a very ugly seriousness: they could both get killed if they were not careful.

'He's trying to unnerve us—scare us out of hiding,' Skylark neighed, beginning to panic. 'He knows we have to leave tree-cover before I can fly—he wants to force us out before the cloud-vapour becomes too thick!'

Col had no time to agree before another two hailstones crashed into trees close by. Skylark reared.

'Let's stick to our plan,' said Col, clinging on as he tried to soothe his jittery mount. Pulling himself together, Skylark stopped trying to throw his companion. As one, the pegasus and rider moved forward, not towards the farmhouse, or even in the opposite direction as Skylark had first suggested. They headed for the source of the missiles.

The cloud-fog grew thicker as they progressed, snaking around the tree trunks. Above, the branches creaked in protest as a strong wind bent them into submission. Col could not be sure when they reached the fringe of the plantation, no longer seeing more than a few metres in front of him. This was perhaps the most risky moment in his plan—he had to hope his sense of direction was as good as he thought.

'Come on, come on, throw another one!' he muttered, straining to look up.

A rapid succession of heavy thuds some way behind them told him that a salvo of hail had fallen into the trees, but it had passed too high for him to tell exactly which direction it had come from. He began to think his plan was going to fail. Surely one of these lethal missiles would find them if they didn't do something quickly? He wondered if they should not just make a dash for it from here. He could tell Skylark was struggling to contain his fear and Col was beginning to catch a sense of panic himself. But then a streak of light shot across the sky, disappearing with a hiss into the trees.

'That's it!' Col slapped Skylark on the shoulder with delight. 'We've got him!'

'He must be really mad at us if he has started on lightning bolts,' commented Skylark with a joyous whinny, relieved now that the waiting was over. Col did not reply: he was too busy calculating the distance to allow himself to relax his concentration from the task ahead.

'Right—let's go. Remember, stay on the ground—do *not* fly.'

Skylark gave a shiver of distaste: he did not like the indignity of acting like his landlocked brethren, but he followed Col's orders nonetheless. He broke into a canter over the rough ground, alert to every slight course adjustment from Col. He galloped directly into the teeth of the wind, his mane whipped back, slick with rain. Ten metres and they began to see what they were looking for: standing in the mist before them were two huge pillars of denser cloud, great thick trunks the colour of iron. But these were not trees: they were legs. Lost in the clouds above was the rest of the weather giant.

As Col had planned, Skylark took off as soon as they spotted the giant and flew to hover at knee-height. Keeping close to the creature, the pegasus circled slowly and silently, watching for every change in direction the giant made, countering every buffet of wind with skill. It would be a disaster if they so much as brushed him with a wingtip; success depended on remaining undetected.

Above them in the mist, Col could hear two raised voices—a high voice of a girl and the lower tones of a man. Shirley and her mentor must be riding on the giant's shoulder to give him instructions. That was not fair, Col thought bitterly. He wasn't getting any help, so why should Shirley?

'I can't see them,' he heard Shirley say, shouting above the storm.

'Here, give me those binoculars.' A pause. 'No, they are nowhere to be seen. Probably still skulking in the trees.'

'What shall I do now? I'd like to wake them up a bit.'

'Tell our friend to send a barrage—that should flush them out.' Col could hear the pleasure with which Mr Coddrington gave this advice.

'Oh, but isn't that a little dangerous?' Shirley asked, but without sounding unduly worried by the idea.

'Only a very slight risk. I'm sure they must at least be positioned on the edge of the plantation somewhere, waiting to make a break for it. We'll startle them out like pheasants before the beaters.'

There was a moment's quiet during which Col supposed Shirley was speaking to the giant and then he saw a vast grey hand appear through the clouds above. Skylark had to dive sharply to his left to avoid colliding with the outstretched fingers. The giant took something from a scabbard on its thigh and the hand disappeared into the fog above.

The cloud was suddenly illuminated by white light as six or seven bolts whistled overhead, landing simultaneously with an almighty explosion. Shirley squealed. Col heard Captain Graves's voice exclaiming:

'I say, Coddrington, that's completely out of order! What if you hit them?'

'Don't fuss, Graves,' shouted the assessor. 'They'll be all right.' He added reprovingly in a lower voice to Shirley, 'That was a bit more than I anticipated, Miss Masterson.'

'That wasn't me!' she protested. 'That was the giant's idea. I just asked for a barrage like you said.' There was a pause as the two weather giant companions scanned the skies around them. 'I still can't see them!' Shirley said, a hint of petulance quivering in her voice. 'Do you think they have slipped away already?'

'I doubt very much they're still in the trees after that display, Miss Masterson. Perhaps we should move from this position and head for the house. We can cut off all approaches from there, even if they have managed to circle behind us.'

The giant began to move. It took all of Skylark's skill at flying and Col's talent for anticipating obstacles for them to avoid colliding with the legs. The creature headed across country, taking the quickest route to the farmhouse in the hope of preventing the elusive pegasus from reaching safety.

'Ready?' Col gave Skylark warning. 'When I say the word, go for it!'

Voices had begun again overhead.

'We could stay here,' Shirley called out. 'We're so near home, we'll see them coming from any direction with no problem.'

Oh no you won't, thought Col, with excitement coursing through his veins. 'Go!'

Skylark broke out of his spiral, heading for the dim shape of a building directly in front of them. They burst out of the ring of cloud into the weak sunlight and clattered down into the farmyard. As hooves touched concrete, a shriek overhead told them they had been spotted.

'There they are!' Shirley was shouting. 'I saw them before they landed—I really did, Mr Coddrington!'

A whistle blew twice and Col looked up to see Captain Graves on Firewings gliding down to land. A great cloud mass rose above the roof of the house. Col could see the indistinct shape of a huge man, his lower limbs densely wrapped in cloud—no doubt because of all the weather he had been brewing. Rearing out of the vapour was the upper torso, reminding Col of the anvil-shaped storm clouds that bubble up in summer.

Yet the giant was more solid than that—a kind of distilled concentrate of cloud with great dark circles for eyes and a hollow mouth which was open in a howl of frustration, blowing the surrounding trees vigorously as the cry swept across the farmyard.

'Well done, my boy!' Captain Graves exclaimed, jumping from Firewings's back. 'Unusual tactics but very effective.' He lowered his voice. 'And as for *their* tactics—quite unsporting. I'll be having words with them later.'

A grey fist swept out of the sky to the ground, releasing two people from its grasp.

'Shall we call it a draw, Michael?' Mr Coddrington began speaking the moment his feet hit the earth. 'Miss Masterson spotted them before they landed—that would have been fatal to the mission in a real life situation.' Shirley nodded, giving Captain Graves an apologetic smile. Col seethed at the injustice of this suggestion, but fortunately Captain Graves was not to be swayed by smiles.

'Really, Ivor, I think this round belongs to Col and Skylark. Their performance was outstanding, totally foxing even an old hand like yourself.'

'I don't know about "totally foxing" as you put it,' replied Mr Coddrington tersely. 'As I explained, I was only on hand in case Miss Masterson ran into difficulties. It was her they were up against.'

'Oh yeah?' muttered Col to Skylark. They knew better.

'In that case, I hope you will mention to her that such dangerous gambits as blasting apart half a forest are not approved under the rules of the game. No, I'm sorry but I am firmly of the opinion that this one goes to the pegasus and rider. Miss Masterson will doubtless get her chance for revenge at the next match.'

'Don't worry, I will,' she said bitterly, giving Col a spiteful look.

Col and Skylark followed Captain Graves and Firewings as they marched smartly out of the farmyard, heading for the stables. Glancing back, Col saw the weather giant was dispersing in a swirl of mist like clouds blown away by a stiff wind. Left in the yard, Mr Coddrington and Shirley were talking, heads close together, looking thoroughly unhappy with the verdict. Col had known Shirley for several years through the Society, but it was only today that he realized quite how ruthlessly competitive she was. And as for the weather giant, it had shown itself quite capable of turning the full force of its armoury of weather weapons against others when given an opportunity; he and Skylark would have to watch their step next time they played against that creature.

13
Dragon

When Eagle-Child and Connie arrived back at the farmhouse, they found Mr Masterson, shotgun slung casually over his shoulder, on the lookout for the universal. Connie was beginning to feel like a parcel being handed around. No one seemed to leave her alone for a minute. A few quiet moments to absorb what she had learnt would have been very welcome just now, but that did not appear to be an option. She was looking forward to the time when the excitement about her celebrity status would calm down and life would return to normal.

'Ah, Connie! We've not been introduced, but I've heard all about you,' he said gruffly, steering her firmly in the direction of the house. 'Come and meet my daughter—have some tea.'

Connie glanced up to Eagle-Child but found that he was already disappearing back to the wooded valley.

'Don't mind him,' said Mr Masterson, following her gaze. 'So far he's refused all hospitality. Camps out in the woods, you know. Nothing but a bit of canvas between him and the stars.' This clearly bemused Mr Masterson, whose corpulent frame gave every indication he enjoyed his creature comforts. 'Come on in. Shirley's already got some other friends over to tea. They all want to meet the universal companion.'

Connie would have preferred to slip away with Eagle-Child but there was no prospect of wriggling free. Frogmarched into the kitchen, she looked more like a prisoner under arrest than a guest for tea.

Shirley Masterson, her pale blonde hair gleaming in the firelight, was presiding over a table laden with sandwiches, cakes, and scones. An older girl with auburn hair and a scattering of freckles sat at her right, and a familiar tousle-haired boy on her left.

'Here she is,' blustered Mr Masterson, 'told you I would round her up for you. I'll leave you young folk together.' He stamped out, whistling for his sheepdog as he went.

'Take a seat, Connie,' said Shirley softly. 'Col, you know . . . ' Col nodded slightly, not meeting her eyes. 'And this is Jessica.'

'Jessica Moss,' added the girl in a clear voice. 'Companion to Selkies; in Sea Snakes, of course.'

'Sea Snakes? Selkies?' queried Connie, sliding on to the bench beside Jessica rather than taking the chair next to Col. She felt the now familiar tingling of being among Society members and realized for the first time that each one had their own energy, like a different musical key.

'Boy, you are green, aren't you!' Jessica exclaimed, but in a friendly tone. 'Col said you didn't know much about us.' Col was now looking out of the window as if he was not listening to the conversation. 'Sea Snakes—that's the Company of Reptiles and Sea Creatures. I bet you don't know what we call the others either, do you?' Connie shook her head. 'Well, there's High Flyers—winged creatures, of course—and Two-Fours—two and four-legged creatures—and Elementals—that's sort of obvious. We use these names as shorthand.'

'And selkies?'

'Ah, now, you must meet some if you don't know what they are,' Jessica said eagerly, thrusting a plate of cakes at Connie. 'They're simply the best! Selkies are seals in water, people on land— one of the changeling species.'

Connie was intrigued. 'Will you introduce me sometime?' she asked, taking a scone and buttering it. Her encounter with Storm-Bird had left her feeling ravenous, as if she had burnt up a lot of energy as well as frazzling a bush.

Jessica looked proud. 'Of course—though, I should warn you, I've only just begun my own Orpheus programme with my mentor, Horace Little. I don't know much yet.'

'Better change the subject, Connie,' broke in Shirley in her sweet-toned but assertive voice, offering her a silver bowl of jam, 'or we'll be here all night talking about selkies. Anyway, I can tell you all you need to know about them—they're all fish and flippers.' Jessica laughed politely, not letting herself be offended by Shirley.

'And what's your companion species, Shirley?' Connie asked, realizing that this was the etiquette of the Society. She took a big spoonful of strawberry jam and spread it thickly on her scone as she listened to the answer.

'Weather giants—particularly storm giants,' Shirley said.

'She'll tell you next,' said Jessica, nudging Connie, 'that companions to weather giants are very rare, whereas companions to selkies and pegasi are common.'

'So there aren't very many of you?' Connie asked.

'No,' said Shirley smugly.

'But not as rare as universal companions,' Col interjected. Connie could not tell if this was meant to be a conciliatory gesture to her, or an attempt to take the wind out of Shirley's sails. Possibly both.

'Of course not,' Shirley retorted, 'we all know that.' Anger crackled in the air between the two of them.

Uncertain how to defuse the tension, Connie tried to change the subject. 'And who's your mentor?'

'A Mr Coddrington—from the Society's headquarters in London,' Shirley said with a mirthless smile. Connie shuddered, remembering that she had last seen that smile on Mr Coddrington's face. She wondered if his charge was beginning to adopt his ways, or whether Shirley had always been like this. 'He's fantastic— so unlike all the old members around here. He really understands what it's like to wield power through our companion creatures. It's a bit like being a god, he told me, and he's right.' Shirley laughed but Connie didn't find the idea the least bit funny. Shirley seemed a bit too much in love with the idea of all that power for her taste.

Jessica coughed. Connie guessed she didn't like the weather giant companion's arrogance any more than she did. 'It's great to have you with us,

Connie,' said Jessica brightly, changing the subject as she made a grab for a plate of fish paste sandwiches in front of her. 'It will be really something for our branch of the Society to have the only universal! Just think what they'll all say at the Tintagel gathering!'

'Tintagel?'

'The Society's annual get-together in November, on bonfire night,' Jessica explained. 'It's a really big thing. It's by the sea this year—thank goodness. We Sea Snakes so often get a poor deal when they go and arrange meetings in the middle of moors or up mountains. We'll all be going; it's always great fun. You'll be able to meet my companion, Arran. In fact, why don't we get together sometime soon and go for a swim? Then you'll know more of us before you get to Tintagel. It'll make it less daunting.'

'Daunting?'

'Come on, Connie: the first universal of the millennium! You can hardly expect to slip in unnoticed!'

'I s'pose not,' said Connie glumly. Naturally shy, she did not enjoy all this fame.

'So, will you come for a swim?'

'Yes, I'd like that,' said Connie, cheering up at the idea of seeing a selkie. 'But I'm a rubbish swimmer.'

'That doesn't matter—as you'll find out,' said Jessica, as she licked fish paste off her fingers with almost seal-like appreciation.

Evelyn was due to collect both Col and Connie, which meant they had to wait together in the Mastersons' porch. Suddenly Connie was tired of fighting with Col. She tried to make conversation.

'Jessica's very nice, isn't she?'

'Hmm.' Col was thinking about the weather—and what it had nearly done to him today.

Discouraged, Connie watched rain dash itself against the path, wondering if she should try again.

'How was your training? Riding a pegasus must be incredible!'

'Fine.' He did not want to start explaining all that had happened during his training session, not at the moment anyway. He was still shaken by the realization that Shirley could have killed him as she played at being god with Mr Coddrington.

Connie gave up. Let him be like that then. She had not done anything wrong: he was just being stupid.

As she lapsed into a resentful silent, Col became aware that he now had a golden opportunity to apologize—no witnesses, no excuse to put the moment off any longer. It did not come easily to him.

'Connie?' he began.

'What?' she replied shortly.

'You know about all that stuff last week?'

'What stuff?' she asked, not intending to make it any easier for him.

'What I said last Sunday.'

'So?'

Just then Connie's phone rang. She flipped it open and took the call. Col watched, exasperated, as she listened intently to the caller, her face becoming etched with concern.

'You what!' she exclaimed. 'No way!' Col wondered what had happened to make her so agitated, his thoughts immediately leaping to Kullervo. 'Of course, I'll come round as soon as I get home.' She ended the call.

'What's up?'

'That was Jane,' she said angrily, slipping the phone back into her jacket. 'Her dad's been given the sack by Mr Quick.'

'What?' Col asked stupidly. At least it was nothing worse, he thought. 'Why?'

'Because of us, of course!' she snapped. 'You may not have noticed, but Jane has been worried sick ever since we visited the company. Her dad's been having a hard time because of us getting mixed up with Axoil in the press and stuff.' She spat the words out at him, finding a vent for her own guilt by turning on him.

'That's rubbish: they can't sack him just because of us!'

'Mr Quick's not put it like that, of course,' Connie said heatedly. 'He's just said that Mr Benedict's contract will not be renewed next year. But he made it very clear that he doesn't want any spies on the inside.'

'But Mr Benedict didn't tell us anything!'

'We know that—Jane and her dad know that— but that doesn't matter to Mr Quick. This is an easy way for him to punish us for getting the story about O'Neill's . . . accident.'

'Hardly an accident, Connie. Murderous sirens, you mean,' said Col brutally.

His tone nettled Connie. 'You just don't understand them. They don't see it as murder. It's just what they do.'

'And you're defending them?' he asked incredulously.

'No.' She felt very awkward. 'But I understand them.'

'Vile things,' Col muttered. 'I don't think they should be allowed to stay at the Stacks any more, doing what they do.'

'And you're to decide where and how they live now, are you?' Connie's eyes were glistening with fury. She felt a swoop of anger as if siren song was blazing through her veins.

Col realized his apology had gone badly wrong—but then he no longer felt the need to say sorry, with her being so stubborn about the sirens.

Three rapid hoots down the lane and the growl of the Citroën heralded the arrival of Evelyn.

'Can we do anything to help—to help Jane, I mean?' Col asked gruffly, holding Connie back before she made a sprint to the car.

'As if you care!' she said, shrugging him off. 'I think we've probably done enough damage already.'

She darted out of the porch, dodging the raindrops, leaving him to ponder this turn of events. Taken aback that Connie had suddenly turned on him like an angry bear, he walked slowly to the car, oblivious of the downpour that had transformed the path into a sludgy torrent. Living with the universal in their midst was far more complicated than he could have imagined when he first heard the news.

The following Saturday, Connie found Dr Brock waiting for her at the Mastersons' farm, yawning broadly in the weak morning sunshine.

'Sorry, my dear,' he said, stifling his yawn, 'but we dragon-riders keep strange hours. I've just been on patrol with Argot.'

'Patrol?'

'Hunting for Kullervo. Preparing for the arrival of the winter storms.'

'Oh.' Her heart began to beat fast as her thoughts leapt back to her aunt's hints about the death of her great-uncle and the wild passion of the sirens for causing death and destruction. She remembered the lost men, the first casualties of this new war between humans and the mythical world. 'What's the Society doing about him—about Kullervo—and about the sirens?' she asked, seeking reassurance. 'Shouldn't I go out to them again? Why won't you let me?'

Dr Brock avoided a direct answer. He began to lace up his riding gauntlets, shiny semi-transparent gloves made from the skins shed by dragons when they moulted. The scales glistened like circles of polished steel. 'We've set a guard on the most likely locations where he might conceal himself in our area and called up our fighting forces. The problem is that, as he's a shape-shifter, we don't know what form he'll assume. We have to rely on our instincts to warn us if he's here. Meanwhile, everyone is to be drilled in evasion techniques. Some members are learning combat skills.'

That sounded all very well, but not reassuring. 'And what about me?'

'You?' He shot her a worried look.

'Well, aren't you going to teach me to fight?' she asked, feeling she should not really have to spell it out for him. 'What if I meet him when I next go to visit the sirens?'

Dr Brock gave her a stern look. 'You are not to visit them, Connie. I thought we'd made that quite plain to you.'

'But . . .'

'The missing men are not your responsibility. Leave the sirens to Signor Antonelli,' he said in the harshest voice she had heard him use so far. 'You will be taught to resist—not to fight. And we're keeping a close watch on your home to ensure he doesn't reach you there.' He sighed, his tone mellowing. 'But it is bad that this has come so soon in your training—bad that Kullervo knew about you even before we did. You've taken a step or two, but even the most experienced companions have been defeated by him, overwhelmed by his hatred. I fear you'd stand little chance if you . . . Well, enough said for now.' He broke off abruptly and started walking.

His unfinished remark nagged at Connie. What she couldn't understand, after the desperate search for a siren companion, was why they were not

253

letting her anywhere near the siren colony. Everyone knew Signor Antonelli could do nothing. It was up to her, whatever Dr Brock said. Fortunately, no more workers had gone missing, but surely it was only a matter of time? The sirens had promised to wait until the winter storms for Connie to help them. Autumn was almost over. There wasn't much time left. She did not have to look very deep inside herself to find the imprint of the sirens' rebellion against everything the Society had tried to tell them. They were defending their territory the only way they knew how. If everyone carried on blocking her, she would have to take matters into her own hands, Society rules or no Society rules. But perhaps that was a thought best kept to herself for the moment.

'Where're we going?' Connie asked, changing the subject as Dr Brock struck out on a path leading towards the moor.

'To see the dragons, of course.' He also seemed relieved to leave the grimmer matters behind them. 'They can't stay in the farmhouse,' he said, whistling a brisk tune as he strode off up a steep hill, before taking a right turn into a densely wooded patch not far from the dell where she had encountered Storm-Bird. 'We're going to the old quarry,' he explained, beginning to scramble up some stones set like steps in the hillside. Connie followed him up a slope littered with tumbled rocks. They pushed their way through a thicket of wizened gorse bushes, until they came out upon the lip of a cliff. The quarry sank away before them, creating a great stony bowl amidst the lush fields. From their vantage point, they looked down upon the trees growing in the quarry bottom; they had a few leaves still clinging mournfully to their lichen-covered branches like bunting left over from a summer fête. At the foot of an escarpment opposite lay what at first glance looked like a huge moss-covered boulder. Slowly, Connie realized that this was not a rock but a dragon stretched out in the sunshine. Dr Brock chuckled at her exclamation of wonder.

'Dragons, unlike other reptiles,' he explained, 'do not—strictly speaking—need to bask in the sun to maintain their body temperature: they are not prone to going dormant in the cold as they have their own central heating. But they like the sun, nonetheless, and enjoy it when we are blessed with a few fine days like today.'

He went ahead, turning occasionally to help her clamber down the quarry side.

'But if they're creatures of fire, how is it that the Society places the dragons in the Company of Reptiles and Sea Creatures when they could belong to Elementals?' asked Connie, breathing hard with the exertion.

'It's a question that would occur to a universal, Connie, and a good one,' Dr Brock replied. 'But consider the dragon further: it could belong to winged creatures, to two- and four-legged, as well as to elemental creatures. But dragons, long ago, elected to be part of sea creatures and reptiles as they felt their essence most closely adhered to things reptilian. You see it is the creatures, rather than the human companions, who place themselves in the companies. In fact, it is their decision where we companions are placed.'

Making their way through the trees, Connie and Dr Brock emerged at the foot of the escarpment. Propped up by the side of the dragon was Kinga, deeply asleep.

'She's sharing Morjik's dreams,' Dr Brock whispered with a strange gleam in his eyes. 'And outlandish dreams they are too, as you may find out for yourself. Morjik and Kinga are asleep now and only at night will they fly together.'

'Why only at night?' Connie asked softly, watching as the dragon heaved a huge sigh, emitting a cloud of fragrant rose-coloured smoke. She could barely resist touching him, eager for the encounter to begin.

'Because even in an isolated place like Dartmoor, a flying dragon might not go unnoticed. Argot and I once got "buzzed"—I think the expression is—by an air force jet when we were flying above cloud. Fortunately, we never heard any more about it because, I suspect, the pilot was too embarrassed to report what he thought he saw. In normal times it is much safer to fly at night—dragons can pass then for large bats or a light aircraft—depending on how high they are and on the prejudice of the onlooker, of course.'

Morjik shifted slightly; one red eye opened a crack. His horny scales shone wetly in the morning light, shot through with a hint of gold like a tree whose leaves are just on the turn. His vast, sage-coloured wings were folded to his sides like closed silk fans. His long tail curled around so that his jaw rested on its pointed tip. Dr Brock bowed to him and said aside to Connie:

'Morjik has suggested that your encounter with him takes place in two stages. Today you should learn to read his thoughts and feelings; one night, when you and he are ready, he'll summon you for a ride.' Kinga sat up and stretched, yawning. She nodded to Connie and got up to make way for her. Morjik slowly opened his eyes and snorted another puff of smoke, this one silver-white. 'Sit with your back to him, Connie; he is ready,' Dr Brock prompted.

Not needing a second invitation, Connie placed herself as Kinga had done and relaxed against the dragon's hide, delighting in the warmth of his body and the feel of the calluses and bumps of his skin against her leather flying-jacket. Immediately she felt Morjik's presence, familiar from their last encounter. His was a vibrant life-force, passing through her like a rush of fiery breath, sweeping her along with it. A heat ignited in the pit of her stomach, a fierce blaze that threatened to engulf her if she could not contain it. Morjik's presence fanned the flames. She felt her whole being exposed in an instant, stripped of any covering she might have held up to hide behind. She both hated the vulnerability he had uncovered and loved the cleansing power that filled her, knowing it would bring new growth as green shoots peeped up from the ashes.

But this scouring also laid bare Morjik's soul to her and she began to sense his distinctive nature in more detail. Age—Morjik was very old. To him, the lives of his companions passed like the bloom and wilting of a summer flower: he continued while they faded into history. Words were few and rarely used; why be swift to speak when you had centuries to say all that you need?

As she learnt about the dragon, Connie felt his thoughts probing her nature: the dragon found her young and untrained like other humans, but different from them too.

'You are broad like an ocean, Connie; not narrow like a rushing stream as my companions have been in their short, hectic experience of life,' he was saying to her. 'Lack of boundaries can be a strength; but, Little One, do not expend yourself in an attempt to do everything and be everything. Live your life for each precious moment you have; do not hasten through it as so many do.'

Connie treasured his words, turning them over in her mind like jewels that glittered as they caught the light. Then Morjik took her in hand and led her down the paths of his dreams. She saw strange colours—ones she had never seen in her world— whirling in intricate patterns like a kaleidoscope. Long spirals led her into the fiery centre of his thoughts, where the furnace tested all words and feelings, burning up the impure and the redundant, until only the necessary and true emerged.

'Connie?'

She woke with a start to find Dr Brock shaking her shoulder.

'It's time to go. You've slept for several hours,' he explained, helping her climb stiffly to her feet. Morjik still slumbered, his eyes fully closed now, but Kinga had gone. 'Did it go well?' Dr Brock asked anxiously.

She shook herself, trying to drive away the sleep that still lingered in her head, clouding her thoughts.

'It was incredible—like a journey into the depths of the earth.'

Dr Brock nodded with understanding. 'Hmm, yes, Morjik is old and his dreams are complex,' he reflected. 'Other dragons, like Argot for instance, dream of the sky and flight—a journey to the stars. You may perhaps experience that too one day. Come, let us go back now: such journeys need to be taken in short stages to begin with.'

As they approached the farm, Connie spotted two people walking slowly down the path ahead of them: a tall, thin figure inappropriately dressed for the country in a dark brown suit, and a slight girl with platinum blonde plaits. They were deep in talk. Connie, to her dismay, saw that Dr Brock was endeavouring to overtake them. She hung back.

'Ah! Ivor. Miss Masterson. Successful encounter, I trust?'

'As always.' Mr Coddrington's smile was like a chilly winter's day. He and Shirley exchanged self-satisfied looks.

'I'm glad I've caught you,' continued Dr Brock. 'Kinga's calling a meeting tonight to discuss progress on locating Kullervo. We're expecting the selkies to report back today—Horace will be here to debrief us.'

'Kullervo?' asked Shirley, catching at the name eagerly. 'So it's true what the weather giants are saying?'

'What are they saying?' Dr Brock said with a slight frown, glancing at Mr Coddrington. The latter said nothing.

'That he's coming—that the mythical creatures are going to strike back against humans who have been harming them.' Shirley spoke with barely disguised enthusiasm. 'And why shouldn't they? They'd be right to do so—and why shouldn't we help them? Mythical creatures had all that power in the past. People feared and worshipped them. You can't blame them for wanting to get it back. I think we'd all be better off if humans learnt to respect and fear them again.' Connie could see that Dr Brock was alarmed, but even though she had little liking for Shirley, she could not help but think she had a point. Indeed, she felt rather grateful that Shirley had dared speak these words aloud. She wondered what Dr Brock would find to say in reply.

'I know they say such things,' Dr Brock said levelly, looking across at Connie as if he sensed her interest, 'and that they have already unleashed their anger across many parts of the world. With what result? I'll tell you: deaths, mainly amongst the poorest people and most vulnerable animals, and destruction of habitats. Is that the kind of fear and respect you want?' He lifted his eyes to Mr Coddrington's emotionless face, perhaps expecting some assistance from Shirley's mentor on so important a matter. 'And did this bring about one iota of change amongst those humans who take decisions about how we treat our world? No. I shudder to think how bad it would have to be before stiff-necked humanity changes its ways. No, that is not the way we teach here in the Society. Is that not right, Ivor?'

'Of course, Francis,' said Mr Coddrington but with little conviction. 'That goes without saying.'

But part of Connie still sympathized with Shirley's question and she felt there must be more to be said. Everyone had been telling her to fear Kullervo, and she *was* afraid, but no one had explained exactly why. As Shirley said, maybe he was just standing up for the mythical creatures. Was that so very wrong? What wouldn't she do to preserve a place in the world for creatures as marvellous as Morjik, Windfoal, and Storm-Bird? The Society so far had been fighting a losing battle and, much as she admired Dr Brock, she wondered how he could be so sure that he was right. Yet some of Kullervo's allies, the weather giants for example, were wrong to wreak such destruction on the most vulnerable. Where did the balance of right lie?

14
Rock Dwarf

'Connie?' It was her aunt at the bedroom door next morning.

After the soul-expanding dreams of the dragons, Connie found it difficult to get up for her training at the Mastersons' and had been lying for a long time watching the light reflected from the sea ripple across her bedroom ceiling.

'Do you want me to cancel?'

Cancel? Turn down the chance to meet another mythical creature? No way: she must be joking!

'No thanks,' Connie replied, swinging her legs on to the cold floor. 'I'll just get ready.'

Her aunt laughed. 'I thought as much.'

* * *

Amidst the cars and a horsebox parked in the farmyard stood a small, cloaked figure: it was Gard, the rock dwarf, clad as usual in deepest black.

'Welcome, Universal Companion, welcome to my temporary home,' he said, shaking her hand in his powerful grip.

Connie was a little surprised that, on touching his cool black hand, she sensed nothing from him now, not like the first time they had met.

'Follow me,' Gard said with amusement in his voice, as if he at least could read her thoughts and was laughing at her wonder, 'and you will then learn how to encounter a rock dwarf. We are not so easily read as others you have met.'

Gard led Connie back to the quarry where she had been the day before. Climbing down a different part of the cliff face, they came upon a log shelter hidden amongst the trees, where two other rock dwarfs were sorting through piles of stones, tapping some with a silver hammer, chipping at others with a chisel. To one side, Connie noticed Frederick Cony asleep in a deckchair, wrapped in a blanket, a hat pulled low over his eyes.

Gard sat down in front of a pile of copper-coloured rocks and gestured to her to sit opposite him.

'Now, let us work,' he said, handing her some tools.

Connie picked up a hammer and chisel and began to copy him. To begin with she felt very awkward at the task and could not see what she was supposed to achieve.

'What are we doing?' she asked after ten fruitless minutes had passed of tapping on the rocks in her lap.

Gard grunted. 'If you mean "what is this for?" then the answer is that we are sorting out some rocks for the dragons. Your friend Dr Brock has something up his sleeve for the annual meeting of the Society. If you mean "why are we doing this together?" then the answer is inside you, if you seek it out.'

Connie sighed and applied herself again to her task. As she entered into the monotonous repetition of lift, tap, place, lift, tap, place, her mind began to wander. She became aware of the grass under her, the earth pressing against her feet, the immensity of the globe of rock extending for miles and miles beneath her. It was then she sensed something else; there was someone else present in her thoughts, sharing the same patch of ground, tapping on the same rocks. She looked up and saw that Gard was watching her carefully.

'So you have found me at last, Companion,' he said. 'It is not through the touch of flesh that one encounters an elemental, but through the materials that make us both, through the earth that sustains and nurtures us. Listen again.'

Connie closed her eyes and tried to recapture the sense of his presence she had briefly held. In the darkness, she heard a whispering; it grew louder as she concentrated her mind on Gard's rockiness, his earthiness. Entering into the thoughts uppermost in the rock dwarf's mind, she sensed many layers underneath, as if he contained aeons of historical time and had seen seas cover land and retreat, watched glaciers freeze and melt, each leaving their trace within him. His first thoughts were for her at the moment: he was wondering about her abilities, remembering those universals he had met in the past. She sensed that Gard's memories stretched back to ages beyond humans, to the very birth of the planet, but yet he did not seem ancient like Morjik: time for Gard was not endless years strung together like pearls on a necklace, but an eternal moment.

Going deeper, she found the next layer of preoccupations concerned one she had been trying to forget: Kullervo.

'You thought I was here only for you,' Gard chuckled. 'Indeed, you are partly right, as you are bound up with our thinking about this dark spirit of malevolence. What is he planning?'

The next layer down, Gard was deeply saddened by the frailty of Frederick Cony. Memories of Frederick as a young man, striding mountainsides with Gard, energetic and indomitable, entwined with images of the elderly man, sleepy and tired.

'He is passing away,' Gard was thinking, 'like many others before him, his body will remain a memory in the earth, but his spirit—where will that be?' Connie's eyes pricked with tears as she understood the desolation Gard felt when he saw his human companions disappear beyond his knowledge into the death he would never know. The tears fell down her cheeks, leaving salty trails.

'That is enough, Universal,' Gard said in a voice like the whisper of sand.

Connie knew there were many more strata to be explored, stranger and richer, and she longed to linger.

'Another time, Universal,' Gard answered her thought. 'You have learnt enough for today. Now you know how we rock dwarfs can always sense you as long as you are standing on the earth; and, as you gain in skill, you too will be able to find us, even if we are on the other side of the world, or deep in its belly.'

Connie opened her eyes and found that she had completed a pile of rocks without even being aware.

'Give those to Dr Brock,' he said. 'Tell him they are a present from us both to help him make a stir at the parade.'

Connie sat by the cars watching the Society members packing up for the day. Her thoughts circled back to Gull-wing and her sisters as they so often did. It was silly that she, the universal, was being stopped from seeing them. They were no threat to her. They needed someone to persuade them to listen to what the Society had to say. She'd only had one brief go at talking them round. She just had to get back out to see them.

Looking over to her aunt's Citroën, she saw that Evelyn was chatting to Mack as he stowed his diving equipment in the boot. For once, Evelyn wasn't watching her niece.

If only, thought Connie, I could get away from everyone, I could then go and see the sirens.

But if she was going to do this, she would need some help. Even if they were not the best of friends at the moment, surely Col would see past this when he understood the need?

'Col, can I help?' Connie found Col in the stables. Whistling cheerfully, he nodded without

269

looking at her and hefted the saddle off Mags's back. She picked up the currycomb. 'I've got something to ask you.'

Col looked up. 'What?'

Taking refuge in grooming Mags's coat, she braced herself to make her request.

'I want to go and see the sirens. You see, I left so abruptly that I don't know if they'll keep their promise not to strike again. I've got to go and reassure them that we'll help them.' Col said nothing, but Connie could feel that his eyes were on her. 'But I can't get there unless someone takes me—unless you take me.'

'Why not ask your aunt—she has a boat too,' said Col in a measured tone.

Connie twisted her fingers in a lock of the pony's mane. 'I don't think she'd take me,' she said quietly.

'Then I won't either, Connie.' He hated turning her down. He must sound a real coward to her.

'But, Col, it's a matter of life and death—not just some silly whim of mine!'

Col sighed. What could he say without saying too much?

'Don't you think they might have a very good reason for keeping you away from the sirens at the moment? Maybe, just maybe, you don't know everything that's going on?'

Connie could feel herself getting angry. The pony began to shift his hooves restlessly in sympathy. Her tone was bitter when she replied: 'But if people aren't telling me everything, how am I supposed to make the right decision? From where I'm standing, it seems pretty clear cut: more men will die unless I do something about it!'

'I'm sorry, Connie,'—and he really did sound sorry—'I can't take you to the sirens.'

Throwing her currycomb in a bucket, Connie left the stable, her slight figure fading quickly into the gathering twilight. Col laid his head on Mags's neck and breathed in deeply. Mags twittered in response.

'Don't you start,' said Col to the pony. 'What else could I do? If she goes near the sirens with Kullervo hiding out there, there'd be much more than a few human lives at stake.'

The pony snorted.

'I'm not treating those deaths as if they didn't matter!' Col replied. 'Do you think I like standing by, waiting for the next attack, any more than Connie?'

The pony nudged him towards the door.

'You want me to go and apologize? Well, think again. Connie's hardly going to listen to me today after what I've just said. No, that has to wait.'

But Mags had other things on his mind than apologies. The universal must not be left alone. His master was acting like a stubborn mule neglecting his duty.

'Things were all right until she came along,' said Col irritably. 'Now look at us: you're mad at me, I'm feeling terrible, and they still expect me to protect her from the most dangerous creature known to the Society.'

Mags shook his mane.

'I know it's not her fault,' Col relented. 'But I just wish . . . ' This was stupid. He took Mags by the halter to lead him to the horsebox. 'Come on, boy, let's just get on with what we've got to do.'

The next day at break Connie found Anneena sitting on a broken swing in the corner of the playground. Jane was standing in front of her, talking animatedly. She swung round to Connie when she heard her approaching.

'Tell her, Connie!' Jane exclaimed in relief, sounding as if her friend had come to her aid just in time. 'Tell her she mustn't!'

'Mustn't what?' asked Connie, leaning against the frame of the swing as her eyes sought out Col playing football with the boys. She had noticed that he had looked over to her a couple of times as she walked alone across the asphalt but he had turned away when he saw that she had seen him.

'She mustn't go to the docks to try and get proof. It's too risky.'

'Proof of what?' Connie asked, not yet understanding what all this was about, her mind still on Col.

'I'm going to see if I can find out why all these men disappeared,' said Anneena stubbornly. 'Something must link them. It's like Col said, Jane: it's bound to be a faulty machine or something. People just don't keep falling into the sea by chance.'

'Col said?' marvelled Connie. 'But I thought you're not talking to him?'

'I'm not. But this is work—that's different. He was over here just before you came out. He said his dad had told him the other day that Axoil have a bad name all over the world for safety.'

'But you can't just go marching into the docks: the whole area's fenced off,' Jane said reasonably.

But Anneena was not in a mood for being reasonable.

'I'll go on Saturday evening: it's pretty quiet at the weekend. I'm sure I can talk my way in or slip in unnoticed.'

Connie understood now why Jane was so concerned. What was Col playing at getting

Anneena all steamed up like this? Surely his dad hadn't really said that about Axoil?

'You're mad. What if you get caught?' asked Jane.

'I won't get caught.'

Jane was almost tearing her hair out in frustration at her friend's obstinacy. 'But what exactly do you think you can find out in any case?'

'Something is happening to those men and happening to them at work. If I can find any proof, then Axoil will have to take action. They might even be closed. We can't let them get away with pretending that none of this is their concern.'

'Does Rupa know what you're planning?' Connie asked with horrified curiosity. She couldn't imagine Rupa allowing her little sister to put herself in danger even for the story of her career.

'Of course not,' Anneena said as if the question was preposterous. 'She'd try to stop me if she knew.'

'You should listen to her,' said Jane. Anneena glared, unmoved from her determination.

Connie silently cursed Col.

'Anneena, you mustn't go. You can't do anything. Promise us you won't.'

Anneena looked shifty. 'I'll think about it.'

'Promise!' urged Jane.

'Well, if you won't come with me . . . '

'We won't,' said Connie firmly.

'Then I suppose I'd better not go on my own.'

Connie glanced over at Jane, coming to a tacit understanding. This was as near to a promise as they were going to get from Anneena. They had just better make sure they kept a close eye on her from now on.

15
Arran

Evelyn came into the kitchen, throwing her keys on to the table along with the post.

'Any plans for the weekend, Connie?' she asked casually, while watching her niece out of the corner of her eye as she waited for the answer.

'I'm going to Chartmouth with Jessica and Arran to learn to swim with the selkies,' Connie said, picking out a postcard from her brother from amongst the pile of brown envelopes. He'd sent her a picture of a Cambodian pit viper: he was an enthusiast for gruesome facts about poisonous snakes—not a taste she shared.

'Good. Jessica's a sensible girl: she'll look after you. How're you getting there?'

'Bus,' said Connie, again wondering why her aunt was so keen to know every little detail of her movements.

'OK,' said Evelyn. 'What time'll you be back?'

'About six, six-thirty at the latest.' Connie glanced up at the clock: she had better run. 'If that's OK with you, that is?' She pulled on her coat and slipped some money into the pocket of her jeans.

Evelyn nodded. 'Make sure you stay together. Ring if you run into any trouble.'

'I will!' called Connie as she slammed the back door behind her.

Connie spotted Jessica leaning on the arm of a tall youth dressed in close-fitting dark-brown clothes; the selkie and his companion were waiting for her at the bus-stop outside the lifeboat station. She got up from her seat to get off.

Arran turned first, having sensed the universal's approach. Connie came to a sudden stop on the top step of the bus. She felt she had just been hit in the chest by the slap of a cold wave.

'Hello, Universal,' came Arran's voice in her head.

Connie gasped for breath as if coming up for air after a long dive. Jessica hit Arran on the arm, to get him to stop whatever it was he was doing to the universal, and his presence was gone from Connie's mind as suddenly as if he had bobbed back under the surface. Someone nudged her impatiently in the back and she jumped down from the bus, steadying herself to be ready for a more conventional introduction.

'Hi!' Arran's spoken greeting sounded almost a bark. 'Sorry about that. Couldn't resist.'

'This is Arran, Connie, as if you couldn't guess,' said Jessica, gesturing proudly at her companion. 'A selkie from the family of the common seal.' Connie looked into Arran's face and could not help but smile back into his soulful dark eyes. He had the longest lashes of any person Connie had ever seen—but then, he wasn't a person, she reminded herself. His thick brown hair was swept back from his forehead: it shimmered as if slightly oiled. He was undeniably handsome. Studying him, she had the sensation she had plunged beneath the surface once more and was now swimming with him in the eddying currents of a seal's life. Her skin was tingling with liquid energy. She could feel how it was for him, how he was eager to be back in the sea, slicing through water, leaving only a trail of bubbles in his wake, on the track of a silver herring winking in and out of the weed. To him, the pavement was as awesome as a rough sea to a man: a place of danger where he was clumsy and slow. Arran was itching to take her into his world, to kick off the disadvantages that hampered him on land and show her the element of which he was a master.

'Connie, are you listening to me?' Jessica asked her, giving her a shake. 'Ouch! You stung me!'

'What?' asked Connie in confusion. 'Oh, sorry: it's the static—it happens sometimes when I encounter others.'

Jessica shook her hand in the air to ease the smarting pain. 'I suppose you were taking a dip. I was talking to you but you were miles away.'

'Er . . . sorry,' said Connie weakly. 'What were you saying?'

'I was saying,' said Jessica, with a tolerant smile, 'that we should go to the beach at the end of Milsom Street. It's more than a bit grotty, being too near the docks to attract visitors, but fine for our purposes.'

'OK. Good plan,' Connie said.

'Come on then: what are we waiting for? It's getting dark already. We'll lose our chance to swim if we hang around like this.'

Jessica set off at a brisk pace, heading south.

'Come on, Universal,' said Arran in his bark-like voice. 'You heard her: let us go before I get you into any more trouble!'

He held out his hand. His fingers were long, particularly the index, and tapered together into a point like a flipper. Hesitating for a second, Connie took it. The returning tide of his presence washed up her arm and filled her with frothing delight. She gave a bark of laughter, which he joined in. A passing couple walking their dog turned to look at the pair in astonishment.

'Hurry—before we attract any more attention,' said Arran, pulling on Connie's arm.

They set off together after Jessica, reeling in a strange shuffling gait along the pavement. One of the dog-walkers turned to the other and whispered something that sounded very much like 'drunk at their age—how shocking!'

'Stop it!' Connie laughed, dragging him round the corner and out of sight of their audience.

Jessica was waiting for them. They were at the end of the residential streets, making for the no-man's-land beyond Milsom Street, where the holiday cottages gave way to industrial units and an abandoned petrol station. 'Arran,' she chided, 'we'll never make it unless you remember you've got legs at the moment.'

After a few more strides, Arran found his land-legs and they began to make swifter progress.

'It is a real honour to encounter you, Universal,' he said humbly as they approached the beach.

'The honour's mine,' Connie said with all honesty. What was she compared to him, a changeling and marvel of the sea?

'You are a unique creature,' continued Arran. 'I sense the sea in you. Do others find their own element when they bond with you?'

'I don't know. I hope so.'

When they reached the shoreline, Connie gave an involuntary shudder. A once wild part of the coast had been tamed under man's yoke. Twisted steel girders writhed out of broken concrete sea defences like amputated limbs showing rusting bones. The shingle was fouled with litter—plastic bags, cans, an old shoe.

'This is where you swim!' exclaimed Connie. If it had been her, she would have chosen a cleaner, prettier spot.

'Sometimes,' said Jessica, sniffing. Connie caught it too: there was a distinct scent of diesel oil on the breeze. 'It's actually quite a good spot because no one in their right minds comes here. Once you swim out beyond the outflow from the city sewer, it's OK.'

'The sewer!' Connie was liking the sound of this less and less.

'Don't worry. Arran knows a safe way round that. Are you ready for a swim?'

Connie looked about her: rubbish, sewage, and oil—this wasn't at all how she had imagined her first encounter with the selkies would be. 'Um . . . '

Her phone rang. Relieved to have an excuse to put off the moment when she would step into the freezing sea, she pulled it out with a murmured apology. It was Jane.

'Hi!' Connie was glad that her friend could not see her.

'Connie, it's me. Anneena's gone,' Jane said, her voice tight with concern.

'Gone? Gone where?'

'Where do you think? I only left her to go home for tea and then found she'd made excuses to her mum and gone off. She said she was going to meet you. You know she doesn't have a mobile, so I can't reach her. She hasn't gone to meet you, has she?'

'No.' Connie had made no arrangements to include Anneena on her dip with the selkies. 'How long has she been gone?'

'At least an hour.'

They were both silent, working out that Anneena had had more than enough time to put her harebrained scheme of breaking into the terminal into effect.

'What do you think we should do?' asked Jane. 'I mean, the worst thing that could happen is that she will get caught and sent home with a telling-off, isn't it?'

Connie gazed out to sea and gulped to ease the lump in her throat. A bank of sea-fog was creeping inland, swallowing up headlands, ships, and rocks like a slow-motion tidal wave.

'I hope so, Jane. Look, I happen to be in Chartmouth myself at the moment. I'll see if I can find her and stop her doing anything stupid.'

Jane sounded relieved. 'Thanks, Connie. Let me know how you get on.'

Connie put her phone back into her pocket and met the curious gazes of Jessica and Arran.

'Trouble?' asked Arran.

'You could say that,' said Connie. 'I think one of my non-Society friends has gone and done something really stupid.'

'What?' asked Jessica.

'I think she's broken into the terminal. She wanted to see for herself what was happening to the men that had gone missing. I don't think it was deliberate but Col put her up to it. He told her some rubbish about faulty machinery.'

'But that's the official Society story,' said Jessica, 'to divert attention from the truth. Col's dad thought it up. It was agreed on last weekend because some reporter won't let the story alone and they were afraid she was going to go out in a boat searching for clues. They wanted to protect the sirens.'

'What? Nobody told me!' Connie fumed. She could strangle Col—and the rest of the Society. 'Well, she believed him enough to go and take a look for herself. And the mist is coming in.' Just then, Connie felt a small vibration in her bones as if a tuning fork had just been struck deep inside her. 'Jessica, Arran, I think the sirens are coming!'

Jessica looked as panic-stricken as Connie felt. Arran, however, remained calm.

'It's clear enough, isn't it?' he said, wrinkling his nose to sniff the wind. 'The Society dropped her into the mess; we'd better get her out of it. Jessica, don't forget to block your ears.'

'Where are we going?' croaked Connie.

'Into the terminal, of course,' said Arran coolly, as if he did this kind of thing all the time. 'I know that place like the back of my flipper—from the sea, anyway.'

'I think there's a back gate on Milsom Street,' said Jessica. Her face was pale but she looked determined. 'That's our best bet.'

'What are we waiting for?' asked Arran buoyantly, starting off at a run. The girls followed him until they came to a halt by the back entrance. The lights of the office buildings and the refinery shone feebly in the fog on their right. The cranes and containers of the dock were now on their left.

'That's where she'll be,' said Connie, nodding to the waterside. 'She'll be looking near where the men went missing.'

The fog rolled in more thickly and ate up the nearest stack of red containers. It had one benefit: it hid them as they slipped under the automatic barrier past the security guard's cabin.

'Right. No time to lose. Let's get looking,' said Arran. Before they could stop him, he ran off towards the docks.

'Arran!' Jessica's voice carried eerily in the damp air. 'Stop!' But Arran ignored her. 'Look at him! Anyone would think this was all a game!' she said exasperated. 'We'd better go after him. He doesn't know about security cameras and all that. Someone's bound to see him.'

If they don't hear her first, thought Connie, but she said nothing. The two girls hurried off in pursuit but he had disappeared into the fog. The tingling in Connie's bones had become ringing: the sirens were getting closer. The two girls reached a tall crane that leaned over the dock like a yellow heron about to dip its neck in the water, its summit swathed in shifting feathers of mist. They flattened themselves against it, looking around for any sign of human or seal.

'Anneena!' Connie called out.

Nothing.

'Arran!' shouted Jessica.

'I'm going to look for your friend in the harbour,' came the reply.

He was very close. Connie and Jessica kept low as they half crawled to a coil of cable at the water's edge. There was Arran, lying on his belly, his arms by his side.

'Arran, no!' Connie exclaimed, rushing to his side. 'You've got to come back with us. They'll be after us any minute now. There are security cameras and all sorts of things around a place like this.'

'There's no time for that!' said Jessica, glancing over her shoulder apprehensively.

'Too late: I'm changing,' said Arran. With a trembling motion like a light wind wrinkling the surface of a pool of water, the selkie's clothes shivered into a thick pelt. His arms fused to his sides, leaving only two hand-shaped flippers. Legs joined together as his feet transformed into a tail. Connie sat helpless, yet marvelling, as his big dark eyes grew so round that the whites disappeared. Whiskers sprouted from his nose, which itself was rapidly thickening into a snout. His jaw jutted forward, sharp teeth erupted from the gums. The change complete, Arran rested his head on Connie's lap, allowing her to stroke his smooth neck. She could feel the layers of insulating blubber under her fingertips.

'This is me,' he told her. 'This is what I'm really like.'

In the distance a klaxon began to sound. They could hear the thump of running feet along the quayside.

'Come with me. I'm off to find her for you,' the selkie said.

'I can't,' whispered Connie. 'I can hardly swim a width.'

'I can't leave Connie,' said Jessica firmly.

'I'll help her,' urged Arran. 'They'll catch you if you stay here.'

But they had left it too late.

'Oi! Here's more of them! Mo, over here!' bellowed a man bursting round the edge of the coil of cable, brandishing a torch. He stopped as he came face to face with the seal and hurriedly backed off, disturbed by the needle-sharp teeth that Arran bared at him.

A second man pounded over from the opposite direction.

'This place give me the creeps, Ben: first, men chucking themselves in the drink, now kids coming to sightsee,' Mo said, wiping the sweat from his face.

'Not just kids,' said Ben, nodding down at the seal. 'Careful. Don't move, girl: I'll scare it off for you.' He started to flap his arms. 'Shoo! Get away from her!'

There was only one course open to Arran. With a parting lick of Connie's fingers with his rough tongue, he slid over the side of the dock and disappeared below the water with barely a splash.

'You all right?' asked Ben, holding out a hand to help Connie to her feet, still shaken by what he had seen. 'You shouldn't be in here, you know. It's not safe at the best of times.' He looked nervously about him. 'Especially not safe when the mist comes in.'

'We're sorry,' said Jessica. 'We just followed the selk—the seal. We were worried he might hurt himself on the machinery.'

'You should've told us first, love,' he said. 'I'd better take you to the office. We'll have to report this. What d'you think, Mo?'

But his colleague was not listening. His hands were hanging limply by his sides, his jaw slack.

'Jessica, block your ears!' hissed Connie. Jessica stuck her fingers in her ears, a panicked look on her face.

'Mo, snap out of it!' said Ben, clicking his fingers under his friend's nose. 'Hey, stop fooling around. This is not the time or the place to play around.'

Now Connie could hear it too. A song insinuated itself into the island in the fog that surrounded them until it filled the whole space. It wrapped around them, wooing them to come to the singer, to sink into the cool wave-sheets of the marriage bed of the sea. A light breeze like the gentle caress of a smooth hand brushed her cheek, coaxing her forward. She shook herself, casting off the lure of the song like a dog shaking water from its coat after a bath.

She turned to the two men. Mo had stumbled forward and was walking slowly towards the edge of the dock. Ben had a pathetically broad grin on his face. He too began to move towards the water.

'Stop!' Connie screamed. She might as well have been shouting at stone for all the impression she made on them.

A new, more urgent tune unlooped from overhead.

'Come! Come!' crooned the siren. 'My arms are soft; my embrace is sweet.'

Connie looked up. On the very top of the crane, she saw the dark outline of a single siren, head bent forward to pipe her victims to their doom.

'Shut up! Leave them alone!' Connie cried.

But it was useless. The siren too was lost in the spell woven by her song. A predator on the hunt, it would take more than puny words to turn her from the scent of her prey. Connie ran forward and grabbed the back of the jackets of the two men but all that achieved was to find herself being towed nearer and nearer the edge as well. Jessica couldn't help her: she needed both hands to stop her ears.

'Think!' Connie hissed to herself. 'You're the universal. You must be able to do something.'

If the predator was to be turned, it would need a new, more powerful scent to follow.

Connie let go of the men and closed her eyes. The murmur of the breeze; the creep of the fog; the lap of the waves: each joined to create one key for her melody. The universal began to sing.

Flight over waves. Moonlight silvering wings. Glint of fish in the shimmering depths of the sea. Red rock. Nest.

The siren faltered as a new song rose out of the fog beneath her. Here was her home—her true companion—her wing-sister.

Forget the mortal men—their brief lives are beneath your notice. Salt on lips. Scales twinkling on the sand. Sea-grass bending to brother wind.

The siren began to reply, loosening the bonds on her prey and casting the links to Connie. It was Feather-breath. She had left her sisters, not content to wait as the sirens had promised when Connie had visited them.

Home to the nest, to sleep, to rest, sang the universal, her song smoothing the jagged emotions of the siren, lulling her like the murmur of the sea itself.

Yes, to rest, sang Feather-breath.

A thick band of fog coiled around the crane, hiding the pinnacle from view. When Connie opened her eyes, she knew that the siren had gone.

Two men were staring at her with confused expressions.

'You, you were singing!' stuttered Mo. 'Did you hear her, Ben? She was singing—right weird it was.' Mo suddenly looked down at his feet and realized that he was standing on the very edge of the dock. He swore and jumped away from the drop. 'What on earth . . . ! Let's get out of here!'

The girls said nothing but let the two men escort them to the security guards' office by the back gate. Where was Anneena, wondered Connie? She hadn't fallen under the song before Connie had had a chance to divert the siren, had she? Jessica gave her an anxious look, clearly thinking the same thing. They entered the office.

There, sitting defiantly on a plastic chair in front of a battered old desk, was Anneena.

'Connie! What are you doing here?' Anneena exclaimed, leaping to her feet.

'Know each other, do you?' Ben asked. 'Thought as much.'

Mo picked up the phone and had a hasty conversation with the person on the other end.

'I've told the management. They'll be here directly,' he said, putting the phone down.

They sat in awkward silence until they heard the purr of an engine outside, followed by the slam of car doors. Mr Quick entered, incongruously dressed in a well-tailored dinner jacket. He had on a black tie, and an expression to match on his face.

'What's all this, Colman?' asked Mr Quick abruptly. 'I've got my guests arriving for the reception in quarter of an hour. I can't afford a crisis just now.'

'Crisis is over, sir,' said Mo respectfully. 'We've caught the intruders.' He waved over at the girls sitting behind the door.

'You!' spat Mr Quick, wheeling round on them. 'What on earth are you doing here?'

'They haven't said,' replied Mo. 'That one refused to answer any questions.' He pointed to Anneena.

'But I know, sir,' volunteered Ben, raising his hand gingerly.

'And what do you know?' sneered Mr Quick, rounding on him.

'Those two said they were seal-watching and followed one in here. I saw the little one,' he gestured to Connie, 'with a seal on her lap, sitting as large as life over by the crane. She was trying to get it out of here, she said.'

Anneena shot a sharp look at Connie.

'Seal-watching?' asked Mr Quick sceptically. 'This is a dock—not a zoo.'

'I know, sir, but I swear there was a seal. Right up on the quayside, it was.'

'Ben's right, sir. I saw it too,' Mo chipped in. 'It dived into the water and then she . . . ' He glanced at Ben.

'Then she sang to it,' Ben finished apologetically.

'Sang to it?' asked Mr Quick incredulously. Anneena's jaw dropped.

'Er . . . yes, sir,' confirmed Mo.

'I've heard of train spotters, but not seal spotters, especially not the singing variety,' said Mr Quick with a sceptical curl to his lip. 'I find it hard to believe that you're here because of a passion for seal-watching.'

'No?' said Jessica in a tone that suggested she thought him of limited intelligence if he did not understand the attraction of seals. 'Actually, it's not uncommon to find harbour seals—also known as the common seal—*phoca vitulina*, if you want the Latin name—near docks like these. What is rare is to find one this far south: they usually stick around the east coast.'

'We haven't time for a natural history lesson, young woman,' he snapped, waving her aside like a bothersome fly. He turned to Mo. 'I've got the mayor arriving in a few minutes' time and I don't want these girls anywhere near the refinery or the docks by then, understood? Take their details and turn them out. I'll be writing to their parents to complain. If we find you here again, I'll call the police, do you hear me?' He bore down on Mo, stabbing his finger into his chest. 'And you'd better do a better job of watching the gate next time, or you'll find yourself out of a job. I'm beginning to think I'm surrounded by imbeciles.' He turned on his heel and left the office.

Chastened, Mo walked the girls to the gate and saw them off the premises.

'Good story!' said Anneena as soon as he had retreated into his office. 'I hadn't a clue how to excuse myself without giving the game away. That seal story was brilliant.' She looked at Jessica admiringly. 'That last bit was the finishing touch— Latin and everything. I'm Anneena by the way.'

'I know you are,' said Jessica with a smile. 'We were looking for you. It wasn't a good idea trying to get in there, you know.'

'I didn't get in. They caught me at the gate. You got much further than me. Did you see anything?'

Connie looked quickly at Jessica. 'No, nothing special,' she said.

16
Tintagel

November arrived, bringing with it the biggest event in the Society's year: the annual meeting. Creatures and their companions were heading to Tintagel from all over the country, taking advantage of the fireworks and bonfires of November the Fifth as a cover for their arrival. People were too busy watching the skies for flashes and bangs to notice an over-flight of dragons and pegasi. Connie sat next to Jessica in the minibus carrying the Hescombe members west, feeling both excited and apprehensive. She was eager to see a gathering of the whole Society for herself but she could not help remembering Jessica's words about the universal not going unnoticed. The last thing she wanted was the attention of strangers.

'Ready?' asked Jessica, as if she had read Connie's thoughts.

'Not really,' admitted Connie. 'I feel a bit sick.'

'That's just nerves. Don't worry, you'll love it.' Jessica could tell from her friend's face that she had not convinced her. She changed the subject before Connie worked herself up any further. 'Did you get into much trouble?'

'You mean for going to the docks? Some. My aunt's grounded me for a week. She seemed more bothered that I'd gone near a siren again than that I'd saved two men from drowning. I just don't understand her sometimes.'

'Ah, yes,' said Jessica vaguely, not meeting her eye. Connie had the weird feeling that Jessica understood her aunt even if she didn't.

Silence fell between them for a few minutes. Connie could sense Evelyn's eyes boring into the back of her head: since the letter came from Mr Quick complaining about Connie's trespass at the docks, Jessica was no longer regarded as such a safe friend for the universal by her aunt. Col must also have heard about their adventure by now. He was sitting a few rows behind with the dragon-riding twins—she wondered what he thought of it all. Did he know that he had been partly to blame for sending Anneena in search of dodgy machinery?

Well, she wasn't going to hear what he thought about it from him, was she? The frosty atmosphere between them had gone on for so long now she didn't think anything could thaw it. With a sigh, she flicked some crumbs off her new brown flying-suit. She wanted to keep it in pristine condition for her first ride on Morjik that night.

'What's Tintagel like?' she asked, her thoughts turning to tonight's event.

'It's an ancient castle ruin by the sea—right on the edge of a cliff,' Jessica replied. 'It's well-known as a place of myth and legend—home to those dragon-butchering knights of King Arthur.'

It was dark as the minibus bumped into the car park—a field borrowed from a friendly farmer. There were already scores of cars and buses lined up under the trees: Connie could see people queuing like a crowd for a big match, all talking excitedly and greeting old friends with enthusiasm. She followed her party past the registration desk—'Society members only beyond this point' a sign read—and down a steep torch-lit path leading to the beach. The flames leapt into the darkness, casting dancing shadows upon the eager faces of the people crowding down to the sea. Connie let herself be swept along, a thrill of anticipation bubbling inside her.

Almost at sea-level, in a valley between two cliffs, the crowd slowed as each member took their place in the queue to climb the steep steps leading up to Tintagel castle. The ruins perched on the top of a spit of land—almost an island—a wide, flat-topped dome of rock that jutted out to sea. Underneath, the waves had tunnelled persistently over the centuries, trying to sever the castle's frail tie to the mainland and cast it adrift on the water for ever. Connie could see the gaping mouth of a cave that yawned at the base of the cliff and hear the boom of waves smiting stone. The ground seemed to tremble under her feet on the verge of surrender to the power of the sea.

Mounting the wooden steps as quickly as she could, Connie emerged on to a grass-covered courtyard. Entering through an archway, she touched a grassy tussock peeping out of a crevice of one of the walls and sensed that the ancient turf was eagerly waiting for the celebration to begin. Surrounded on three sides by tumbled castle walls like jagged, broken teeth, Connie looked nervously over the low wall on the fourth side. It barely concealed a gaping black void and a perilous drop down to the waves. Far below, Scark circled above the wave crests. Connie smiled to see that he too had flown in for the celebration.

'Not that way!' called Jessica. 'We've got to go higher!'

Higher? thought Connie with a shudder. She hated heights.

'The meeting's to take place on the very top—follow me.'

Connie trod in Jessica's footsteps up yet more stairs and on to the flattened summit of Tintagel. She began to breathe more easily now she was no longer near the cliff-edge. Arriving at the top, she saw that the crowd had formed itself into a square, in the midst of which was a huge bonfire—as yet unlit. A cold breeze blew in from the sea, carrying the sound of the waves to Connie's ears. Tonight, the sound seemed charged with meaning; Connie's hair was sparking, her skin tingling. It was as if Tintagel had become a great harp, with taut strings of unseen energy stretching from wall to wall, resonating harmoniously with every breath of wind.

'You can feel it?' Jessica asked excitedly, grabbing her hand and squeezing it. 'It's the sea creatures: they're here too. Arran and the other selkies are out there.'

Connie returned the pressure: yes, she could feel it. Here, surrounded by all these Society members, she felt secure and completely at home. She knew she was grinning with pure happiness—she couldn't help herself. She looked around the hill top. There were hundreds of people gathered but even they seemed lost on the vast plateau. It made her realize just how few people were left to protect the mythical creatures.

'Is this everyone?' she asked Jessica.

Jessica nodded. 'Uh-huh. There used to be thousands of us in Britain but the Society's been dwindling for years—fewer gifts are being identified so its membership's in decline. That's why you are so important, you see. They've been calling you the turn of the tide in the Society's fortunes. They say that if the universals can come back, why not others?'

Jessica's confidence in her was misplaced, thought Connie. It would take more than one person to make a difference. She quickly found a seat beside Jessica with the Sea Snakes and tried to make herself inconspicuous. They waited. Everyone, sharing a common instinct, fell silent. It was then that the mythical creatures made their entrance. The first Connie and Jessica knew of their approach was the drumming of hooves on soft turf, deep percussion to the humming vibration of the wind. On to the summit from the west swept a stampede of animals, all shapes, colours, and sizes. At their head was Windfoal, dipping her gilded horn as she passed the bonfire in a majestic circle; behind her, bellowing, neighing, roaring in a cacophony of sound, came centaurs, pegasi, bull-headed minotaurs, rams with golden fleeces, great bears, giants, and many other creatures that Connie could not name. At the same time that these beasts entered the field, creatures from the three other companies were also arriving. Opposite the Two-Fours, Connie saw a cloud of flying animals swirling down from the east, led by a dark shape flashing and flickering with white fire—Storm-Bird. She could see little of the group arriving behind the Elementals, but she had no difficulty making out the squadron of dragons zooming in from the night-sky in a great arrow formation, led by Morjik. As they swept over the bonfire, Morjik let out a great gout of flame and it burst into life.

Once the mythical creatures had taken up position with their companies, eight figures walked or flew forward to stand in the centre.

'They're the Trustees,' Connie whispered to Jessica, pleased for once to know something about the Society that her friend did not.

Kira Okona held up her hand and an expectant silence fell over all those present.

'Welcome,' the companion to unicorns said in a loud, clear voice, 'in the name of the Trustees and the worldwide family of the Society for the

Protection of Mythical Creatures, I welcome you all to a very special celebration. We have rarely been among you on your bonfire night; but then, never before have we had the arrival of a universal companion to celebrate.' A murmur of wonder rippled through the crowd. It grew to a rumble like thunder and suddenly burst out into cheers and laughter. Connie hid her face in her scarf. She could feel the creatures present seeking her out. All around her, members were hugging each other; some were crying with joy.

'Who is it? Where are they?' she heard pass from person to person. Jessica looked across at her once, winked, and then stared resolutely ahead, keeping her knowledge to herself.

Kira held up her hand and the noise slowly died down. 'Please, my mythical friends, do not try to bond with the universal: there are too many of you!'

Laughter fluttered across the square. Connie felt the presence of hundreds of creatures subside back to the tingling energy she had first experienced.

'And my human friends, our universal is still young and, how can I put it, a little camera-shy? You will meet her when she is ready, so please be patient.'

Connie felt relieved. For one awful moment she thought she was going to be dragged up to the front and singled out for everyone to look at.

'But, on a sobering note, we have also come to ask you to remain watchful. It is no coincidence that with the return of a universal has come the resurgence of our greatest enemy. As you will already know from the alert sent out to your chapters, the shape-shifting creature Kullervo has returned and is expected in this region by the time the winter storms arrive.' From the crowd's silence, Connie could tell that this was not news to anyone there, but a chilling reminder. 'However, let us not be troubled by such dark thoughts this evening. Tonight is a night of celebration— celebration of all our gifts and of the bonds that bind us to our companions. So, in the time-honoured custom of your country, let us celebrate with entertainment provided by the four companies. Tonight it is the turn of the Company of the Four Elements to open our festivities.'

Beckoning to the north of the circle, Kira fell back to sit with the Two-Fours. All the other Trustees, except the rock dwarf, rejoined their companies. Gard waited as a troop of hooded rock dwarfs marched forward, each carrying a set of chimes on a wooden stand and a small silver hammer. They set these in a circle around Gard and, throwing back their hoods, prepared to play.

Connie gasped: she had not seen Gard's face before as he had kept it hidden in the depths of his

303

hood. She had been expecting the dwarfs to resemble the bearded little old men she had seen in her books of fairytales and was completely taken aback. The dwarfs, though human in form, were more like rock-hewn statues come to life than men. Some had a blue-black, smooth surface formed into angular features like basalt, others had powdery white, soft contours like chalk; one striking individual appeared to be made from rock crystal and shone luminescent in the flickering light; Gard himself had a coal-black sheen to his craggy hands and face.

With a solemn bow to the audience, the rock dwarfs began to play. Striking the chimes in intricate order, they produced music that seemed to have been formed out of the materials of the Earth itself, making Connie think of hammers tapping in deep mines, of the rumble of rocks falling down mountainsides, the tinkle of gem-stones pouring on to a treasure-house floor. It was not music as she was used to—you could not say it was either harmonious or beautiful, but it was mesmerizing with its insistent beat and strange clashing notes. All too soon for Connie, the music ended and the dwarfs bowed as those assembled applauded with varying degrees of enthusiasm.

'Thank goodness that's over,' Jessica groaned.

'You didn't like it?' asked Connie, amazed.

It was Jessica's turn to be surprised. 'Meaning you did? I couldn't make head or tail of it. A jumble of grating and ringing sounds that seemed to go on and on: how could you like it?'

Connie laughed. 'Well, it didn't sound like that to me!'

'Hmm,' Jessica brooded, 'perhaps this is what the universal gift is all about. But if it means having to appreciate such awful music, then maybe you aren't so fortunate after all.'

The rock dwarfs left the arena to the enthusiastic applause of the Elementals and polite claps of the rest. Their place was taken by a band of young people from the Sea Snakes.

Jessica nudged Connie. 'Now, this will be more like it! Now the dancing can start.'

The band—two fiddles, a flute, a drum, and a guitar—began to play a tune, loosely based on a Scottish folk song, but they added their own harmonies, soaring above the melody or throbbing underneath as a bass accompaniment. Closing her eyes to concentrate on what she was hearing, Connie realized that they were trying to capture their experience in Sea Snakes—the wash of the sea and the thrill of dragon-flight. Then other youngsters broke from the ranks of Sea Snakes and began to dance. They held hands and wove in and out of each other like the tentacles of some great sea beast. Connie found herself pulled off the ground by Jessica and attached to the end of a line. As the dance swirled around a bend, her feet almost lifted from the ground, so fast was her chain going. The dancing got wilder. Creatures and companions massed around the bonfire—banshees writhed with Evelyn in their midst; fire imps flickered in and out of the flames, their companions jumping after them; pegasi flew in great looping circles overhead, their riders shouting and laughing. Col and Skylark dived towards Connie then swooped at the last moment out to sea. Bears stood on their hind paws and danced clumsily with their companions, growling to the music. Mr Masterson galloped by on the back of a great boar, his face shining with delight. Connie's chain of dancers finally stumbled over each other and finished in a pile of giggling, breathless bodies.

'Enough, enough!' laughed Kira over the hubbub. Windfoal neighed, summoning the creatures to return to their sides of the square. Slowly order was restored and Connie found herself back amongst the Sea Snakes, her arm linked to Jessica on one side and to a boy she didn't know on the other. They staggered back to their places, grinning at each other.

'I'm exhausted,' Connie panted to Jessica.

'So am I. That was wild!'

Dancing over, the celebration drew to a close. A quieter mood stole over the crowd as a procession of ten dragons and ten riders entered from opposite ends of the field. At the head of the lines were Dr Brock and Argot. Connie sat up eagerly: she had heard many hints about the surprise the doctor had prepared and she could not wait to see what he had in store. Red, chestnut, slate blue, grey, green: the dragons seemed to glow in the darkness. The riders bowed to their mounts and then vaulted nimbly into their seats. The dragons beat their wings in unison and flawlessly took off together.

'That's very impressive!' Connie exclaimed to Jessica.

'Just wait—there must be more. Synchronized flying we've seen before, but Dr Brock has promised us something special.'

The dragons circled around the castle in a great wheel. Then, on a signal from Argot, they dived down to the campfire. As the dragons plummeted back to earth, they opened their jaws and breathed out a waterfall of silver sparks. The crowd gave an appreciative murmur as the beautiful rain drifted slowly down, winking out as the sparks touched the ground. The riders leant forward and gave their mounts something in their mouths before the dragons rose again. Each creature took a place on the rim of the great wheel. Flying at a gentle pace, the dragons turned their heads and let out streamers of red flame. From below, the effect was of an enormous red circle blazing in the night sky.

Suddenly, two young dragons zipped in from the north and released a salvo of flashes and explosions. Flares shot into the sky and burst in popping streaks of gold and red. There were shrieks and cheers from the watching crowd as the sound reverberated from cliff to cliff.

Then came the finale. The dragons broke from their wheel and plunged down upon the heads of the spectators below, showering them with gold, emerald, and topaz sparks, building a great firestorm until the dragons could be barely glimpsed in the fizzing and spitting explosions above. Then all went black. The crowd craned their necks to spot the creatures in the darkness above but they had vanished. Next, as if out of nowhere, there was a great rush of wind and the dragons split in pairs five ways, showering green sparks over the Two-Fours, tawny-gold over the Elementals, orange over the Sea Snakes, and blue over the High Flyers. The final pair flew over the bonfire and spun a silver circle of fire that hovered for a moment before fading.

'Ha!' Jessica cried appreciatively. 'They've honoured each company, including yours—the silver circle, the compass, is your sign.'

Connie was touched. While content to remain anonymous amongst the Sea Snakes, she was pleased that Dr Brock had honoured her gift in this way. He had certainly made good use of Gard's rocks. She had spotted that the riders were feeding the dragons different minerals to produce fireworks out of their fiery bellies.

The crowd went into a frenzy of appreciation, applauding, whistling, and shouting as the dragons landed as perfectly as they had taken off.

'Trust Dr Brock and Argot to bring it to an end with a bang!' Connie laughed, joining the standing ovation with the others.

17
Kullervo

Silence after celebration. As the last revellers filed back to the car park, Connie was left in the arena in happy anticipation of one of the encounters in her training to which she had been most eagerly looking forward. Scark pecked at a sandwich crust a stone's throw away, keeping a wary eye on her. He seemed to like to know where she was these days, Connie had noticed, like a fussy parent.

'It's all right, Scark,' said Connie softly. 'I arranged with Dr Brock that Morjik will fetch me for my first night flight once all the other animals and people have gone. We're going to fly back to the Mastersons' house. You really don't need to follow me around like this: I'll be fine.'

Scark gave a sceptical squawk and tossed the crust to one side.

Waiting as Morjik said farewell to his fellow dragons, Connie could hear the waves washing on the rocks below, barely disturbed by the slight cold breeze blowing from the sea where Shirley's weather giant was rumoured to be in residence. Enchanted by the perfection of the night sky, she thought it was a fine evening for a dragon ride. Why could she not see the stars like this at home, she wondered, marvelling at the constellations wheeling overhead? She could see so many more here than at Hescombe where the lights from the refinery and from Chartmouth leached their twinkle from the sky.

Connie flashed her torch idly around the meeting place: it was empty now and she had only the glowing embers of the bonfire for company. The dying light cast stark shadows on the broken walls that teetered precariously on the very brink of the precipice. Checking her watch, she found that it was only five to eleven; Kinga had warned her that Morjik would take some time saying goodbye: dragons, though solitary creatures, relished the opportunity of their rare meetings for passing on the knowledge and news of their kind. Resigned to a long wait, she sat down on a fallen pedestal at a safe distance from the cliff-edge.

There she watched the inky folds of water edged with white collapse on to the rocks far below and drain away, to be replaced by another wave on the same eternal journey.

'Miss Lionheart?'

Connie almost jumped out of her skin. She had not heard anyone approach until a voice spoke close by her ear.

'Mr Coddrington.' Connie's voice shook. 'I'm here with permission—a dragon ride—a lesson.'

'Do not be concerned, Miss Lionheart. I've not come to question you, but to tell you that the lesson has, unfortunately, had to be cancelled. We've had reports of a low-flying aircraft in the vicinity. I've been sent to bring you back safely to the minibus.'

'Oh thanks,' she said flatly, hurrying to get to her feet.

'But perhaps we could have a little conversation now?' he continued, standing between her and the path back to the car park.

'About what?' she asked, edging to one side to manoeuvre round him.

'Well, things did not exactly get off to a good start between us, did they?' he said with an unconvincing attempt at a friendly tone. 'I thought we should let bygones be bygones and begin over again . . . ' Though he continued to speak, she was finding it hard to concentrate on what he was saying as a buzzing began in her head. He must have noticed for he was now looking at her as if he was assessing her again, smiling his cruel, thin smile.

The buzzing grew louder, becoming so intense she felt as if something was drilling inside her skull.

Connie put her hands to her ears. 'I'm sorry, Mr Coddrington, but I'm not feeling very well. Can we talk about this tomorrow?'

He was replying, but Connie could only tell this because his mouth was moving. All sounds were now blocked by the noise in her head, augmented by a shrill whistling that was building into a shriek. Her knees buckled and Connie fell forward onto the grass, clawing at the earth in agony. She knew what was happening: she was being assailed by the presence of creatures trying to link with her. She could not tell how many, nor what species, but they were crowding into every corner of her mind, crawling all over her like an invasion of ants.

'Stop it,' she yelled. 'Make them stop it!' But the presences did not relent—instead she felt herself being grasped by claws and lifted off the cliff. She clung to the grass but merely ripped tussocks up by the roots as she was dragged away.

'No, no, leave me!' she begged both the presences invading her mind and the creature carrying her off. A seagull screamed a protest in her ear. 'Mr Coddrington! Help!' A leap into the night sky and the beast was airborne. Struggling to gain a glimpse of her captor, she squirmed around and saw above her the shadowy bat-like wings and long whipping tail of a black dragon. Looking down, Connie realized that they had flown out to sea and were now turning back towards land. Paralysed by fear of falling from the beast's talons, she ceased trying to escape and hung limply, sobbing with pain and confusion.

The journey was mercifully brief. Reaching the top of a high cliff, the dragon swooped down to land. With consummate skill, it came to rest lightly on the ridge, despite being burdened with its prisoner.

'I see you have caught her—just like a salmon in a fish-eagle's grip,' laughed a smooth voice. 'Put her here, Charok.'

Connie dropped out of the dragon's claws. She screamed as she tumbled over the cliff-edge, only to come to land in a nest of branches, bracken, and twigs a few metres down. Winded and grazed, she lay for a moment, though sickened by the foul stench of the debris beneath her. Steeling herself, trying desperately to silence the voices in her mind, she raised her head, scraping her hair from her eyes. Before her loomed a vast midnight-blue eagle with a hooked beak. Its eyes glinted, one yellow, one gold, as if it were considering her as a morsel to be devoured. She cowered back, scrambling to her feet, crunching on the bones of other meals as she did so.

'Do not be afraid, Universal,' cackled the bird, 'I do not eat such as you. You are a mere mouthful; my hunger cannot be sated by flesh. No, you are here as my guest. Welcome. Forgive the unexpectedness of my invitation but I had no choice. I could not hope to speak to you while you were surrounded by all those humans and I have waited long for my opportunity. You have been well guarded. It was kind of the Society to organize such a big meeting in so remote a spot, allowing me to gather my forces unobserved.'

'Get them to stop,' was all she could manage to say in reply, meaning the noises still drilling into her skull.

'Oh yes. I apologize for my friends' eagerness: they all want to meet you—as do I.' The eagle let out a piercing screech that echoed off the cliff. Immediately the invasion ceased. Though feeling groggy, Connie was now able to take in her surroundings. She was trapped in a nest on a rock ledge. Above her perched the black dragon, its red eyes glowing like coals, surrounded by other creatures, all looking down on her. She could not tell what manner of creatures they were—glimpsing a silhouette of a thin arm here, a flash of bared teeth there, her imagination supplying the rest in the shape of banshees, ghouls, and werewolves. Behind them stood a darker shadow blotting out the stars, armed with an iron-tipped club: Shirley's weather giant.

'Who are you?' Connie whispered, her throat constricted with fear.

'Do you not know?' the eagle mocked. 'You a universal and not know!'

The bird bent forward; Connie backed away, but she had nowhere to go except over the edge of the nest and down into a black chasm below.

'Do not be afraid. I will not harm you—much,' the bird said ominously.

Connie stopped moving and waited in terror as the bird touched her with its beak. Immediately, a rush of emotion smote her. Swept up in the vortex of the creature's mind, she felt hatred, anger, malice, and despair ripping into her. It was as if she had suddenly fallen through the bottom of the world and was spinning in an endless void with no star to relieve the utter darkness.

The eagle lifted its beak and instantaneously the sensations left her. Connie panted, trembling from head to toe.

'Do you still not know who I am?'

'You're a mythical creature but no bird,' Connie began weakly. Her perceptions were starting to clarify. 'You're not like any other I've met: you are broad—like an ocean.' As she said those last words, she recalled Morjik saying something similar about her. If the creature resembled a universal, what did that make it? 'You're Kullervo.'

The bird ruffled its wings, pleased by her discovery.

'It cannot be hidden from you, just as you could not be hidden from me,' it said. 'I am all things; but one name I have is, indeed, Kullervo.'

As she watched, the great eagle reared up, spread its wings, beating them as it shifted shape into a cloaked figure, taller than even the weather giant, rising up to the clouds. A mist swirled around him, clinging to him, like ivy to a tree. Only his eyes remained the same, burning above her, acid yellow and lava gold, with black slits for pupils, like twin stars.

'This is how legend speaks of me.' Kullervo's voice thundered in the clouds above. 'A dark shadow on the edge of man's world. But I am no longer going to live in the margins. I am coming nearer; my anger cannot be turned back.' He dropped his arms and bent towards Connie. 'And you must help me.'

'Me?' Connie gasped, wondering what a being of such power could want with her.

'Yes.' As he spoke, Kullervo was diminishing in size like water pouring into a transparent vessel until he stood only a metre taller than Connie—taking a form so sharply defined that she could trace the veins in his muscular arms. He was now like a living statue of a satyr carved out of blue-grey marble by a master sculptor. 'You've no need to be afraid. Ha!' he laughed scornfully with a toss of his handsome head, stamping his cloven hoofs. 'I can read your mind, Connie: I know what you are thinking. You are thinking of all the warnings and terrible things you have heard about me from those fools in that precious Society.'

That had indeed been what Connie was thinking; she was alarmed that she could not hide her thoughts from him.

'They have had you so worried, have they not? They have been stopping you at every turn—keeping you in the dark. That's not how I would treat you. I know you are special. You're clever. I know you've seen through their lies.' His voice had sunk to an urgent whisper, sounding both sorrowful and gentle. His words entered her thoughts like a light breeze filtering into a stuffy room, tempting her to leave these confines and taste the fresh air with him. 'It is time to put away your fear. You know I am right. The mythical world must act to save the Earth from humanity.' Connie raised her head and looked into his eyes— it was not cruelty she saw now but pain: his eyes were the eyes of all the creatures she had known who had been mistreated or hunted into oblivion by humanity.

Connie shook her head automatically but part of her heard in his words her own thoughts. Hadn't Shirley said the same? Wasn't Axoil just a small part of what was destroying the Earth and had to be stopped? It was hard now to remember all that Dr Brock and others had told her. All she could think of was the dark soul before her. He contained such power—such rage—it was as if the anger of the whole Earth seethed inside him. Was he not right to be angry? Should she not help him?

'Come see with my eyes, Universal!' he said softly. He reached out his hand. Connie paused and then took it tentatively in hers. This time she was ready for the wave that swept over her and she tried to imagine herself swimming with his dark mood rather than being swamped. Kullervo was showing her the world as humans had made it— once fertile plains gasping for water; ice melting under a hot sun; floods bursting the banks of rivers. She began to waver: she could see these things his way. Had not her own heart prompted her to ask what use the Society was in the face of all this death and destruction? The world would be better if it was scoured clean so it could teem with life once more, not gasp for its last breath under man's smog. Mankind needed to be taught to respect the mythical creatures by seeing their power unleashed.

Just as she was about to slip into the current of his mood, surrender herself to his force, her mind snagged on something, caught despite itself on an unseen obstacle. Beneath the surface, she sensed he was hiding something from her. What was it? He was right that humanity was criminally foolish in its headlong pursuit of gain, but did not Kullervo revel in this destruction? Did he not feed off the imbalance in nature created by humanity, spinning the world into yet more cycles of devastation and death? Did he not seek the end of mankind itself?

The moment she saw this, Connie realized that she must not allow him to perceive that she had read more deeply than he intended; but his was such a powerful mind, how could she keep anything from him?

An island—I need an island, she thought to herself. Painfully, against the tide of his perceptions, Connie imagined herself piling stone on patient stone so just the tip of dry land emerged above the waves. On this frail isle, she placed her secret. Then Kullervo released her hand, the floodtide receded, leaving her knowledge untainted by his mind.

'You understand,' he said with a smile. 'I can sense that, Universal—and you will agree with me in time.' He spun away from her, lifting his face to his supporters, arms outstretched. 'She understands, my friends, as I said she would!' he cried triumphantly.

Before he spoke, Connie had already turned her mind to escape. Even if the Society was wrong, she knew now that Kullervo was not right. Sooner or later this interview would end in her refusing to help him, but she could not see how she could escape with her life unless she could summon help. She peered over the edge of the nest cautiously: nothing but a ledge and then a sheer drop to the waves clawing at the cliff bottom many metres below. If only someone knew she was here! But who would? Unbidden, Gard's face appeared in her mind. As long as you are standing on the earth, we rock dwarfs will know where you are, he had told her. If she could stand on firm ground, would that alert Gard to her danger? Surely it was worth a try?

'Are you ready to pledge your allegiance to me?' Kullervo asked, swinging back to face her, holding out his arms as if preparing to embrace her.

'I'm afraid,' she replied, trying to buy herself some time. 'I need to think about it—about what you've said.' She swung one leg over the side of the nest, trying to gain a foothold on the narrow rock ledge. 'Your ideas seem so new to me.' Her boot caught a hold and she filled her mind with her memory of Gard's presence, managing it only for a second before the presence of Kullervo dashed down on her once more.

'What are you doing? Get away from there!' he boomed, his gentleness cast aside. He thrust out a powerful fist and hooked her roughly by the jacket. Lifting her up as if she weighed no more than a doll, he dangled her carelessly over the edge for a moment. 'There is no way you can escape from here unless you have wings,' he mocked. 'Do you still want to go that way?'

A small white dart plunged out of the night sky to peck at Kullervo's fiery eyes, screeching with fury. It was Scark.

'What? Protecting your human chick, are you?' crowed Kullervo. He batted the annoyance away, sending Scark crashing into the cliff with a sickening thud. The bird slid into the nest and fluttered to his feet, wing drooping at his side. Undaunted, he attacked the shape-shifter's cloven hoofs, screeching with anger. Kullervo looked down with amusement at the tiny creature scratching at his feet and raised his hoof. Connie realized what he was about to do. Thrashing helplessly in his grasp, she opened her mouth and screamed and screamed, 'No!'

Fixing his eyes on her and smiling, Kullervo stamped his foot hard on the seagull, crushing the life from him.

'No!' Connie's cry tore at her throat until she had no voice or breath left. She kicked and punched, but couldn't reach him.

With a cruel laugh at her grief, Kullervo dropped Connie back on to the floor of the nest, and once more assumed the form that towered over her. A chorus of howls rose from the onlookers. Connie cradled the broken body of her friend, moaning in despair. Scark was still warm, but even as she held him she felt his heartbeat fade and his wings sag. His spirit had flown, never to return. Scark had come to save her. She was the reason he was dead.

'My followers grow tired,' announced Kullervo. 'You do not have long to make up your mind. Kullervo's wrath is coming in any case: you either join me and ride out this storm, or you perish with all others who stand in my way—like this bird of yours.'

Connie remained crumpled at his feet. Her situation seemed hopeless. She did not know what to say.

'But I'm still a child,' she pleaded, sobbing again. 'Please let me go.'

'You are a universal. And I have no pity—just as mankind has no pity on the world.'

'But not all of us are like that. Some of us want to stop the destruction. I don't want to join you. I just want to go home,' she cried out in desperation.

'Your home is by my side—there or nowhere.'

Kullervo swirled his cloak about him and raised his arms to strike her, but a harsh screech above distracted him from his purpose. The black dragon had launched itself into the air.

A green flame streaked across the night sky and bore down upon Kullervo's encampment.

Morjik!

The black dragon rose to meet him. They clashed in mid-flight, scorching each other with bursts of fire, the shock of their collision echoing like a thunderclap. All eyes turned to witness the combat as the beasts wound themselves together, shrieking, writhing to find a hold that would bring the other crashing down. In an instant, Kullervo assumed his eagle shape and launched himself off the nest to aid his servant. Lightning seared the dark, narrowly missing Morjik, as the weather giant added his might to defeat the interloper.

Transfixed by the fight above, Connie did not see the pegasus until it landed behind her.

'Climb on!' Col hissed in her ear, grabbing her arm to pull her to her feet. This was her one chance. She had to take it, even if it meant leaving Morjik to battle, outnumbered by Kullervo and his followers. But what use was she in any case? She scrambled on to the pegasus and clung on to Col's waist one-handed, still clutching Scark.

'But Morjik,' she shouted desperately as Skylark swooped off the ledge.

'Help is coming!' Col replied, urging Skylark away from the nest as fast as he could fly.

A fizz of light and a blinding flash erupted a foot from Skylark's nose. Connie closed her eyes seeing the jagged trail of the lightning still etched on her eyelids.

'Keep low,' ordered Col grimly. 'The giant's seen us!'

Skylark dipped sharply to the left, avoiding by a hair's breadth a ball of ice as it exploded on the cliff face, showering them with tiny shards of rock. Connie twisted to look over her shoulder just in time to see Morjik diving at the giant's head, jaws blazing white-hot fire. Above him, Charok and the eagle ripped at him with furious swipes of their claws. The giant threw a second bolt which went wide as he fended off Morjik's attack, but the flash revealed the pegasus to Kullervo. Turning in mid-air, the eagle sped towards them, screaming to his followers to join him. Skylark was flying as fast as he could burdened with two passengers, but his speed would be no match for Kullervo's.

'Col,' she screamed, 'behind us!'

Col glanced over his shoulder and saw the pursuit was on.

'Dive!' he urged Skylark. 'Dive!'

Skylark dropped like a stone towards the waves, his riders clinging to his back, barely able to hold on as he hurtled down. All went wet, cold, and damp as they plunged into the ring of cloud the giant had spun to conceal the camp. Connie could no longer see the waves but she could hear them breaking on the rocks below.

'Climb now!' commanded Col.

Still wrapped in the obscuring blanket of vapour, Skylark levelled off and began to beat his wings, straining with the effort to gain altitude as fast as possible. Connie could swear she heard the rush of passing wings close below them, followed by others, but she could see nothing.

As they broke out from the top of the weather giant's storm cloud, Connie saw a squadron of dragons silhouetted against the moon, led by Storm-Bird and Argot. Half peeled off in pursuit of Kullervo. The rest rushed to Morjik's aid. It was like the opening of the celebration, but this time in deadly earnest. With brilliant precision, they flew like two arrows into the cloud and were gone. Connie heaved a sigh of relief: with such forces on his side, Morjik would surely be victorious. Kullervo would be beaten back.

'Where are we going?' she shouted into Col's ear.

'I've orders to take you to the Mastersons' farmhouse. You'll be safe there.'

'Orders?'

'Well, you didn't give us long to find you but we were ready. When we heard that you'd been taken, Dr Brock guessed what had happened. We prepared a rescue party—I was to pull you out while the others acted as a diversion, and I'm to take you to the farm—but we didn't know where you were exactly until that rock dwarf suddenly shouted out that you were at Deadman's Cove.'

'Scark found me first.'

'I know. I'm sorry, Connie.'

Connie shivered and clung more tightly to Col, relieved beyond words to be amongst friends again. She let herself sob on to his shoulder, the fingers of one hand caressing Scark's bloodied feathers as she clutched the battered body to her chest. She cried until she had no more tears left.

Now they were flying swiftly but calmly over Dartmoor, Connie began to nod with tiredness, her reserves of energy all spent, her mind numb with sorrow. Letting her thoughts wander, she stumbled clumsily into the dialogue between the pegasus and Col. Compared to her dazed, grief-stricken state of mind, they were sharply focused; united in concern for their passenger, alert to pursuit, flying with one mind: a perfect team.

'She senses us, Col.' Skylark had noticed her presence.

'Sorry, I can't help eavesdropping. I've not yet learnt to control my gift,' she apologized, feeling as if she had walked into a room without knocking.

'I understand, Universal,' Skylark replied. 'You are welcome here, is she not, Companion?'

To Connie's relief, there was no hesitation from Col.

'Of course she is. Connie, I've a confession to make.' He paused. Connie felt Skylark give him a mental nudge. 'I let you down—never really gave you a chance. I'm sorry.'

'He's trying to tell you, Universal,' broke in Skylark, 'that he's been a fool.'

'Thanks, Companion,' said Col sourly. 'Now my friend here has explained my feelings about myself so clearly, will you accept my apology? Can we start again?'

It was the second invitation to make a new start that Connie had received that evening, but this was one she was eager to accept. Even in her weary state, she appreciated how difficult it had been for proud, popular Col to make an apology to her and admit that he had been wrong.

'Course,' she replied. 'And I'm sorry that I had a go at you about Jane's dad. I should never've said you didn't care.'

'So, friends then?' said Col.

'Friends,' she agreed, her head dropping forward against his shoulder. Her thoughts were slipping out of focus: she could no longer hear their silent communication. Exhaustion and shock were finally catching up with her.

'Grab her before she falls!' warned Skylark, sensing her distress. 'She is losing consciousness.'

Just in time, Col caught Connie as she was about to release her grip around his waist.

'We must land to put her in front of me,' he told Skylark, but his mount was already circling down to find a convenient spot. Once on the ground, Col was shocked to see how white Connie's face was—she looked drained of life, like a waxwork image.

'She needs help: we must fly like the wind!' he urged Skylark as they took off once more, Connie now slumped over the pegasus's neck. Col took charge of the gull's broken body. 'Whatever has Kullervo done to her?'

* * *

Col and Skylark landed with their burden by the farmhouse where Evelyn, Jessica, Mrs Clamworthy, Dr Brock, Gard, and the remaining Trustees were waiting for them anxiously. Skylark trotted forward to stop by the steps up to the house, panting hard, his flanks glistening with sweat, legs close to buckling with the effort he had just made.

'Thank God,' Mrs Clamworthy exclaimed, 'you're unharmed! How's Connie?'

'He killed her seagull. She's in shock or something. Take her someone!' Col called. Dr Brock darted forward and caught Connie as she slid off Skylark's back. Evelyn let out a wail of distress. 'She's been like this for some time,' Col explained, his voice cracked with concern. 'Should we call an ambulance?'

Kira hurried forward and wrapped Connie in a blanket. 'Bring her into the house,' she said calmly. 'She'll have the best care she could wish for in Windfoal.'

The party filed quickly into the house, leaving Col and Skylark together in the yard. He placed Scark reverently on the back seat of his grandmother's car then turned to pat Skylark's neck affectionately.

'You were brilliant!' he complimented him.

'And you were brave,' the horse nuzzled him back.

Leading Skylark with his hand resting gently on his mane, Col sought out the warmth of the stable and a well-earned rest for his steed.

18
Sword and Shield

The sweet smell of hay and the warmth of a tartan cloth—Skylark twittered with pleasure, comfortable in his stall. Nudging Col softly, he released his companion to go back to the farmhouse, as they both knew that Col would not be able to sleep without news of Connie. Col found most of the Hescombe party sitting with Mr Masterson in the dining room around a shining, dark-wood table, talking in low voices. Evelyn, however, was striding angrily to and fro, casting challenging looks at the disapproving portraits of previous Mastersons gazing down on them from the walls. The youngest clan member was leaning against the door, dressed in a floral dressing gown and slippers, looking in.

'Is Connie OK?' Col asked Shirley.

She shrugged. 'Think so.'

Taken aback, Col turned to look into Shirley's face, but she did not meet his eyes. Her expression was one of boredom, as if she was uninterested in the events of the night—indeed, she was acting as though she was more annoyed to have her house invaded by uninvited guests than anything else. He could not waste time on her if she would not give him a proper answer so he pushed his way past and into the room.

'Ah, Col!' Dr Brock rose as he came in. 'We were waiting for you. As the last person she saw, Windfoal thinks you should be there when Connie wakes up. Come with me.'

Dr Brock took Col up to a grand bedroom with heavy red velvet curtains, just beginning to glow with pale pink light in the rising sun. Col saw Connie asleep in a four-poster bed under a canopy, her hair spread out across the pillow. She no longer had the marble sheen that had so alarmed him a few hours ago; instead, her face had regained its usual colour and she seemed to be having a pleasant dream as a smile flickered across her lips.

'She's been sent to sleep by Windfoal,' said Dr Brock, 'who's protecting her from all bad memories while she dreams. They'll come back when she wakes—indeed, I need her to remember because we must know what she's seen and heard.' He sighed. 'Our vigilance failed. It means that it's time for us to tell her all. We can no longer keep it back from her without putting her in worse danger.'

Col and Dr Brock took seats in a pair of saggy armchairs either side of an empty grate. Despite himself, Col found he was yawning. He rubbed his eyes roughly with his knuckles.

'Is she all right? I mean, what did Kullervo do to her tonight?' Col asked, still haunted by his glimpse of Connie on the moor and the shattered body of Scark.

'I think he almost killed Connie,' Dr Brock replied softly, 'when she refused to help him in his plans to bring havoc upon the human world. But thanks to you, and to others, she's been saved. But it has been at a great cost: not only has one brave bird died for her but we've had news that when Morjik drove Kullervo and his creatures away, he was badly wounded by lightning burns. Even now he is being brought back by the dragons. He is close to death.'

'Morjik! Scark!' It was not Col but Connie who had spoken. The two turned round to find her sitting bolt upright in bed with a wild look on her face.

'Lie still,' said Dr Brock, rushing over to prevent her getting out of bed. 'Kinga is doing all she can for Morjik. Don't worry, there's strength left in the old dragon yet.'

Connie reluctantly lay back on the pillows, but tossed her head fretfully, still distressed. Nothing would bring back Scark. It was as though she had woken to a nightmare. Her wonderful gift had turned ugly and she did not want to think about it. She wanted to go back into the sleep where everything was calm and beautiful.

Col came to her side and touched her hand. 'How do you feel?' he asked.

'I'm fine,' she lied, returning his gesture with a slight squeeze of his fingers, 'just confused—and afraid—afraid for Morjik.'

'Confused?' asked Dr Brock gently.

'Yes. He—Kullervo—seemed to want me on his side. I'm not sure why he didn't just kill me,' Connie replied, withdrawing further under the covers as if afraid to hear the answer.

Dr Brock rubbed his chin and looked away, working out what he should say.

'I'm not an expert on these things, but I think, Connie, that if the universals have one companion species in the mythical world, it's Kullervo. You are counterparts—he in his world, you in ours. He knew about you before anyone else did. You see, he has always been on the watch for your kind, ever since we managed to hide the universals from him in the last world war. He's been waiting and searching for a next one, to take them before we could conceal them from him. He was ready for you, when we'd stopped watching.'

'But I don't want to be companion to such a vicious creature!' Connie protested.

'Quite so,' said Dr Brock, laying a comforting hand on her arm. 'I said you were counterparts, not that you would have to be a companion for him. In fact, it would be very bad news for us if you did want to join him: with you as a channel, he could magnify his power a hundredfold. At present he acts in our world through his followers as his own power is still confined to the mythical world. He needs a universal companion to open the door for him.'

'That means he'll be coming back for me!' she said desperately, sitting up again. She wanted to run away from being a universal, go back to the time when she had never heard of such a thing.

Dr Brock again restrained her gently. 'For you—or for the next universal to be discovered. I know it's hard for you to hear this, Connie, but it's better that you are fully aware of the danger you face rather than run into it heedlessly. We should've told you earlier but we thought you weren't ready. You must understand that he's prepared to wait for an accomplice. He will try to turn you but, if that fails, he would rather you were dead than alive to resist him. You also pose a threat to him, you see, if you survive in opposition to him.'

'How?' asked Col, horrified. This was the first time he had heard this. Connie again looked as ashen-faced as she had on the moor a few hours ago. She had just realized that she was trapped— trapped as a universal. The wild thought that she could run from this truth had been a delusion.

'We're not sure, but the stories about Kullervo say that he can only be defeated by an equal and opposing force of good. Now, I'd say that our Connie here was good through and through, wouldn't you?' Dr Brock's eyes glistened from under his white brows at Col. 'She's the nearest thing we have to that force.'

'But I can't do anything against that . . . that monster,' Connie said incredulously. They all seemed to expect so much of her and she hadn't even been able to stand on her feet before Kullervo. She hadn't been able to save Scark.

'Maybe not yet, but your training has only just begun. Are you able to tell me about him, Connie?' Dr Brock asked quietly. 'No one before has seen him and lived, you see, so we have to know all we can about him in order to fight him.'

Still shaking, Connie took a deep breath and recounted the events of the night in a halting voice. When she reached the part where she had touched Kullervo a second time, she was reluctant to say how close she had come to giving in to him. Now ashamed of her weakness, she did not dwell on this part of the encounter. Tears streamed down her face as she retold the death of Scark.

Col listened with growing alarm as she described the shape-shifting spirit that had imprisoned her. He thought her incredibly brave to stand up to him as she had. 'He's gone, hasn't he?' Col asked Dr Brock when she had finished, hoping that his friend would at least be able to find some temporary comfort.

'For the moment. The dragons beat him back tonight and he was last seen travelling to the north in the midst of the weather giant's cloud. There'll be bad weather in the Irish Sea today, I'd say.'

The mention of the weather giant brought another event of the night to Connie's mind. 'Dr Brock, you must do something about Mr Coddrington! I think he's on Kullervo's side.'

Dr Brock looked shocked. 'Ivor Coddrington on Kullervo's side! I don't like him, I admit, but I can't believe it even of him. He's been in the Society for years!'

'Even so,' Connie persisted. She told him how Mr Coddrington had waylaid her at the castle;

how he had done nothing when she had been carried off by the black dragon. 'I think he failed me in the assessment because he was doing as Kullervo asked. Kullervo wants to keep me out of the Society. If you don't believe me, ask Mr Coddrington!'

'This is a serious charge, Connie,' Dr Brock said doubtfully. 'Ivor Coddrington has served the Society faithfully through many previous crises; he's deep in the confidence of the Trustees, knows all our plans.'

Connie felt too weak to argue. 'Just ask him.'

'But it was Ivor Coddrington who alerted us to your disappearance!'

This took the wind out of her sails. Had she got it wrong? Perhaps she had let her personal loathing of the man cloud her judgement? 'It can't have been!' she protested.

'But it was. I was there when he ran back to the car park to tell us that you had gone—so was Col.'

Connie gave up. With so many witnesses against her, how could she explain that she just knew by a deep instinct that he was not to be trusted? She turned her head away from them, wanting to go back to the peaceful sleep where such matters were not her concern.

'She's had enough,' Col murmured to Dr Brock, getting up to go.

'Yes, we've stayed too long. Sleep well, child: no one will find you here.' Tenderly, Dr Brock smoothed Connie's hair off her forehead and then the two visitors quietly withdrew from the bedroom.

That evening, when Connie awoke refreshed from her ordeal, her training began in earnest. The time to initiate her into the deeper knowledge of the universals had come. Closeted with six of the Trustees in the hay barn, she was learning how to control bonds with more than one creature at a time. Kinga and Morjik were absent because of the dragon's wounds, but they were not far away. Morjik was lying in the lambing shed next door, deep in a dragon-dream of pain and suffering, watched over by Kinga. The attack by Kullervo had wrought another change amongst the Trustees: Frederick Cony, who up to now had spent most of his time asleep or resting, had been galvanized into action and was taking Connie's training very seriously.

'My uncle Reginald,' he told Connie as he sat perched on a hay-bale, his grey hair shining like wet granite in the stark electric strip-light overhead, 'was the last universal in this country before you came along. He died ten years ago, but he told me much that might prove helpful.'

Kira was impatient, striding fretfully up and down the straw-strewn floor with the pent-up rage of a caged lioness. 'Frederick,' she said, 'we must help Connie block those attacks. As long as she cannot defend herself against them, she's vulnerable to Kullervo. We cannot protect her day and night in Hescombe: she has her own life to lead there.'

'Of course we must, Kira,' Frederick agreed, 'but there is more to the skills of a universal than merely blocking out hostile presences.' He addressed himself to Connie again. 'My uncle told me that once the universals were known as the healers and warriors of the Society in the days when we fought battles on behalf of the mythical creatures. The universals even had their own company in the Society and there was always a universal amongst the Trustees—the ninth and leader of us all.'

'But we only have one evening to give Connie some emergency aid, not years,' Kira said anxiously. Restless, Windfoal pawed the ground with an ebony hoof and twitched her ears forward expectantly, her coat like dazzling silver foil in the bright light.

'Then let us get started,' said Gard gruffly, giving the companion to unicorns a stony glare. He did not like to see his companion criticized by anyone, particularly when he rejoiced to see some of his friend's old spirit had come back.

'Righto,' said Frederick briskly, taking charge. 'If you would be so kind, Connie, please stand in the centre of our circle.'

As Connie stood in the middle of the hay-bales, they were all aware that one point of the compass stood empty. Without Morjik, the energy of the circle was out of balance. Windfoal whinnied sorrowfully; the crystal tones of her lament echoed in the rafters. Storm-Bird rumbled like the sound of a distant storm rolling across the plains.

'Now,' Frederick continued, 'I remember my uncle telling me that the basic tools of the universal consisted of the sword and the shield. I can only describe what he said to me as, of course, I have never experienced any of this myself: you will have to do the rest.

'He told me that the shield kept the universal free of encroachment from unwanted presences. He said he always imagined holding a great shield over his head so that the attack was deflected away. The most accomplished universals could even make the attack rebound on the perpetrator—this was one of the most effective weapons of the warrior. I suggest we try it now as this, I am told by my respected colleague, is the most urgent need,' Frederick said, casting a wry look at Kira.

Connie felt full of self-doubt, sure she was going to fail, yet she knew there was nothing for it but to try. She now understood that she had a duty to others as well as herself which meant that she had to learn to protect herself from Kullervo; she did not want any more creatures to risk their lives coming to save her. She took a steadying breath. 'Right, I'm ready,' she said.

Silence fell in the room. The air began to tingle with energy—energy that Connie could almost see flowing towards her. A stream of silver sparkles unwound from the unicorn's horn; jagged white light whizzed from Storm-Bird's wingtips; iron-grey links clattered to the ground from the rock dwarf's mallet and rippled to her feet. She recognized instantly their different natures—gentle, stormy, adamantine. Reminding herself that she should be resisting these encounters, she groped inside her mind for some sign of the gift she was said to have and stumbled upon something in the dark—something that was growing like a bulb putting out its first shoot in early spring. Slowly, a faint outline of a shield took shape in her mind. She held it aloft. It worked: the thoughts were held off.

'Now, try harder to reach Connie,' said Frederick, watching the girl closely as her brow furrowed with the effort.

The creatures began to batter against her shield; it was becoming heavier and harder to hold up. An insidious wave of gentle calm crept over the rim and caressed her mind: the unicorn had broken through. As if a dam had burst the others were close behind, filling Connie's mind with their presence. She was borne away, twirling hopelessly like a leaf on the flood.

'Oh!' exclaimed Connie, grabbing hold of her hay-bale before she collapsed. The presences immediately withdrew.

'That was very good, Connie,' said Frederick. 'You must not expect too much of yourself at first. Could you see what to do?'

'Yes,' Connie panted, 'but I wasn't strong enough to keep hold of the shield.'

'Maybe not yet, and not with such powerful minds as those before you, but you will grow in strength and skill. The second tool—the sword—may help you do this.'

'And what is this sword?' Connie asked doubtfully. She'd never held a sword in her life.

'Uncle Reginald described it as the chief state of mind of a universal. In fact he used another image to convey what he meant: he said it was like being a sea into which all rivers emptied—a great estuary where cold waters, warm waters, fast and slow moving, all mingled. You never lost yourself because you were the sea, but you could sense the presence of each individual without confusion.'

Connie was still filled with doubts. 'But what has this to do with swords?'

'Sorry, my dear, I can't remember,' said Frederick apologetically.

'It is the next stage,' Gard broke in, creaking as he got to his feet. 'The universal can unite those forces and, if all are willing, direct them. It has been many ages of man since I have done this. We rock dwarfs do not like mixing with others out of our element, but when needs must, even we have allowed universals to direct our powers.'

'Then let's try,' said Connie, wondering where all this was going. She had experienced power being wielded through her when the Storm-Bird had blasted the bush. Was that what it would be like?

Once more an expectant hush fell in the barn. Connie tried to clear her mind and imagine herself as a great sea, but a sunny peaceful one, not dark like that which she had sensed in Kullervo. The three presences were creeping up on her and she pictured them as three tributaries blending into her waters. As her attention flagged for a second and the image wavered, she reminded herself that Morjik had said she was broad like the ocean: it should require no effort to be what she was by nature.

'Poor Morjik!' It was not Connie's thought but Windfoal's that she heard.

'We should help him.' That was Gard.

'The power of lightning can heal as well as harm,' added Storm-Bird.

Then the four paused in wonder: they could all encounter each other directly for the first time.

'Healer as well as warrior,' said Gard.

As one, the four realized what they should do. They began to search for Morjik. Connie found his presence at hand and gradually stretched her thoughts out to him.

'Universal,' came the answering thought, 'I am weak and wandering far in my dreams.' The ancient dragon sensed the others with her. 'But who are these with you?'

The Trustees declared their names and offered their gifts—peace from Windfoal, strength from Gard, and energy from Storm-Bird. Connie felt their powers pulsing through her like molten metal pouring into a mould; with an effort, she concentrated her mind, channelling the offerings so that none went astray. She felt she was holding a tool of great power, comprising the twisted steel of the unicorn's healing, the sustaining power of the earth, and the dynamic force of the clouds. Bringing it down upon the dragon, cutting through his hide like a diamond-edged scalpel to reach the canker within, she sensed the powers passing through every fibre of the dragon's body, a cleansing force rooting out the filth left by Kullervo and his followers. Finally, Morjik heaved a great sigh and settled down to a dreamless sleep. On Connie's signal, the four withdrew their presence and broke their bond with each other, confident in the knowledge that they had given deep healing to Morjik and he would now recover swiftly.

'So that was the sword,' said Frederick. Connie opened her eyes to find him smiling at her. 'We witnessed what was happening through our bond with our mythical creatures.'

'You have an amazing gift, Connie,' said Eagle-Child. 'Through you, we can hear and see each other as clearly as you do. Now I understand how the unity of the Society was preserved throughout the centuries. Why had we forgotten this?'

'Why indeed?' said Frederick. 'My uncle never mentioned that the sword could be so shared. I fear it had become a little-used weapon by his day. The Society had disintegrated into dissent as the industrial age took its toll and he spent most of his life in hiding.'

Connie was feeling exhausted. If she could have put words to her feelings, she would have said she felt like the shore when the tide has gone out—washed up and scattered with stranded thoughts.

'Perhaps they no longer had the energy to use it,' she said. 'I can see that it's a skill that cannot be used very often. I'd be worn out if we'd gone on much longer.'

'And you were already tired from your encounter with Kullervo,' added Kira. 'We must be more careful of our universal, friends.'

'Then it's bed and sleep,' said Frederick. 'But, before you go, I think I can say that you have completed the first stage of your training successfully, can I not, fellow Trustees?'

'Indeed you can,' concurred Kira. 'You've much more to learn, Connie, but you now can take the next steps yourself.'

Eagle-Child nodded gravely and added: 'Yet I fear it is not a success we can allow others to learn about. If we can, we must stop Kullervo getting wind of the fact that you have these skills: he may think you are a more desirable ally—or captive— than ever. But I'm beginning to wonder if we can keep anything about you from him. He seems to know more about you than we do.'

With that disquieting thought, Connie rejoined Evelyn in the farmhouse. Over a sturdy casserole with dumplings cooked by Mrs Masterson, Mr Masterson volunteered to drive Mr Coddrington back to the station at the same time as he dropped the Lionhearts at home. Connie sincerely wished he hadn't. With the assessor still hanging around Hescombe, she doubted it would be long before Kullervo heard every last detail of her progress. She therefore kept very quiet at the table.

Mr Coddrington, however, was in full flow. 'I hate myself for not being able to prevent your abduction, Miss Lionheart,' he said loudly so that all the table could hear. 'But what could I do against a fully-grown dragon? I tried my best, I assure you, but you were gone in an instant.'

'You mustn't blame yourself, Ivor,' interrupted Mr Masterson. 'None of us could have done any more.'

'Well, at least I was on hand to raise the alarm. That was fortunate—most fortunate,' Mr Coddrington concluded, giving Connie an apologetic smile.

19
Storm

After the events at Deadman's Cove, Connie knew that life would never be the same again. She buried Scark at the foot of the cliffs he so loved, watched by a despondent flock of gulls. His daughter, Mew, picked at the sandy mound, unable to comprehend her loss. Connie knew how she felt.

The Society members settled back into an uneasy calm. Kullervo had disappeared again and there was no sign of any further attacks from the sirens. Despite this, Connie knew it must only be a matter of time before they struck: Gull-wing might be able to curb her sisters at Connie's request for a little while, but it surely would not be long before Feather-breath or one of the others gave in to their instinct to hunt their persecutors again? Besides, she had not come up with a solution to the threat Axoil posed to their home— she felt she had failed them.

A more mundane threat also remained. Jane's dad was anxiously seeking a new job before his contract expired at the end of the year; so far with no success. It looked as if Jane and her family would have to be on the move in January, a prospect that dampened spirits as the four friends finalized their display about the local oil industry.

'What I want to know is why there have been no more accidents,' remarked Anneena, stapling a picture of the Stacks to the display board. She sounded almost disappointed.

'Perhaps the company has learnt their lesson and fixed their faulty machinery,' suggested Jane.

'Doubt it,' muttered Col.

'Now, what do you think of that?' asked Anneena, stepping back to admire their work. 'Do you think Mr Quick will appreciate it?'

'I think he will just love it!' said Col with a broad grin.

The first hint of new trouble came from an unexpected direction. One Saturday in early

December, the phone rang. It was Connie's parents announcing their intention of spending the Christmas holidays in England rather than in Manila as originally planned. Connie heard Evelyn making a poor show of pretending to be pleased as she attempted to make her brother's family feel warmly welcome. A trickle of ice-cold anticipation ran down Connie's spine. She was delighted that she would be seeing her parents far sooner than expected but she knew too that this was going to complicate matters even more.

'But what shall I tell your father when he arrives?' Putting the phone down, Evelyn looked horror-struck at the thought she would have to explain to her disapproving brother all about the threat to his daughter's life.

'Nothing,' Connie said with a shiver, trying to drive away her anxiety. To distract herself, she picked up a tea-towel and began to dry the dishes. 'You see, if you tell Dad, he'll forbid me to have anything to do with the Society, but now Kullervo knows about me, that'll put me in more danger than ever. I need the Society and I need to learn how to use my gift if I'm to defend myself.'

Evelyn could not think of an argument against this suggestion and as it excused her from a difficult conversation with her brother, was more ready to agree than Connie had expected.

'I draw the line at telling lies, Connie,' she warned. 'If your father asks a direct question, I'll have to tell the truth.'

'Of course—and so would I,' grinned Connie. 'But how likely is that if he doesn't know the first thing about Kullervo—or mythical creatures for that matter?'

Mr Johnson's class set up their display in the entrance hall the morning of the final assembly of term, under the banner 'Our Local Community'. Prominent amongst the projects on local history, traffic schemes, and fishing was the four friends' collage of information about the Axoil refinery. Mr Johnson came over to inspect the finished product and coughed nervously.

'Er . . . isn't it a little . . . a little confrontational?' he murmured to Anneena.

'That's exactly what it's meant to be, sir,' she replied happily. He stood back to consider it from a distance. 'You asked us to do a subject of local interest and that's what we've done. If you think about it, how else can we guess what the local environmental impact will be if we don't look to international examples? And you said you'd support us . . .'

Mr Johnson groaned. 'Yes, but I didn't expect it to be quite so . . . quite so one-sided.'

Anneena hadn't been able to resist Col's suggestion that they accept Mack Clamworthy's offer to help collect all the old stories about Axoil around the world. He had told Col he was more than happy to 'dish the dirt' on the company run by his old playground enemy. The collage reporting accidents and pollution scandals was far from flattering to their visitor.

'You're not going to ask us to take it down?' challenged Anneena, giving the teacher a defiant stare.

'Er . . . no, but . . . well, we'll see,' Mr Johnson said awkwardly. 'Now, let's go back to the classroom and keep our heads down.'

After lunch the school was summoned to the assembly hall. Col filed in with Justin and took a seat at the back. Sitting at the front was Mr Quick, hunched on a seat too small for him like a black vulture before the ranks of brightly dressed, twittering children. It was painful to see his smile—it was more like a skull's grimace: there was certainly no good humour behind it. Col was not the only one to wish he could wipe that expression off his face for him.

'Wait till he sees our display,' Col muttered to himself with grim satisfaction.

'Boys and girls, settle down please!' called Mrs Hartley over the hubbub as she bustled in from the foyer. 'Now, as I'm sure you are all aware, we have a very special guest with us today. Mr Quick from Axoil is here to announce the winner of the playground competition and present us with a cheque. Thank you to all those who entered—we had lots of lovely entries, didn't we?' Mrs Hartley looked to Mr Quick for confirmation but his grin had slipped and he was staring with something like malice at Rupa who had just come in and was standing by the door with a photographer.

'Er . . . yes,' he said abruptly when he realized that Mrs Hartley was addressing him.

'So now I'm going to announce the winner. If you're the lucky one to be chosen, we'd like you to stay behind after assembly so we can take your picture in the display area with Mr Quick.'

Col winked at Anneena who grinned back, bobbing restlessly in her seat to get a better look.

'And the winner is—Ursula Jones from Year Four. Well done, Ursula!'

The school clapped politely as a pigtailed girl shuffled to the front to receive her certificate.

'We selected Ursula's design because she had the unusual idea of a climbing frame shaped like an oil tanker. Mr Quick's little joke is that we should paint it in the Axoil colours!' Mrs Hartley tittered with laughter; her guest grimaced at Ursula who was smiling nervously back at him.

'That's no joke,' muttered Col to Justin. 'I bet the creep really wants it done up like that.'

Mrs Hartley was speaking again. 'We've put up Ursula's design in the display area for you all to see. Well done, Ursula, you can return to your seat.'

At the end of assembly the children streamed out of the hall. Connie followed Anneena, eager to see if Mr Quick had spotted their collage yet. They bumped into Col who was glaring furiously at the little huddle of press in the entrance hall.

'Look!' he burst out. 'They've only gone and taken our stuff down and put up that design for an oil tanker!' He was incandescent with rage, not even attempting to keep his voice down.

Hearing the disturbance, Mr Johnson appeared at their side. 'I feared something like this might happen,' he said, his eyes flashing angrily. 'She must've done it as soon as she saw we were inside the hall.'

Mrs Hartley scented trouble and glided over to the group. 'It's all going so well, isn't it!' she gushed. 'I had to take down a few things, Terry, to make space for the winning picture, but I'll make sure they go up again as soon as we've finished here.' They showed no signs of moving, so Mrs Hartley was forced on to a different tack. 'Terry, you'd better get back to your class so you can dismiss them. Parents are already arriving to collect their children.' She waved vaguely to the main entrance where in fact there was not a single person waiting, before returning to intercept Rupa who was searching in vain for her sister's work. Mr Quick was now posing for the cameras, his arm around Ursula, both holding an oversized cheque with quite a few noughts.

'Come on,' said Mr Johnson wearily. 'I suppose I should have guessed this would happen.'

He beckoned them to follow him back to the classroom. Connie tugged Col's arm, fearing he would do something rash.

'Come on, Col. Axoil won't always have the last word.'

Signor Antonelli moved over to Dr Brock's tiny house to make room for Connie's family. Connie had been seeing less and less of the Italian recently as he was busy heading up the task force to deal with the sirens. Signor Antonelli had told her that he was teaching the dragon riders to deflect attacks by the sirens with minimum force as he was sceptical that anything they could do now would persuade the sirens to take a peaceful path.

'*Carina*, 'ave you 'eard from them? What they do?' he would ask her every time their paths crossed. Connie had resumed sending messages, this time via Mew, but had received only ambiguous answers in return.

'I don't know. I really do think I'll have to go and see them again,' she told him.

'No, no!' he protested, taking her hand in his. 'You no risk zat!'

'That's what Dr Brock and the Trustees said as well,' said Connie. She looked out of the kitchen window at the still winter's day. No sign of any storm yet, nothing to herald the arrival of Kullervo in the area as the sirens had told her. 'But what else can I do? I can't just sit on my hands waiting for the sirens to take another life or hit a bigger target, like a tanker or something.'

'*Pazienza!*' Signor Antonelli counselled, wagging his finger at her. 'The *universale* is *più importante* than even this little stretch of coast— *più importante* than exposure of *le sirene.*'

Connie groaned. Everyone was telling her to sit tight but it did not seem right to her to put herself above the lives of the sea creatures and birds that would be affected in any disaster. What about Mew and her flock? She felt doubly responsible for them now Scark had gone. How could she live with herself if she found Mew floating in oil on her doorstep? What about the people that worked for Axoil? What would she feel if another man went missing? Yet, with her family arriving and no one in the Society willing to take her out to the sirens, she did not have any choice for the moment but to act as if things were normal. Trips to see the sirens were completely off the menu.

Her parents and brother Simon arrived later that day to celebrate Christmas with Connie and Evelyn. Simon was moving to a new boarding school in England after the holidays, having been expelled from his school in Manila because of a mysterious incident with a snake. This development had necessitated the sudden change of Christmas plans but neither her parents nor Simon were forthcoming about the details. Connie wondered if Simon was growing more like her as he got older— she could certainly relate to someone having wildlife problems in the classroom.

It was odd to fall back into her everyday role of daughter and older sister after spending the autumn getting accustomed to her new identity as the only universal. It did her good not to worry about the future, her time being totally taken up by shopping for Simon's new uniform with her mother, rambling with her dad and brother, and eating together as a family every evening. She suppressed her worries about the sirens and Kullervo, trying to maintain a convincing performance for her parents that she was behaving perfectly normally and nothing out of the ordinary ever happened in Hescombe.

Evelyn was on her best behaviour with her brother's family, keeping her eccentricities well hidden, even managing to seem interested when Connie's mum, her brunette hair flawlessly arranged, nails manicured and clothes co-ordinated, attempted a conversation about fashion and make-overs. Connie, knowing them both well, could tell that her mum was trying to drop her sister-in-law a heavy hint that she could do with some attention in the style department, but Connie also knew that Evelyn was too thick-skinned to notice the implied criticism. In any case, Connie had long since decided her aunt's eccentric style did not need any alteration.

Mr Lionheart, a giant of a man with a mane of black hair, which he kept tamed with copious amounts of hair-cream, questioned Connie closely about her activities with the Society while they strode the coastal path together. He seemed reassured by the description of riding lessons.

'I even learnt some geology,' Connie added, keeping her back firmly to the Stacks, visible from the headland. That impressed her father: any society that kept the children to their studies even at the weekends was sure to get his approval.

On Christmas Eve, Evelyn volunteered to cook them a special supper. The Lionhearts were gathered around the kitchen table, which was decorated with white candles, a pyramid of sweet-scented tangerines, and a vibrant red poinsettia in a gold pot. Connie's father beamed jovially at everyone, having already downed a generous gin and tonic, and reminisced with Evelyn about Christmases when they were children. Connie's mum listened politely, but her attention was really taken up with the maddening disorder that was her sister-in-law's dresser—old glass bottles and mismatched cups piled haphazardly in front of cracked plates. From time to time, as distressing burnt smells wafted to her from the stove, she wrinkled her nose and fidgeted in her seat, finding it difficult to resist the temptation to interfere with Evelyn's culinary endeavours. Simon slumped on his elbows, disappearing, like the dormouse in the teapot, into the hood of his favourite sweater—a garment that he refused to be parted with unless his mother wrestled it from him to wash. The smell of freshly singed salmon attracted Madame Cresson into the kitchen. She leapt on to Simon's knee and put her paws on the table.

Alarmed at such flagrant evidence of her peculiar household, Evelyn spoke sternly to the cat: 'Leave the table immediately!' Madame Cresson merely glowered at her.

'Go on, puss: do as you are told,' said Simon, pushing her gently away. To Connie and her aunt's surprise, Madame Cresson obeyed without a murmur and slid out of the cat flap. Unless Connie asked her, the cat rarely did as she was told. Connie and her aunt exchanged a meaningful look.

'You've got quite a way with animals, Simon,' Evelyn said, keeping her tone even, while turning the fish over in the frying pan.

'I s'pose I have. It's been like that this year. They seem to like me now Connie's not about so much,' Simon said.

'What? All animals, Si, or just cats?' Connie asked, trying to hide her excitement. Simon was looking a bit embarrassed: he knew his dad was not keen on this kind of talk.

'Dunno really,' he muttered. Then, changing the subject, he said, 'I like your friend Col: he's cool. And having your own pony—and a boat!'

'Don't you get big ideas, lad,' his dad butted in. 'No room for a pony at your new school.'

'Well, if Simon wants to spend some of his holidays with us here,' Evelyn slipped in quickly,

'I'm sure Col will let him ride his pony. Don't you think so, Connie?'

'Oh yes!' Connie agreed, knowing what her aunt was thinking. If they could spend some time with Simon, they could see if he would be a likely candidate for undergoing an assessment. Not with Ivor Coddrington though, Connie made a mental note.

'That would be very kind of you, Evelyn,' said Mrs Lionheart, 'but you've already taken on so much with Connie . . .'

'It would be no trouble at all,' Evelyn replied quickly, shovelling the charred salmon on to plates and slapping them down in front of her guests.

'Well, we'll see how things go during term,' said Mr Lionheart, giving his supper a doubtful stare. 'You never know, Simon may want to stay with some new pals. After what happened in Manila, it's perhaps best he mixes with normal people.'

That night, Connie could not keep her mind on anything but her little brother. Could he have the gift too? If so, it should be kept very quiet or he would be in danger. What likelihood was there that there would be any members of the Society on hand to help at his boarding school? With a new worry to add to her existing problems, Connie spent a restless night, plagued by a series of dreams in which she was running after Simon as he bounded away from her like a cat. All the while she was aware of a shadow in close pursuit, threatening to overtake her and swallow them both up.

On New Year's Eve, Connie was in her bedroom preparing for a party over at Jane's when a headache exploded in her temples with completely unexpected ferocity. She sat down on the bed abruptly.

'What's the matter, darling?' asked her mother. She had come up to help choose an outfit for her daughter and was half-buried in the wardrobe in the vain hope of finding something that she thought pretty. 'Your face is as white as a sheet.'

'Headache,' croaked Connie, hands clutched to her temples.

Mrs Lionheart came over to the bed and smoothed Connie's hair off her forehead. 'Migraine, I expect. I used to get them all the time at your age. Nothing for it, I'm afraid, but to lie in a darkened room and wait for it to pass.'

'But the party . . . '

'You're certainly not going out in this state. I'll stay with you.' Mrs Lionheart gave a resigned pat to her own newly styled hair.

'No, don't do that,' said Connie. She knew her mother had been looking forward to the party all day. 'Look, I've got my phone. I can ring if I need anything. The Lucases next door can keep an eye on me. I'll sleep it off.'

'All right. If you're sure. I'll come back early to check on you.' Connie's mother smiled and stroked her daughter's cheek. 'I hope you feel better soon. I'll bring up some painkillers.'

Pills taken but head still pounding, Connie buried herself in her pillow. Through the fog of pain, the next thing she heard were raised voices in the hall.

'I think I should stay.' That was Evelyn.

'No, no, Connie was most insistent that we all go. She'll ring if there's a problem.'

'But . . .'

'Evelyn, do you really think I don't know my own daughter? She'll be fine. All she needs is sleep. I'll pop back later to see how she's doing. I've already spoken to your very nice neighbour: she'll look in to check on her.'

'But . . .'

'We can hardly go on our own to these Benedicts, Evelyn,' Connie's father said gruffly. 'Don't even know them. It'd be terribly rude not to go this late in the day.'

'I suppose . . .'

'Well, that's settled then. Let's go or we'll be late.'

The house seemed very quiet now that her family had finally gone. The wind was picking up. The hot water pipes creaked and gurgled. Her bedroom was very dark. Despite her headache, Connie began to wish she hadn't refused her mother's company tonight. It was not a night to sit in shadows. She switched on the bedside light and leafed through Col's present of *The Odyssey*—but that was no good: it only reminded her that she hadn't succeeded in getting back out to the sirens again. Casting it aside, she turned on her radio for company.

'Attention, all shipping. There are warnings of gales in Sole, Plymouth, Portland, and Wight. Severe gales and blizzard conditions expected soon along the south coast.'

The mention of the approaching storm unsettled her for some reason. She did not know when Kullervo would strike. What if it were tonight? But then, what could she do? She had been forbidden to go out to the sirens and her head was pounding. She was having difficulty even thinking straight.

There was a tap on the window. Looking out into the darkening skies, she saw Mew perched on the ledge, her feathers ruffled by the strong wind. Connie's heart gave a lurch, recognizing that this was the sign she had been waiting for. Opening the window quickly, she let in an icy blast and one cold seagull. Mew hopped on to her dressing table and began to flutter her wings, sounding her ear-splitting wail.

'What brings you here?'

Mew screeched insistently, aggravating her headache with her penetrating cry.

'Do you have news?'

The bird tapped her foot.

'What about? About the sirens?'

Tap.

'They're up to something?'

Tap.

'OK, OK. Calm down—let me think.'

Connie stroked Mew's head thoughtfully as she started to put the pieces of the puzzle into place. Mew thought something big was about to happen. Slowly Connie made the connections. The buzzing in her head? She'd felt this before. Hadn't it happened long ago—the day before her assessment and her visit to the sirens? The trip to the Stacks was the first time she heard about Kullervo. But he had known about her before that. Perhaps even then he had been closer than she thought? So was it really a headache? It might be a warning. What if Kullervo was nearby? Was there a mythical creature in the area, a hostile one trying to disable her with its presence? If so, then she should be able to clear her head by practising with the universal's shield. Closing her eyes for a moment, she steadied her mind and mentally drew a picture of a round shield. Slowly raising it, she waited. The buzzing faded as if someone had turned down the sound on a radio. She had her answer.

What had the creature been that had caused the noise in her head? She had a residual impression of a swirling, incorporeal being, foggy and cold. She then remembered the weather forecast: the approaching storm—how could she have been so dim?—it must be the work of a weather giant! Kullervo had timed his attack to perfection. Shielded by his most potent ally, he had broken out of hiding and was heading into Hescombe. Was he intent on punishing her for her refusal to join him? Perhaps he planned to have his revenge by goading the sirens to wreck the first tanker they could find right outside the universal's front door? That would be like him. But if so, that meant the sirens were going to act without coming to her first. Yet what could she do to prevent them? The answer was obvious. Kullervo would expect her to be kept at home by the Society since his attack on her. He wouldn't anticipate that she would try to stop him. How little he knew her. She wasn't about to turn in meekly for the night when lives were at stake. He'd already claimed Scark's life; he wasn't going to take any more if she could help it.

She grabbed her mobile and punched in a number.

'Col—it's Connie. I've news.' She could hear a babble of voices in the background—he must be at Jane's party too. She quickly told him what she knew. 'Look, Col, you know that I'm the only one who can deal with the sirens so I'll have to go out to them. I've got to try and stop them. I'll need you to take me there. Will you do it?'

Col, at the other end of the phone, was thinking rapidly. 'But I thought the Trustees told you not to go out to them?'

'Col, I can't sit by while the sirens do this—I just can't. Look, I've had more training since I last met Kullervo—I'm better prepared. I've got to do this. Please help me.'

Col hesitated. He had let Connie down once before when she had needed him, he did not want to do so again, but neither did he want to rush into danger without taking sensible precautions. 'Look, Connie, I'll take you but we need help—we can't cope with Kullervo and the sirens on our own,' he said. 'I'll tell your aunt what you said—she can fetch Dr Brock and the others.'

'What about the ships? What if there's a tanker out there right now? I can't see the sirens letting such prey slip past them with Kullervo to egg them on. Shouldn't we try to warn the company, or the coastguard, at least someone?'

'Look, Jane and Anneena are here. I'll see if I can think of something to put them on the watch without letting them know too much. I'm sure Rupa will help. It's going to be difficult getting any attention for a disaster that hasn't happened yet, but it's worth a try.'

'Look, Col, whatever you do, don't tell my parents what we're up to. They wouldn't understand and they'd certainly try to stop me.'

'Perhaps I should stop you,' said Col grumpily, 'but I've got a feeling you'd never forgive me if I tried.'

'Too right.'

Ending the call, Connie pulled on some thicker clothes and bundled herself up in waterproofs: it would not be fun going out in *Water Sprite* on a night like tonight. Mew cried to be released, so she let the gull out of the window. The bird disappeared into the squally darkness. Connie dashed downstairs to grab her boots, hopping across the hall in her haste to get them on. Slamming the back door behind her, she ran down the street, slipping several times on the ice until she made herself go more slowly. Snow was falling, not in gentle fat flakes, but stinging grit-like fragments of ice driven into her face by the wind. She clambered on board *Water Sprite* and tried her best to get it ready for sea; a few minutes later, Col joined her.

'The others are coming,' he panted as he jumped down into the boat beside her. 'Your aunt's furious, of course. She'll skin you when she catches up with you. Your parents are in the dark as instructed. Mr Benedict was starting them on his homebrew as I left so I think they're safe for a few hours.'

'What about Axoil?'

Col gave a grim smile. 'I've told Anneena and Jane that Dad's had a tip-off from the union that the company's using the holiday to take away the dodgy machinery without anyone noticing. I told them that if they took Rupa with them, they should be able to catch Axoil red-handed. It's the best I could do.'

'Got some ear protectors?' Connie asked. He nodded and cast off.

As soon as the boat left the harbour, Connie began to have second thoughts. The sea was heaving, whipped up by the approaching storm into angry hills of water. Rags of clouds scudded across the sickly moon, driven by the relentless wind as if fleeing some danger hidden in the darkness. The little boat was having difficulty making headway.

'Will she manage this?' she shouted to Col.

'Yeah, she'll weather it,' he said confidently. 'Stay in the cabin—I don't want to lose you overboard to a rogue wave.'

Painfully, the boat ploughed its way across the short stretch of water between the harbour and the Stacks. Connie began to worry about what she would do when they reached them: no one could land on the Stacks without wings, and with all the noise created by the storm, could she attract the sirens' attention? She would have to feel out for their presence like she had for Morjik, but, with the interference from the other presences, that was going to be doubly difficult. Taking some calming breaths, she tried to focus on her shield, imagining herself holding up a bright, shining silver one, engraved with the points of the compass. The shield held: the buzzing disappeared and her head was clear again. All she had to do now was hold them off so she could use the sword when she got closer.

A thump on the cabin door alerted her to their arrival. She poked her head out, only to receive a faceful of spray as a wave crashed against the side of the boat. Col was already wearing his scarlet ear protectors.

'Can't get any closer,' he shouted. 'Too risky.'

Wiping the salt from her stinging eyes, Connie saw that they were about fifty metres from the

Stacks. The sea was lashing against the rocks, battering them hard. Closing her eyes, Connie concentrated on the song of the sirens, trying to remember its peculiar quality, its particular curves and dives. The creatures were there—she could tell—but they were not listening to her. Beyond their song, she sensed a dark presence enveloping them, drowning their will in his to bring about destruction.

'Gull-wing!' Connie whispered. 'Feather-breath!' But there was no answering call: Gull-wing and her sisters were drunk with the new song of death and devastation Kullervo was teaching them and had no time for the soft harmonies of a human companion.

Opening her eyes, Connie tapped Col on the shoulder. 'It's too late,' she mouthed. 'He's already here.'

'I know,' Col shouted back and pointed to the horizon. There—a blacker shape against the dark skies—was the silhouette of a ship sparkling with lights, a great tanker the length of a football field, churning its way heedlessly down the Hescombe Channel. But that was not all: revealed by a crack of lightning, Connie saw nine figures on top of the Stacks. They had their backs to Col's boat and were gazing out to sea. The eight smaller forms she recognized as the sirens; the ninth—a vast eagle standing beside Gull-wing—was undoubtedly Kullervo. The sirens opened their wings and launched off the Stacks, recklessly riding the gusts of wind coming from the west.

'No!' Connie screamed to the sirens, trying to cut through the evil song they were singing, to make them see sense before it was too late. They couldn't even hear her as they were so intent on completing their plan. But someone else heard the disruption: the eagle turned round and spied the little boat rocking violently on the swell with its cargo of two small passengers. His reaction was immediate and immense. Connie felt a great tidal wave of hatred and malice bearing down on her. Clutching Col's arm for support, she closed her eyes and bent her full force upon raising her shield above her head. Darkness. Hate. Loathing. The foul tide broke over her; Kullervo's presence brought her to her knees, but she kept the shield secure. On seeing her crumple to the floor of the boat, Kullervo crowed with delight, and eagerly turned back to watch the mayhem he had unleashed out to sea. With wings outspread, he leapt off the rock in pursuit of the sirens, thirsting to see death at close quarters, regarding the puny powers of the universal a matter of no importance compared to the feast that was about to begin. So he did not see Connie pulled up by Col and shakily regain her feet.

20
Kraken

'We're too late,' Connie sobbed. 'They're going to drive that tanker on to the rocks and drown all those sailors.'

Dismayed, wretched in their powerlessness, Connie and Col watched Kullervo disappear into the gloom.

'*Water Sprite*, ahoy!' A shout from the stern turned the pair's attention to matters closer to hand. Another boat had arrived: Evelyn had brought Signor Antonelli, Horace, Jessica, and Col's grandmother to assist them. They could not get too close because of the bucking waves and the howling wind and their ear protectors made it nearly impossible to converse, but Connie, pointing the others out to Col, heard enough to know that they too had seen the sirens and Kullervo set off for the tanker.

'I have an idea that may save the sailors,' bawled Horace across the water as he stripped off his life jacket. Jessica had already dumped hers on the floor. 'Take our boats as near to that tanker as you dare go. We're going to get some help.'

Connie stifled a scream when she saw Horace and Jessica dive over the side of the boat and disappear under the water.

'Don't worry, Connie,' Col yelled. 'They must've gone to find the selkies. They'll look after their companions.' Connie was only partially comforted. How could anyone survive the freezing stormy waters of the Hescombe Channel? What about their ear protectors: would they work under water?

Col spun his wheel and followed Evelyn's boat, *Banshee*, further out into the channel. They could now see the sirens wheeling around the ship and, though they were not yet within hearing, Connie could feel they were singing their song by the tingling in her spine.

It seemed to take an age for the boats to cross the stretch of water to reach the tanker. The waning moon did little to lighten the darkness that yawned between them and the ship, its yellow eye distant and cold, gazing unconcerned on the perils below. Most light came from the tanker as it pitched and rolled in the heavy swell, its deck a blaze of lights, illuminating the area in which the drama was unfolding.

'Look—it's the *Cyclops*. She seems to be drifting,' Col told Connie. It was true: the tanker had left its course down the middle of the channel where the water was deepest and was now veering towards the shore.

'What's that?' Connie asked Col, grabbing his arm to get his attention and pointing into the sea. Glimpsed briefly between the wave crests she thought she had seen a head bobbing in the water—no, there were more—tens of tiny bodies struggling in the sea.

'The crew's overboard,' Col said grimly. 'The song's done its work.' He steered *Water Sprite* towards the mariners in the hope that they could pull some out of the water before the sailors sank out of reach. 'We're not going to make it.' The nearest head dipped beneath a wave, arms flailing helplessly, before struggling to the surface once more. 'Come on, faster!' he urged the boat on.

Connie clung on to the rail, battered by the wind and flying spray, and waited for the moment when they would be within range for her to throw a lifebuoy. The sailor disappeared under the water again and this time did not resurface. Connie screamed. Then, to her great joy and relief, a head popped out of the sea near where the man had sunk. Familiar ebony eyes, long whiskers, a sleek snout that glistened in the searchlight: Horace and Jessica had found their helper. Diving beneath the waves, Arran grabbed the sailor's jacket with his teeth, pulled the man to the surface and towed him towards the boats. Reaching *Water Sprite*, he left the sailor to Col and Connie, who hauled him over the side. Once safe, the mariner lay coughing and retching on the deck. Returning to assist the other people in the water, Arran was joined by more selkies, bobbing up out of the water in all directions. Soon this efficient rescue party had towed all the seamen within reach of the boats, leaving them to be pulled aboard *Water Sprite* and *Banshee*. Jessica reappeared above the surface to help Arran with the final casualty.

'Here you are!' she gasped, following the man over the side of the boat. 'Nothing like a bracing dip in December to get the blood flowing.'

Arran barked at her heels in what Connie now knew to be his distinctive laugh.

Last up the side was a cold, but pleased, Horace Little.

'Thanks, my friends,' he bellowed to the selkies, seemingly undisturbed by the violence of the weather which pelted him with freezing spray and whipped his blanket viciously around his legs. 'A great swim!'

Arran and the other selkies bobbed once in the water before diving from view a final time.

Just when Connie dared to believe that the sailors were safe, a screech from overhead gave her a second's warning of the sirens' attack. Enraged to see their prey clutched from the jaws of death, the sirens bore down on the boats with murderous anger. Connie threw herself on to the deck, dragging Col down with her so that they narrowly avoided a siren's talons.

'What can we do now?' Col shouted. 'I thought they liked you!'

She shook her head. 'Not with Kullervo about, they don't,' she muttered, risking a look into the sky, expecting to see the sirens swooping down on her again. But, instead of an approaching death, she saw something that gladdened her heart. 'Look, Col!' She pointed up to where a dragon was grappling with the sirens in mid-air: it was Argot with Dr Brock on his back. A blast of fire, and two sirens fell with wings aflame, screaming as they hit the water. Connie shuddered with the impact, sensing their pain and anger. Danger to themselves had been no part of the plan: the other sirens retreated hurriedly, scooping their injured sisters from the waves before flying back to the

Stacks, shrieking maledictions at the dragon as they went. There was no sign of Kullervo.

Argot flew down until he came to hover over *Water Sprite*, skilfully holding position in the buffeting winds. The bedraggled sailors scrambled for cover, pointing wildly at the dragon and crying out with terror.

'Connie!' Dr Brock bellowed, pulling off his ear protectors. 'I need your help with Kullervo if we're going to save that ship. We've got to board her.' He reached his arm down to her. 'On the count of three, jump up! One, two, three!'

Lifted by a rising wave, Connie leapt to reach Dr Brock's outstretched hand and was pulled up on to Argot's back. Jessica shrieked, fearing for her friend.

'Go, Connie, go!' shouted Col in encouragement. The dragon swept off in pursuit of the ship, which was now hidden in a great mass of dark cloud. Plunging into the heart of the storm on Argot's back, Connie could see that the ship was perilously close to the cliffs that ran between Chartmouth and Hescombe. Spray exploded into the air as each massive wave broke on the rocks. It would not be long before the thin steel sides of the tanker met the stone outcrops of the cliffs. The sharp rock teeth would slice through the tanker's belly, spilling the ship's black bowels into the water.

'We must hurry,' shouted Dr Brock, seeing the same danger.

Despite being pounded by the wind, Argot landed on the wave-washed deck without difficulty: after *Water Sprite*, the tanker was a massive target for a skilled flyer. Connie and Dr Brock scrambled down from his back and pelted towards the bridge. They burst in and found it deserted: a forlorn alarm rang on the wall and red lights flashed to an empty room.

'Do you know how to sail this thing?' Connie asked, looking down on a bewildering array of dials and handles while water pooled at her feet.

'Er . . . no,' admitted Dr Brock, 'but there has to be a first time for everything.'

Connie felt she could be of no assistance with the controls so took up position as lookout at the window. Through the driving snow, she could just make out the dark cliffs ahead. A flash of white light—a bolt of lightning—and Connie saw something else.

'Kullervo's on the cliff top and he has the weather giant with him!' she told Dr Brock.

'I know,' said Dr Brock, intent on leafing through a fat book he had pulled out of a locker. 'I saw him as I flew over. I think the weather giant has changed the direction of the wind to the south-west to bring the tanker on to the shore.

He's probably also responsible for this cloud: no one will see us until it's too late! Let me know if you sense Kullervo coming any closer.' Dr Brock's face was creased with worry. 'And I'm afraid I can make little impact on the ship's course by reading the manual. We need some mythical help.'

'Even dragons can't tow a ship this size out to sea!' Connie replied, her hope ebbing away.

Dr Brock flung the book aside. 'No, but they can send a message.' He rummaged through the locker and produced a bundle of flares. 'Here, take these to Argot and ask him to fire these above the cloud.'

Connie ran back out into the storm to where the dragon was sheltering. The wind was blowing so fiercely it almost knocked her over. Argot spread a wing to shield her as she shouted her instructions.

'Here,' she said thrusting the distress flares into Argot's teeth. 'It'll be just like the fireworks—one touch from your fire and these will go off with a bang. Be careful now.' Argot hesitated; Connie could feel he did not want to leave her and the doctor with no means of escape. 'Don't worry— these will bring help—we'll be fine,' she reassured him, though deep down she was not so convinced herself.

Argot took off and disappeared into the blackness, heading steeply upwards. A shaft of lightning crackled past, narrowly missing the dragon as a fortunate gust of wind threw him out of its path.

'He's gone,' Connie told Dr Brock when she returned to the bridge. 'The weather giant almost got him, but he escaped. But I couldn't see if he'd managed to let off the flares—too much cloud.'

Dr Brock shook his head. 'I fear it will be too late if we don't do something now. We've got to summon some more help.' He looked up at her with a sudden inspiration. 'Of course! What I need is the universal. Connie, have you ever heard of the Kraken?' Connie shook her head. 'It's a legendary sea monster—Col's dad is a companion to this species. He's in the area at the moment so his companion creature must be here too. Can you try and summon it?'

Connie bit her lip doubtfully.

'I'll try. What is it like? I have to know a little about it to sense its presence.'

'A great, many-armed creature that lives in the depths of the oceans, unseen by man except when it rises in storms to devour ships.'

'And this is the creature you want to help us?'

'The Kraken won't want its waters polluted by oil any more than we do. Don't appeal to its better nature: appeal to its self-interest.'

She had nothing better to suggest so it was worth a try. But she would have to be quick, before Kullervo guessed what she was about, as she would have to lower her shield to reach out to the Kraken. Connie focused her mind on the sea, imagining the depths undisturbed by the storm raging above. Diving down into the silence, she sent out her distress call.

'Kraken, you are summoned. You are needed.'

Nothing. She tried again. And then again. Her call echoed around the void, meeting only silence. She was about to give up when a tentacle gripped her departing thought and pulled her back down.

'Why do you wake me?' a cold presence asked her. Its question curled around her, drawing her into itself. She slipped into a world of darkness, lit only by the phosphorescent glow of bizarre sea creatures, strangers to the life on the surface. Huge round eyes bulged at her with an eerie green glow; trails of semi-transparent tendrils flitted by; the electric-blue parachute puff of a jellyfish brushed her, making her smart with red-raw pain from its sting. Lost to her own world, Connie felt a momentary doubt that anything she might say could be relevant to this dweller of the deeps. Down here was as alien as the surface of the moon. But this was not so, she reminded herself: no matter how unfamiliar the Kraken's world seemed, the depths of the sea were not immune to the effects of what happened overhead. This too was part of the same world, an interlinked system in which one part needed the other to survive. Schooling herself to make the effort, she showed the sea beast a picture of all that was happening on the surface.

'I do not care for such matters. Ships wreck every day in my oceans.' The tentacle released its hold, casting her carelessly away.

'Wait!' Connie cried, swimming back down to reach the Kraken before it could sink without a trace from her mind. She grabbed hold of one of the tentacles and showed the Kraken the black oil in the belly of the tanker. She warned it of the pollution that would result if this load were allowed to spill into the water. Then she showed it a picture of the ship safe in Chartmouth Harbour, cargo intact. She received no answer, but she felt movement: the Kraken was surfacing.

'It's coming,' she told Dr Brock as the creature released its hold on her. 'But as for what it's going to do—your guess is as good as mine.'

Hurtling out of the darkness, an enormous arm whipped across the deck like a rope the thickness of a tree trunk. It was joined by another and another. The rails on either side of the deck were crushed like matchsticks in the Kraken's squeezing grip.

'*Cyclops* is in the Kraken's embrace,' Dr Brock marvelled. 'Will it crush us, or help us?'

The tanker ceased to drift towards the rocks and hung for a moment on the billowing seas. Connie swallowed hard: which way would the Kraken choose? She had been unable to read its alien mind, so brief had been their contact. Slowly, the ship turned to the east and began to move towards Chartmouth.

'It's doing it; it worked!' Connie cried.

The wind redoubled in its howling, trying to prise the tanker out of the creature's arms. The sea lashed and piled itself in mountains against the sides of the ship, but to no avail: the Kraken's grasp was stronger than the storm. The weather giant could produce nothing to defeat it once the sea creature had determined its course. Connie felt a dark pulse of power as Kullervo summoned the Kraken to join with him. But the depths of the ocean were so far beyond Kullervo's reach or understanding, his call went unheeded. The Kraken cared only for itself—Kullervo could offer it nothing it wanted.

As the lights of Chartmouth appeared on the port side, Connie prepared to restore her bond with the Kraken to thank it for its aid. This was unwise, for she did not yet understand her adversary. Angry beyond all measure to see his plan foiled, Kullervo sought her out to vent his spite upon her. The shape-shifter was waiting to pounce. Her guard down, the presence of Kullervo swept back and felled her.

'Death! Darkness! Ruin!' he shrieked in her mind, driving his vengeful presence into her so hard that she almost lost her sense of self under the inundation. Connie twisted in agony, trying to block her ears. Dr Brock ran to support her but there was nothing he could do to assist her in this battle.

'No, that's not the way,' whispered a deeply buried instinct. 'Find the shield.' Dropping her hands from her ears, Connie grappled to restore the image of the universal's shield in her mind. She lifted it inch by inch. At first, the shield struggled to hold back the deluge, wobbling and wavering in her grip, but gradually it gained in strength and brightness. She could now feel his hatred battering on the shield's rim, drumming out destruction for her and her kind, but no longer able to touch her.

How dare he attack me, thought Connie, an angry fire kindled inside her like a dragon's breath. How dare he enter my mind without my leave? He has no right to do so. And look at him, waiting out there, relishing all this suffering he has caused! He killed Scark!

Enraged by Kullervo's invasion of her, no longer frightened now she sheltered under the protection of her shield, she felt a great urge to defeat him. It filled her with the strength to raise the shield above her head. How she despised him and all he stood for!

'Go,' she ordered the dark presence. 'I send you back.' There was a great rush of energy, like the opening of a dam of silver water, and Connie felt the evil thoughts rebound from the surface of her shield, propelled back the way they had come. A piercing screech split the night sky; a midnight-blue eagle fell like a stone from the cliff and dashed on to the rocks beneath, losing shape and substance. The storm-tossed sea turned black where the creature had fallen and threw itself in impotent fury against the cliff face, the spray flickering with blue fire. But the shape-shifter was unable to take form again in the chaos of the storm he himself had raised. Kullervo's presence vanished, battered into spray on the rocks, then sucked with the retreating waves down to the depths. His leader gone, the storm-giant immediately dispersed into scraps of cloud and swirled out to sea. Connie could breathe freely again.

'Is he dead?' she panted, seeing that Dr Brock was craning to look out of the window, wiping the glass with his sleeve to clear it.

'He's gone for the moment, but I doubt very much that he's dead,' Dr Brock said sombrely. 'But perhaps that's something you can tell me.'

Connie thought for a moment, putting her scattered wits in order.

'You're right—he's gone, but he cannot be destroyed this way,' she said at length. She knew that the shape-shifting spirit was too subtle to be vulnerable to a mortal's death.

'But you, my dear, you have won a great victory.' Dr Brock helped her to her feet and surprised her with a hug. 'You caught him out with that last trick of yours: he was not prepared to block it. Hoist by his own petard!' he chuckled, turning back to the control desk. 'Come, let's steer this cockleshell into port and see what Mr Quick has to say for himself.'

'But we still have to dock this thing,' Connie said doubtfully.

'I'm not so sure about that—listen.' Over the noise of the diminishing storm, Connie heard an engine throbbing and then a searchlight picked out the deck in a crazy dance as a helicopter struggled in the wind. 'I think we should expect a visit from the coastguard, my dear,' Dr Brock said with no attempt to conceal his relief.

Sensing the arrival overhead, the Kraken chose this moment to release its grip. Its arms snaked back over the side, clearing the deck just in time before the helicopter let down its passengers. Five airmen tumbled from the sky on ropes, slammed down on the deck, unclipped their harnesses, and ran towards the bridge. They burst into the control room in a fizz of radios and jingling buckles but stopped short when they saw it was already occupied.

'What the hell are you doing here?' said their leader, a stocky man with a bristling moustache dripping with melting snow.

'Same as you—just trying to help,' replied Dr Brock calmly. 'I think you'll find we've made quite a good job of saving the crew and preventing a shipwreck, but I'm not sure we're up to docking. To whom am I handing over command?'

Bewildered by the sight of the elderly captain and his young first officer, the man shook his head in disbelief.

'But we've no time to ask questions, sir,' interrupted another member of the team.

'True. You're handing over to my team—the air-sea rescue from Plymouth, Captain . . . ?'

'Brock.'

'Captain Brock.' The officer snapped a smart salute and Dr Brock graciously made way for the professionals.

'*Captain?*' murmured Connie, as she and Dr Brock watched the team place the tanker back under control. The radio now buzzed and crackled with communications flying between the tanker and the port authorities.

Dr Brock winked. 'My one and only chance,' he said. 'I was technically in command even if I wasn't in control.'

Within half an hour, the air-sea rescue team had steered into the calmer waters of Chartmouth harbour. The tanker slid up to its berth by the new refinery and barely bumped against the quayside as it was secured. A textbook docking, Dr Brock pointed out knowledgeably to Connie. A crowd of people on the quayside, lights and camera crews, indicated that the drama out to sea had not gone unnoticed by those on shore.

'It looks as if the others have got here first,' Dr Brock said, nodding to the activity around the two small boats from Hescombe. 'I wonder what the authorities will make of the sailors' stories? First sirens and then dragons. I imagine they'll be breathalysed pretty sharpish.'

21
Aftermath

'SO, Dr Brock,' called the reporter at the impromptu news conference in the security guards' hut on the dockside. 'You and your young friend here—Connie Lionheart, is that right?' Connie confirmed her name with a nod. 'You were out fishing with the rest of your party, saw the tanker in trouble, managed to climb on board, set off some flares to alert the authorities, and steered it safely to port?'

'Yes, that's right,' said Dr Brock with a twinkle in his eye.

'And how did you get on board?' another reporter asked, looking up from her notepad. 'The rescue services had a helicopter—how did you manage it?'

'We got a lift,' Dr Brock said without elaborating.

'You mean your other young friend, Colin Clamworthy,'—it was Col's turn to be picked out by the cameras—'took you to the ship's side and you climbed on board?' she suggested.

'Yes, something like that,' Dr Brock replied. The hut buzzed with excitement as the cameras took a close-up of the athletic elderly man and his young helpers. 'We've been warning for months that the Stacks are a danger to shipping. It's time the government took action and stopped tankers sailing so close to them. Now, if you have any more questions, I suggest they wait until we've had time to restore ourselves with dry clothes and a cup of tea. In the meantime, you should ask Axoil just how close the south coast came to ecological disaster tonight. I think Miss Nuruddin here has the details.'

Rupa nodded, waving a press release over her head. 'I'll give you the full story on the condition you credit my paper,' she told the representatives of the national press who were still arriving in their droves. 'We've got some great pictures.'

As first on the scene, Rupa had inadvertently been in a prime position to cover the story of a lifetime. Faulty machinery forgotten, she now had the disgraceful incompetence of the Axoil crew to report on. So leaving Rupa, with Anneena and Jane beside her, to brief the journalists about the sorry state of Axoil's labour force, both on shore and on board its tanker, Connie, Col, and Dr Brock joined Evelyn, Signor Antonelli, Jessica, Horace Little, and Mrs Clamworthy in an all-night café for a much-welcomed brew-up.

'What have you all been up to?' Evelyn asked, not yet having recovered from the shock of seeing Connie piloting a tanker into port. 'And how are we going to explain this to your parents?'

'To be honest, I don't know,' laughed Connie. 'It's going to test our powers of invention, that's for sure.'

An hour later, Jane and Anneena came running into the café, hotfoot from the press conference.

'We've done it! The story's broken in a more spectacular way than Rupa could've dreamed!' cried Anneena. 'The press are all asking for an inquiry. The inspectors will be down here tomorrow to look into what happened to the missing men. The unions are hopping mad. Mr Quick won't be able to sweep this one under the carpet after that near-disaster.' She paused and gave Connie, Jessica, and Col a funny look. 'And just how did you get involved in the rescue?'

'It's a long story,' said Connie, not wishing to lie to her best friends but also restricted in what she could say. How could she explain sirens and dragons, not to mention Kullervo?

Fortunately, the other Society members came to her rescue. Col began talking loudly about the perilous boat trip, Jessica said something about cold water inducing hallucinations in the sailors, and her aunt gave some sketchy details as to how they had pulled the sailors out of the water—

'You mean they were all in the water?' asked Jane incredulously. 'How on earth did that happen?'

Connie could see that her friends could find no rational explanation for what had occurred. She regretted for the hundredth time that evening that she could not tell them everything. Protecting the mythical creatures by lying to Anneena and Jane seemed a high price to pay just now.

The television burbling to itself in a corner began to broadcast the chimes of Big Ben.

'Happy New Year!' Col said with a grin.

'A very *Happy* New Year for us—but not for Axoil, I think,' remarked Anneena, hugging her friends in turn.

The snow was falling gently, covering the refinery in a softening white shroud. The Hescombe party decided to take their boats back home now that the storm had blown itself out and they wanted to avoid any further questions from the press for the moment. The story seemed to be doing very well on its own in any case. Leaving the confused sailors, jubilant news-team from the *Hescombe Herald*, and irate managers from Axoil to fight it out in front of the cameras, they slipped away from the port before their departure could be noted. As the door of the café banged closed behind them, the first news bulletin of the New Year began:

'Tonight, ecological disaster has been averted on the south coast. In an extraordinary series of events, an elderly man and two children managed to save a stricken oil tanker from running aground . . .'

'Will we be in any danger near the Stacks?' Col asked Connie softly as he restarted the engine. 'I don't want Anneena and Jane to see anything. I think they've been forced to swallow enough already.'

Connie nodded and dipped deep in her mind to listen for the sirens' song. She sensed sorrow rather than rage in their singing; the sirens were absorbed in tending their fallen: they would not be flying again tonight.

'I think the madness has lifted now Kullervo's gone,' she replied. 'We'll be safe enough to pass them by. In a few days, I'll go and talk to Gull-wing and the others and try to reconcile them to our ways. I must see if we can find a way for them to live in peace. At least now they are not likely to be drowned in oil. Maybe I can persuade them to stay hidden if they want to carry on living on the Stacks. I doubt any tanker will go too near them after tonight's near miss.'

Col nodded and signalled to *Banshee* that all was clear. The two boats chugged back to Hescombe, passing over the head of the Kraken who had returned to its slumber.

A week later, the newspaper cuttings were piled high on the kitchen table. Connie and Col leafed through them: *'Tanker terror'*; *'Oil catastrophe averted'*; *'Scandal hits Axoil—shares plummet'*—and their favourite because they knew it had annoyed Dr Brock and made everyone else laugh—*'Plucky pensioner and children save ship!'*

'You know, I feel a bit of a fraud myself,' said Connie. 'We're getting all the credit, but it was the mythical creatures that really did it.'

'Oh, I dunno,' said Col, still buoyed up by a congratulatory phone call he had had from his father in which Mack had not once claimed to have diverted an oil disaster himself before.

Evelyn came in bearing the morning post.

'Are you going to show those to your parents, Connie?' she asked.

'Of course, I'll show the clippings to Mum and Dad—when Dad has recovered from the shock,' Connie said, putting them back into their folder.

'You mustn't worry too much about that,' her aunt said, seeing Connie's glum expression. 'I know your parents weren't too pleased to find out about your "midnight gallivantings"—as your father called them—but I think, with time, they'll come round. With the world singing your praises, they can hardly do otherwise. Still, perhaps it's for the best that they've gone to take Simon to school. I've been afraid for days that some over-enthusiastic Society member will burst in and spill the beans before the entire Lionheart clan!'

'So've I. I think Signor Antonelli would've done the other day if Col here hadn't been on hand to stop him.'

Connie turned her attention to the mail. Most of it was for her: letters of congratulation from Society members; invitations to appear on daytime television; fan mail from environmental campaigners the world over. Two letters stood out from today's crop. She pushed them over to Col who read them with a frown.

'Bit cool, aren't they?' he commented, throwing the note from Mr Coddrington and the card from Shirley to one side.

'Well, you know what I think about him,' Connie said tersely. 'As for Shirley, I expect she's just sore her giant's been expelled from the Society.'

She slit open the last of her letters. Out fell a book token from Mr Johnson. The note read: *'A late prize from the governors of Hescombe Primary School on the completion of last term's project. Well done!'*

'Yeah, I got one of those too,' commented Col when he saw the familiar writing.

Evelyn pounced on the token. 'Ah—academic recognition! Now that may help persuade your parents to let Simon come here at half term if nothing else does.'

'Or it may not—I think some of the details in the press may scare them off completely,' said Connie.

'True. He always hated my involvement with what he regards as a bunch of dangerous lunatics and now he blames me for his own daughter going the same way.'

Connie grinned and gathered up the papers.

'Well, in any case, that's one battle won for the Society,' Evelyn said with satisfaction as she opened the dresser drawer devoted to Connie's collection of letters and clippings. 'The sirens' existence has been kept secret. They are safe for the moment, now an exclusion zone has been made round the Stacks. That would never've happened if it hadn't been for Kullervo—I hope it makes him choke, wherever he is. Anyway, I think it calls for a celebration. How about a visit to my banshees? They throw one hell of a party.'

Connie grimaced at Col as she slipped her bundle inside and shut the drawer with a bang.

'Maybe not. I was only joking,' added her aunt quickly when she saw their expressions. 'In fact, we're invited to Anneena's restaurant for lunch with Jane and her family. The Nuruddins want to celebrate Mr Benedict's new job in Plymouth.'

'And what about a ride later, Connie?' asked Col. 'Skylark and me want to take you for a spin this evening. How does that sound?'

'That sounds great,' Connie replied, 'but there's one thing I have to do before we go. I should've done it already. Wait for me; I won't be long.'

Putting on her coat, Connie stepped out of the house and slid her way down the path to the beach. It was deserted: even the most hardy beachcombers had stayed in today, deterred by the arctic breeze, so no one saw her as she held out her arm, palm downwards, towards the sea, seeking the silent world of the deep.

'Thank you, Kraken,' she murmured to the strange currents that circulated far below the human world. 'Thank you.'

Crunching back up the beach, she paused for a moment by Scark's grave. 'Your flock is safe now. I hope you can rest in peace,' she said in a hoarse whisper. 'Goodbye, Scark.'

'Ready now?' Col asked when she returned to the house still in a thoughtful mood. Connie nodded. 'Let's go then.'

Col, Connie, and Evelyn set off together down Shaker Row, turning their backs on the sea and the midnight blue shadow that was gathering again where wave meets shore.

URGENTLY REQUIRED

NEW MEMBERS SOUGHT FOR THE COMPANIONS CLUB

www.companionsclub.co.uk

The evil shape-shifter has returned. Now, the Society for the Protection of Mythical Creatures is looking for dedicated new recruits to join them in their fight against the dark powers of Kullervo.

Are you a creature companion? Do you have the special powers need to communicate with mythical beasts?

Take our Companion Assessment to see if you have what it takes!

NEW MEMBERS WILL
- be sent a club badge to mark them out as a companion to their mythical creature
- receive regular email updates about official Society business from the Trustees
- receive downloads from their desktops with their own companion symbol
- be able to send comments and ideas about the stories for posting on the website
- be eligible to enter special Society competitions to win fantastic prizes
- and much, much more!

So don't delay.
Visit www.companionsclub.co.uk today.

YOUR PLANET NEEDS YOU!

JULIA GOLDING grew up on the edge of Epping Forest. After reading English at Cambridge, she joined the Foreign Office and served in Poland. Her work as a diplomat took her from the high point of town twinning in the Tatra Mountains to the low of inspecting the bottom of a Silesian coal mine.

On leaving Poland, she joined Oxfam as a lobbyist on conflict issues, campaigning at the United Nations and with governments to lessen the impact of war on civilians living in war zones. She now works as a freelance writer.

Married with three children, she lives in Oxford. *Secret of the Sirens* is her first novel for children, and the first part of the glorious 'Companions Quartet'.